A SHOOTER'S AMBITION

S. Allen

Lock Down Publications and Ca$h
Presents

A Shooter's Ambition

A Novel by *S. Allen*

S. Allen

Lock Down Publications
P.O. Box 870494
Mesquite, Tx 75187

Copyright 2019 by S. Allen
A Shooter's Ambition

Lock Down Publications
Like our page on Facebook: Lock Down Publications @
www.facebook.com/lockdownpublications.ldp
Cover design and layout by: **Dynasty Cover Me**
Book interior design by: **Shawn Walker**
Edited by: **Sunny Giovani**

4

Stay Connected with Us!

Text **LOCKDOWN** to 22828 to stay up-to-date with new releases, sneak peaks, contests and more…

Thank you!

Submission Guideline.

Submit the first three chapters of your completed manuscript to ldpsubmissions@gmail.com, subject line: Your book's title. The manuscript must be in a .doc file and sent as an attachment. Document should be in Times New Roman, double spaced and in size 12 font. Also, provide your synopsis and full contact information. If sending multiple submissions, they must each be in a separate email.

Have a story but no way to send it electronically? You can still submit to LDP/Ca$h Presents. Send in the first three chapters, written or typed, of your completed manuscript to:

LDP: Submissions Dept
P.O. Box 870494
Mesquite, Tx 75187

DO NOT send original manuscript. Must be a duplicate.

Provide your synopsis and a cover letter containing your full contact information.

Thanks for considering LDP and Ca$h Presents.

DEDICATIONS

I dedicate this book to my mother Karen Collins. Another one down, Ma. Plenty more to go. I love you.

ACKNOWLEDGEMENTS

Shout out to my Potna Shack 'B' from Culture City. We the last of a dying breed. Keep your head up; it's almost over! Stackhouse from Clarksville, Tennessee, Kenneth Hobson, KT, CEO Cash, thank you for the opportunity and the knowledge and wisdom you have given me to become a better writer. Shout out to all of the LDP family and talented authors. Too many to name. Who give those behind the wall an outlet outside of the negativity and hard times within the belly of the beast. Last but not least, shout out to all the soldiers behind enemy lines who stuck to the code— you all know who you are. Take this time to educate yourself mentally, and keeping yourself up physically and spiritually, and let God take care of the rest. And to all my fans and the ones who purchased this book, thank you for your support, and trust and believe I'm going to keep dropping this heat.

Shout out to Ca$h and the entire Lock Down Publications family. The game is definitely ours. A special shout out to all of the real men and women behind these walls that stuck to the code. I salute! Last but not least, shout out to all my haters and back-biters. Thank you for being who you are because without y'all it wouldn't but no me. Get on my level!

S. Allen

S. Allen

A Shooter's Ambition

Prologue

The shit that stands out the most from my learned patience of stalking in sniper school is the marksmanship that leads to the bloodshed. Although in sniper school we shot blanks, I still remember the recoil from the 7.62-millimeter round releasing from my barrel and the gun smoke that invaded my lungs. The application of my synchronized mental checklist is forever embedded in me— did I camouflage properly? Did I confirm the sight of my objective, breathe and relax, and last but not least, apply the slight pressure to the trigger mechanism and viola mission completed? Target down and out.

In Iraq, I remember this day like it was yesterday. It was clear and crisp with wind gusts of twenty miles per hour. It was midafternoon when this white Ford F-150 stopped at the road intersection and two dudes got out. This drew my attention to full alert as I sighted them in my scope to get a better view of what the fuck was going on and what were they up to. They couldn't have stopped in a better spot, at least in relation to where me and my squad was posted. They ended up directly in the cross-hairs of my M4 assault weapon.

The driver of the truck jumped into the bed of the truck and struggled to lift something. I could tell the shit was heavy by the way he was slumped over and the struggle he displayed when handing it to the passenger on the outside of the vehicle. The passenger being slightly bigger and possibly in better shape received it and ran to the side of the road.

Sweat poured from my forehead as I immediately recognized that they were planting a roadside bomb. From my training and experience I knew that I had to pop this nigga's top. I tracked him through my scope until he stopped at the edge of the road. This would be my only opportunity; one shot, one kill. I lined the back of his head in the crosshairs of my scope, took a deep breath and applied a slow and steady squeeze. He hit the pavement as I saw his brain explode from his skull and his body jerk. Per stalking class, my position was undetectable. This skill would follow me through the rest of my life and into a city that's plagued with violence, thus, creating me to become a vicious lion stalking my prey in a jungle where it's kill or be killed.

Chapter 1

"Rock, weed, Park!" Young Byron yelled, standing on the corner of Avers and Augusta on Chicago's westside. It was 8:15 pm and the drug block where Byron was the top security, was about to close for the night. At 18 years old, Byron was the top security for the block, which was controlled by the Mafia— a ruthless street gang who accumulated their finances through selling drugs. It was 1993 and Chicago was at its apex of the crack epidemic as the gangs in the city shed blood over the lucrative drug game. Bodies dropped and cemeteries were packed to the fullest capacity, all in the name of the almighty dollar, and the Mafia was taking their piece of the pie.

Byron Hobson wasn't your average street thug. He was smart, ambitious and full of life. Byron was the only child, a product of a dramatic and broken home. At only five years old, Byron's father, Calvin, left him and his mother to fend for themselves, in the form of Calvin pursuing a life consisting of chasing heroin and prostitutes. Byron's mother, Ilena, was forced to be the head of the household, maintaining a job at the Sears Roebuck to provide for her only son. With extremely long hours at work, young Byron was left at home to raise himself. Being that no authority figure was on watch, Byron grew into adolescence and took to the streets as most young black males with no father figure do.

Byron's friend at the time, Lil' Poo, introduced him to the gang. He would always tell Byron he should join the Mafia's because they were about making money. To encourage him more, Lil' Poo always had the newest shoes, the flyest clothes in school, and he kept a pocket full of dead presidents. At 13 years old, Lil' Poo had the money and reputation that Byron desired. After thinking long and hard about joining the Mafia's, Byron made his decision and told Lil' Poo he wanted in. After being blessed into the organization, Byron's young life instantly changed. Selling crack for his gang got him the money, clothes and respect from his peers, but everything in life that comes as easy as crack money also had its faults for young Byron.

Ilena would start to notice him coming in at all kinds of hours of the night, and she also noticed the new clothes and shoes that she knew she hadn't provided for him. "Byron, I know you out there hanging with them gang-bangers. If that's the life you want to live, you will not live it in this house. I did not raise you like that, damnit!"

Ilena would always preach to Byron, but at that time, the only thing that kept Byron at home was his display of his academic skills. Despite being from the notorious westside of Chicago, Byron received all A's and B's in his schoolwork. Math was his forte, and would later help him in life. Ilena had faith in her son that one day he would flourish into something great.

Five years later, Byron was in the hood, still involved in gang activity when Lil' Poo walked up smoking a blunt of purple haze. "Aye, Lord, it's twenty minutes into shutdown and it's still like thirty junkies in the alley waiting to get served." Lil' Poo said passing Byron the potent weed.

"Yeah, I know. You might as well tell Funk n'em to start clearing out the alley. You already know if Billy Good come through here and this shit ain't shut down, he gone have something to say. Niggas might get violated."

"I'm already hip. Rico should be on his way anyway to pick up the money. We don't need no extra shit. Billy Good don't be playing about how his demo ran so let me go holla at them niggas and tell 'em to close it down." Lil' Poo grabbed the blunt from Byron and walked off to go handle his duties.

Avers and Augusta was one of the biggest drug strips on the westside. Crack addicts lined up in the alley waiting to get served the devil's love. Ten dollars would get you a high one never dreamed of, and the Mafia's ran the block with an iron fist. An old-school cat by the name of Billy Good ran the block, and was also the King and Chief for the Mafia's. His blocks were run with a strategic structure that brought the blocks thousands of dollars daily. Avers and Augusta was his most lucrative block, bringing in a $100,000 a day, so everything had to be on point. From the pitchers to the servers, to the security, any signs of insubordination of the rules laid down from Billy Good would surely lead to violations and in some cases terminations.

"Shop closed, shop closed, shop closed!" Byron yelled letting the junkies know they were no more drugs being sold.

Most of the times, some crack addict would try and stay in line begging the dealers to serve them, and in most cases, would end up with the addict being severely beaten with a lead pipe or baseball bat.

Hearing the commotion in the alley, Byron already knew what was going on. Taking the 9-millimeter berretta off his hip, Byron walked through the gateway into the alley as Lil' Poo and Funk were arguing with a crackhead who was begging for a rock. Not in the mood for the trivial games, Byron walked up to the crackhead and pointed the gun at his foot and pulled the trigger.

Pop! The sound of the handgun echoed throughout the broken night air, as the crackhead yelled in agony. "Ahhhhh! Alright, man, alight! I'm leaving!" Tears streamed down the bloodshot red eyes of the fiend as he hopped away down the alley to get away from the dangerous gangstas.

"Man, stop playing with these fiends every night. Every night it's the same shit. They got to know shop closed means shop-fucking-closed!"

"Hell, yeah. It's called training and management, Joe. They fiends but they still gotta abide by the laws of the land." Byron said, tucking the hot 9 back in his waistline.

Lil' Poo let a grin come across his face as he was one to always be with the bullshit. "Y'all trippin'. Let's go meet this nigga Rico so we can get off this hot ass block."

Byron, Lil' Poo and Funk walked through the alleyway and stood in front of the building.

Ten minutes later, Rico pulled up and parked his S-class Benz and honked the horn. A minute later, a man came from the building carrying a black Nike duffle bag containing the day's profit from the drugs. Byron pulled his banger out and watched as the man went to Rico's Benz and passed him the duffle bag through the window. Security had to be tight because there was no room for mistakes dealing with the Mafia's and Billy Good's drug money. Rico was Billy Good's top lieutenant and every night collected the proceeds from Avers and Augusta. After Rico pulled off without incident, the block was officially shutdown.

"What's up, Joe? What y'all about to do?" Byron asked his homies as he lit a Newport.

"Shit, I'm about to go get up with Lord and them in Fifth City and go shoot dice. See if I can hit they ass for a rack or two," Lil' Poo said looking down the block.

"I'm about to slide on this broad up north," Funk replied.

"Where at up north? By them GD's?" Byron asked him, taking a pull of his cigarette.

"Yeah, but they don't be on shit."

"Take this anyway. To be aware and prepared is to stay alive." Byron passed him the 9-millimeter.

The GD's and Mafia's were sworn enemies in the Chi and Byron wanted to be on point. Funk grabbed the gun and stuck it in his Pelle-Pelle jacket. "I'm going in the crib, Lord. I'll holla at y'all in the am."

"Almighty." Funk and Lil' Poo replied as Byron started walking toward his house.

Byron stayed on Avers and Augusta, so his walk wasn't far. Walking in the house, Byron was greeted by the smell of E&J liquor and cigarette smoke as Ilena glared at him through glossy eyes as he closed the door. Drinking was her usual when she came home from work; it helped her ease the tension from living in the poverty of the westside of Chicago.

"Where the hell you been all damn night?" Ilena slurred, standing up to confront her son.

"I was outside with Lil' Poo and them."

"Yeah, I looked out the window and saw you standing on the corner. I bet you out there selling drugs for the gangbangers, ain't you?"

"Nah, Ma," Byron lied.

Slap! The open palm of Ilena's right hand went across Byron's left check, causing a great sting and tears forming in the wells of his eyes.

"Don't you dare lie to me in my face, in my house. I know what the fuck you out there doing. You think I don't have eyes, boy? But let me tell your lil' grown ass this again. You not gonna be around here hanging out, selling drugs and shit. If you want to do that, get out of here. That way, when you get shot or go to jail it won't be on my conscience."

The words Ilena spoke hurt Byron's heart. He knew his mother was stressed ever since his father left, and he also knew he was adding to it. He loved his mother and he knew he was violating their relationship, but he was young, black and trapped in the ghetto and he felt he had no choice but to answer to the call of the streets. Byron looked at his mother's red eyes. "Momma, I'm sorry and I love you," he said as he walked off toward his room to get some much-needed rest.

"That's right, just walk off like your no-good father. Just walk off," Byron heard his mother say as the words hit his back. Tomorrow would be a new day with new opportunities.

Chapter 2

The next day was the first of the month. Every 1st and 15th of the month were the busiest days on Avers and Augusta. Reason being, most of the crack addicts received their government-assisted checks and they rushed to Avers and Augusta to get the best crack the city had to offer. It was 12:00 mid-day and Byron stood on his post directing the traffic to the alley. After the argument with his mother last night, he was tense and for the first time, he felt like dropping out of the gang to take some of the stress off his mother's shoulders. But at the same time, he felt it was too late for him to turn back. He had been a Mafia for five years and the money he obtained from selling drugs kept clothes on his back and food in his stomach. Not to mention, the Mafia's were blood in, blood out, and the only way out was death.

"Rocks, blows, weed, Park!" Byron yelled at a red Corsica that had pulled up.

"Excuse me, sweetheart, we looking for some rock," a skinny black female said from the passenger side.

"Park your car and get out. Y'all know the drill." Byron sneered. It was early in the day and Byron was agitated because he knew from street instincts, police were going to be hot this day, plus he didn't like how the driver of the Corsica, a middle-aged white man, was looking all nervous.

The skinny black chick got out the car and walked over to Byron holding a crumpled up $10-dollar bill. "Here you go, sweetie." She held the bill out trying to give it to Byron.

Byron looked at the money like it contained HIV. "Listen, shorty," Byron said, trying to conceal and control his anger, "go in the alley right there, stand in line like everybody else, and you will be taking care of."

"Alright," the crackhead said and walked off toward the alley, trying to put extra to the switch of her hips.

Byron turned his attention back to the man in the Corsica who had both of his hands on the steering wheel, as sweat profusely poured from his forehead. Byron had a bad feeling in his gut as he watched the man from across the street, but he continued to watch the cars coming down the block and noticed that a tinted Black Chevy Tahoe turned on Avers and Augusta.

The truck came down the block slowly which caused Byron to get on point as he slid his right hand to his waist, now clutching his gun. The truck slowly drove by, but the dark tint obscured his ability to be able to see just who was occupying the vehicle. Being that he knew the block was pumpin', as well as governed by the Mafia's, created a perfect recipe for a dangerous situation, so he had to watch for the jack-boys and rival gang members. As the truck made a left on Avers Byron relaxed a little, turning his attention back to the alley as he saw the skinny black chick sashaying back to the red Corsica. After she got in, her and the driver engaged in what appeared to be an argument over the drugs she had just copped.

Man, they need to get off this block, Byron thought as he made his way across the street to tell the crackheads to get the fuck outta dodge. All of a sudden, the black Tahoe came speeding down the block.

Before Byron could register what was happening, the white man in the Corsica jumped out pointing a .357 at Byron. "Freeze! Chicago Police! Let me see some hands!"

Skirrrrt! The black Chevy Tahoe came to a screeching halt as the doors flew open and four officers hopped out pointing guns. "Get on the ground now! Get on the fuckin' ground, muthafucka!" the officers yelled.

Byron thought about reaching for his gun, but he was sure as he was black they would not hesitate to squeeze their triggers, so he complied with the officers and laid face down on the ground, placing his hands on top of his head.

Byron was snatched off the ground and pat-searched by the white man from the Corsica— Officer Myron Calhoun from the Drug and Gang Task Force. "What do we have here?" Officer Calhoun pulled the 9-millimeter Beretta from Byron's waistline. "Looks like you'll be heading to Cook County today, pal," Calhoun stated, smiling from ear to ear, revealing his coffee stained teeth.

Avers and Augusta was swarmed with Chicago's finest. Byron

saw Lil' Pooh, Funk and a few more Mafia's being escorted by police officers, handcuffed with their heads down, en route to being loaded into a paddy wagon to be driven to Kedzie and Harrison, the sixth precinct.

One hour later, after being fingerprinted and photographed, Byron, Funk and Lil' Pooh were handcuffed to a bench. A lady sitting at a desk in front of them who identified herself as Officer Collins asked the young men questions— age, height, address, etcetera— until another officer approached holding a clipboard. He was black, about 5'4", receding hairline and potbelly with a sneer on his face.

"Uncuff this one right here," he said, pointing at Funk.

An officer uncuffed Funk from the bench and escorted him to the back with the officer with the clipboard.

"Man, Lord, what the fuck happened, Joe," Lil' Pooh asked Byron in a hushed tone.

"Lord, I don't know. All I know is they came from everywhere, Joe; this shit crazy. My mama gonna have a fit."

"Nigga, you need to be thinking about what Billy Good gonna do. Remember when that nigga Boo-Boo fucked up on security, they shot him in his leg. Remember that shit?"

"Yeah, that was messed up," Byron said shaking his head. Byron had a lot on his plate at the moment, and this being his first time in jail didn't make matters better.

Five minutes later, the officers came back with Funk and cuffed him back to the bench. His eyes were bloodshot red and tears were falling from them.

"Uncuff that one," the officer said pointing the clipboard to Lil' Pooh as he did with Funk. Lil' Pooh was uncuffed and led to a backroom.

"What's up with you, Lord," Byron asked Funk, wondering why his friend was crying and shit.

"Man, this shit crazy, Joe," was all Funk could muster before they returned with Lil' Pooh, handcuffing him back to the bench, as his homie too sported a tear coming from his eye.

Byron was nervous as shit when the officer was uncuffing him and leading him to the backroom, where he was then cuffed with his hands behind his back.

"How are you, Mr. Hobson? My name is Detective Wells and I'm going to ask you a few questions and I want some simple answers; you got that?" The officer placed the clipboard on a table. "Now how old are you, son?"

"I'm seventeen," Byron replied

"Who you run with?"

"The Mafia's."

"What you know about somebody being shot in the alley on Avers and Augusta last night?"

"Nothing, sir," Byron answered.

At that precise moment, Officer Wells walked over and slapped the shit out of Byron so hard, Byron stumbled backward and his ears were ringing. "Now, I'm going to ask you again. Who. Shot. The crackhead. Last night?"

"Sir. Sir, I don't know," Byron stuttered.

Slap! Slap! Slap! Slap! was all you could hear in the empty room as Officer Wells' palm made contact with Byron's face. "Get this piece of shit outta my face and make sure he gets charged with that gun."

Byron was led back to where Funk and Lil' Pooh was, cuffed back to the bench, tears also in his eyes, with a full understanding now of what took place with his homies.

After Byron was read his Miranda rights and charged with possession of an illegal firearm, he was led to a holding cell where Lil' Pooh and Funk were. When Byron entered the cell, Lil' Pooh was on the phone and Funk was laying on a bench. Only a toilet, sink and television was in the cell, and it reeked of urine and must. Byron walked over and sat on the bench near Funk.

"What took you so long, Lord?" Funk asked sitting up.

"They charged me with that banga, Joe. I already know my mama gonna put me out. Damn," was Byron's reply.

"Shit, if you would've ran and threw the damn gun, you wouldn't have to worry about that shit. Nigga, you wasn't on point."

"Fuck you mean? I ain't have a chance to run. Nigga, if you

would've ran, your clown ass wouldn't have got caught," Byron retorted.

"Clown? Lord, watch how you talk to me." Funk stood up.

"Or what, nigga? On the Five, I don't see that shit."

"Aye, y'all, chill that shit out. Fuck y'all on?" Lil' Pooh said, rushing to intervene and stand between his boys before shit got real.

"Nah, this nigga need to watch how he talking when he talking to me. Nigga got us caught with some work and got the nerve to pop slick!" Funk retorted, ice-grilling Byron.

"Lord, y'all squash that shit. I just got off the phone and they about to send one of the guys to come pay our bond and get us outta this bitch! Y'all worried about the wrong shit. Y'all need to be worrying about how we gonna pay back this bond money." Lil' Pooh said, looking at his homies as they grilled one another. Lil' Pooh's and Funk's bond was $1,000, and Byron's was $1,500. They definitely needed to be coming up with a plan to pay the Mafia's back. Nothing in life was free.

Funk let a smile plaster across his face. "Yeah, Lord, Pooh right. This shit ain't 'bout nothing. Shit happens." Funk extended his hand to Byron.

Byron looked at Funk's hand for a second before he reached out and the two shook up, the Mafia's way. "Everything almighty, Joe. It's all good!" Byron stated, but knowing deep down within, Funk was faking and not to be trusted, not one bit, but for the sake of the situation at hand, Byron let the issue lay to rest, but made a mental note to check Funk later for his disrespect.

Chapter 3

"Hobson, Montgomery, Banks! Let's go! Y'all just made bond," the short, chubby, Rueben Studdard look-alike guard yelled.

The three were led out the holding cell, given their bond statement and conditions and released from the Harrison Precinct. The blistering cold night's air invaded Byron's face as he zipped up his jacket in attempt to brace for the biting weather.

"Damn, it's cold as shit out here. I wonder who they sent to come get us." Byron said to no one directly as they walked down the stairs of the building.

"I don't know, but if they ain't here in five minutes I'm jumping on the first bus pull-up," Funk replied.

"Oh shit!" Was all that could be heard from Lil' Pooh.

Byron looked up and at that moment he felt his stomach turn. A white 4-door Benz was parked at the curb and a man stood beside it wearing a black hoodie covering his head. Byron knew the car from anywhere, and he also knew the occupants. The car belonged to Billy Good and the dude posted up was Rico, his henchman. At that moment, Byron knew he was in some shit.

Rico opened the back passenger side door and the individual stated, "Get y'all ass in this car," sneering, displaying the diamonds in his mouth which were glistening and bouncing off the street light, thus creating an up-close view of the celestial bodies that illuminate the night's sky. All three paused for a split-second until Rico placed his hand in the pocket of his hoodie. "I'ma tell y'all one more time. Get. Y'all. Ass. In. The fuckin' car!"

All of them knew Rico's work and decided it wasn't worth testing, as it was well established that Rico was indeed Billy Good's Top Gun and his body count was impeccable. All his victims were found with three to the dome, one in each eye and one between the eyes. Knowing Rico's body work quickly formulated Byron, Lil' Pooh and Funk to oblige to his command, with them getting into the backseat without argument or incident.

Once Byron entered the whip, the strong scent of marijuana invaded his nostrils and lungs creating a serene feeling in spite of the uneasiness of Rico's tone and demeanor. The heat in the Benz was welcoming and relaxing, the peanut-butter leather interior was comfortable and wrapped around the contours of your body as if it was a glove. The sound of Al Green's *Love and Happiness* graced the air waves. Occupying the driver's seat was none other than the king himself, Billy Good, live in the flesh.

The serious expression on his face was as stone as the diamonds in his 5-point star chain, which played games with Byron's eyesight, causing him to divert his sight elsewhere only to be captivated by the ice that sparkled on his wrist. He sported a salt and pepper afro that was razor-sharp lined as Steve Harvey's. Everything about the 56-year-old boss exuded money, power and respect. Just assessing the situation at hand caused a tremor down the spine of Byron, as this was the first time ever being in the presence of the Chief himself.

After everybody was settled in, Billy Good merged into the traffic to travel the grimy streets of Chi-Town's westside. Nobody spoke a word as Billy Good turned the volume down and cruised down Kedzie Street for ten minutes in complete silence.

"So, don't nobody got shit to say now, huh? Police raided my fuckin' block, confiscated ten thousand dollars' worth of my shit, and nobody has a muthafuckin' word to say? I just spent money outta my pocket to bond y'all asses outta jail, and nobody don't have nothin' to say?" Billy Good peered through his rearview mirror, locking eyes with Byron since he was designated security. The menacing glare in his eyes was so penetrating and intimidating, it was as if he had actually turned the heater up in the car.

Byron, feeling the heat, since he was staring directly into his eyes, knew that somebody had better say something quick, so he stepped up to the plate. "Aye, Lord, it was my fault. Shit just happened so fast when I was about to react, the cop had his gun in my face."

Billy Good made a left on Avers, let a few seconds pass, then spoke. "I tell you niggas all the time, the first and the fifteenth is sweep day. Y'all gotta be extra on point. The reason y'all was slipping is because y'all don't listen! Lil' Pooh, I expect way better outta you because you been on the block the longest and you know better."

Lil' Pooh just dropped his head, shaking it.

"All three of you niggas gonna be doing security all week, first, second and third shift. If I find out y'all missed a post, y'all already know what it is," Billy Good stated as he pulled up on Avers and Augusta. "Now, get the fuck outta my shit before I change my mind and have y'all violated for breaching security!"

Lil' Pooh and Funk slid out the backseat, Byron in tow.

Just as Byron was about to place a foot on the ground, Billy Good turned to him still wearing a mean mug on his face and commanded, "You stay in the car."

Lil' Pooh had a look of confusion on his face, whereas Byron was perplexed, wondering should he make a dash for it, but decided to face whatever it was as a man. Afterall, he couldn't run too far or for the rest of his life.

Billy Good pulled away, leaving Lil' Pooh and Funk on the curb looking dumbfounded. Rico fired up a blunt of White Widow, took a few tokes then passed it to Billy Good.

After he inhaled the smoke, holding it for what seemed like eternity, he turned his attention back to Byron. Exhaling, he spoke, "I been hearing a lot about you, shorty. Having a lot of complaints about how you conduct your position on *my* block." He passed the blunt to Byron. "You know what that tells me, Lord?"

"What's that?" Byron asked, taking a pull from the blunt.

"It tells me that you must be doing your job. That's the only time muthafuckas complain. Now, I gotta ask you a quick question. Why the hell did you shoot that crackhead last night, because you know that caused the undo heat on *my* block."

Byron thought before he spoke. "Chief, you said you wanted the block shut down at a certain time and the fiend was interfering with Nation business, so I had to make an example so it wouldn't happen again in the future." Byron blew weed smoke through his nostrils, and instantly felt the effects from the potency of the herb, suppressed a slight cough and created a vision of Dreamland, but Byron knew he was indeed a part of the Real World, playing in a man's game.

"Rico, you hear that? Because the fiend was interfering with Nation business, so he shot him." Billy Good let a devilish smirk appear along with a slight chuckle. "You know what, Byron? I been looking for a long time for somebody of your caliber. You remind me of myself when I was your age, always wanting to be on the frontline, always wanna put the work in and enforce the laws of the land, the laws of the Mafia and the body as a whole. The only problem I had was that I didn't want to listen to the OG's who had the knowledge, so you know what? I had to learn shit the hard way."

Byron was all ears, attentive, letting the wisdom and coat-pulling soak into his brain like a sponge to liquid while he passed the blunt to Rico.

Billy Good continued. "Byron, you have the ambition and attitude to flourish into something great in this thing here we call Mafia, but you must take heed and not make the same mistakes as so many others who possessed the same traits. Byron, do you know what status is?"

Byron shook his head, slowly, dazed and slightly paralyzed from the THC that flowed through his bloodstream.

"Byron, status is for men of honor; it's a symbol as an individual being an outstanding member of this organization, for men of high caliber, do you understand?"

"Yes, sir," Byron replied, eyes as red as the color of fresh blood.

"Byron, for you conducting yourself with integrity and dignity speaks volume to me. It lets me know that you make your position, not letting your position make you. Handling your function for the Mafia Nation in the manner you have, I'm blessing you with the reward of Five-star branch elite upon your crown."

Byron couldn't believe his ears. He knew it wasn't April, so it couldn't be any April fool's joke. Instead of being punished for his actions, he was being rewarded. He had heard Lil' Pooh always talking about reaching 5-star status. Shit, Lil' Pooh would do anything for 5-stars— murder anybody to get it— and here it was, Billy Good had just bestowed upon him what so many Mafia's had died for.

"Byron, you are no longer security for Avers and Augusta. Your staff titles and duties have just changed. You will make your own security and staff on Avers and Augusta. You will be in charge of getting *my* money off that block. You are now at the top of the chain of command. I am the only person you will report to. You will carry all of my commands out without question; do you understand me?"

"I understand," was Byron's only reply.

Billy Good pulled up in front of the building on Avers and Augusta where Lil' Pooh and a few hoodrats were standing, johning on one another. "Byron, you now possess a lot of power. Don't fuck this up. Give 'em the bag," Billy Good told Rico.

Rico reached under his seat and retrieved a black Nike gym bag.

"Now, it's a quarter key of crack and fifteen thousand dollars."

"What's this for, Lord?" Byron was most definitely perplexed as he received the bag.

"You got five stars now, Lord. Get yourself and your squad together," Billy Good stated just as stoned-faced as ever. "Now go put that shit up and get up with me first thing in the morning. Almighty."

Byron couldn't help but let the smile spread across his face as he was elated with his new development. "Almighty, Lord," was his joyful response as he exited the Benz with the bag in hand.

S. Allen

Chapter 4

The next day, Billy Good held a meeting at Douglas Park on the westside. It was mandatory for all Mafia's to be in attendance. Over a hundred gangstas stood accounted for, surrounding the operation of Avers and Augusta. Just as he finished with his statement, he motioned for Byron to step into the circle, standing next to him and Rico. "Let it be known now, Byron has five stars within this organization. Y'all will treat him as such, therefore he is at the top of the chain of command on Avers and Augusta and all issues will be reported to him and only him. Almighty."

The crowd of goons responded in unison, "Almighty."

"Avers and Augusta is now Byron's. Anybody who feels different, speak now or forever hold your piece."

Funk had a mug on his face as he spat on the ground.

"At this time, Byron, I am giving you the opportunity to select your staff."

Byron took the floor and spoke. "From this day on, it's a new day on Avers and Augusta. I will oversee all operations on that block and Lil' Pooh will be my first in command."

Lil' Pooh allowed a smile to appear across his hardened face, ecstatic that his guy had received 5-Branch status and elected him as first in command. He knew his pockets were about to swell to capacity.

"Funk, you will be on security, in charge of all the security details. Assemble a security squad and report back to me."

Funk didn't like not one bit of what was transpiring, more so, the matter of him being placed in security. In his mind he wanted to be his own boss and by him being on security staff he would always have to be subordinate to Byron.

Byron, clever as ever, knew exactly what he was promoting. He really didn't trust Funk but felt that he would give him enough rope to hang himself. Byron read the bitterness on Funk's face, but being a man of his position, he would play Poker to weed out the imposters and deal with them accordingly as they were— an enemy of the organization— in order for the organization to function properly. "Y'all know what we on, Lord," Byron declared as he continued addressing the guys. "The objective at hand is for us to get this money up so we can all eat and stay at the top of the game. If everybody do they part and abide by the laws of the land, we will flourish into something great!"

A smile formed across Billy Good's face as he liked the manner Young Byron was displaying on top of his young; electing to utilize the very same words he had spoken to Byron the night before. He knew with Byron conducting the block he would accumulate more riches and not have to worry about watching over the workers. "Tomorrow morning, I want all pitchers, look-outs and pack-runners to meet us in the alley at six to get y'all packs for the day. Almighty!"

Everybody nodded in agreement and simultaneously greeted back, "Almighty!"

At that moment the meeting was adjourned and all you could hear was, "Joe, let's get that money, it's a new day." Byron had been loyal to the Mafia's and all the others knew that, so it was only right that he was blessed with such a position, and now he would show the organization his worth, if there were any who doubted or question his gangsta.

It was 6:00PM when Byron, Lil' Pooh and Funk sat in Byron's basement. Byron's mother would be home in two hours, so they had to take care of the business quickly. Unzipping the Nike gym bag, Byron pulled out the quarter-key of crack that Billy Good supplied to him. Lil' Pooh's eyes got as big as saucers while Funk's jaw just dropped open as if he had lost all the feeling in his face. Both mesmerized from seeing the bulk of crack that laid before their eyes, screamed as if they were a duet, "What the fuck? What's up, Joe? That's how we rollin'?"

"So, what's the plan? How you wanna bag this shit up, Lord?" Lil' Pooh inquired.

"We gone weigh up by the ounce. I say we got nine ounces, we pull nine eight balls off each ounce, break each ball down into three hundred dime pieces, and we'll pull twenty-four thousand, three hundred dollars. Each pack is to be distributed in hundred-dollar packs, leaving as less room for error. Billy Good wants a stack off each ounce, so we give him nine thousand dollars, and that leaves us fifteen thousand. After we pay the workers we should be left with ten thousand dollars, and we'll take and use that toward the next demonstration." Byron began cutting slabs on his plate and weighing ounce by ounce.

"So you mean to tell us we ain't gone get paid?" Funk questioned as he eyed Byron suspiciously.

"Listen, Lord, you gone get paid, but right now our mission is to show this nigga Billy Good we ain't playing no games about this money. When we off the next demo, you gon' be paid twenty thousand dollars, nigga."

Funk's eyes lit up like a kid in a candy store, showing nothing but greed. "That's what's up," was Funk's reply as they began to chop and bag the work.

The next morning, Lil' Pooh and Funk stood in the alley and issued out a few packs to the runners. It was as cold as Alaska, having them feel as if they were Eskimos as all three were hoodied up with their Carhartt gear. After a runner runs out, Lil' Pooh would be there to supply them another as if they were working on an assembly line. Funk was to oversee the security on the corners and make sure that the block ran smoothly. Byron watched the flow and action from his front window— watching as the security pointed crackheads to the alley, the police making their routine pass— however, yelling in code to everyone before any miscues could occur. He watched *his* block get that money and he couldn't help but grin.

His first day of being in command, half of the demo was sold, and he sat in his room fumbling through the $100's, $50's, $20's and $10's. He had never counted so much money at one time and the feeling was intoxicating. He couldn't wait to hand Billy Good his cash, every dime, and at the same time he would purchase his own work. He would help the Nation progress and grow just as he would himself.

Byron's thoughts of success were disturbed when he heard his mother calling his name. "Byron, come here."

He commenced to stuffing the stacks of cash inside a Nike shoebox and placing it in his closet before striding off to see what Illena wanted. "What's up, ma?" He inquired as he entered the front room.

Illena sat on the couch drinking a half pint of E&J. Byron started to notice his beautiful mother's looks fade away. In he earlier, happy days, Ilena was drop dead gorgeous, light skinned with long pretty hair and had a body so well proportioned, Byron's father stayed fighting in school for dudes drooling over his high school sweetheart. But after he left them, Ilena's appearance started to blemish from years and years of drinking and smoking.

Just as Byron was in deep thought of his mother's deterioration, Ilena took a swig of the brandy she clutched in her right hand before she spoke. "So, I got a letter from the police station on Harrison today, or rather *you* got a letter..."

Byron's eyes immediately dropped to the floor and locked on a huge roach that was crawling across the carpet.

"So, you done got yourself arrested for a gun, huh? You got a court date for next week and it's a possibility they gone lock your dumb ass up." Ilena took another sip of the brown, comforting potion before she lit a Newport. "Byron, you really think I'ma keep going through this bullshit with you? You out here running with them gang-bangas and I'm at work, bustin' my ass to make sure I keep a roof over your head, the lights on and food in the fridge for you to eat. You don't pay for shit; you don't help not one bit. But let me tell you somethin', you make your bed hard, you gone lay in it; you hear me boy?" Ilena's words were slurring by the minute from the effects of the alcohol, nevertheless, speaking what was the truth. "What kind of man are you? Don't tell me you a spineless coward like your father."

Byron continued to watch as the roach made its way behind the TV. With a weak attempt he said, "Ma, I was gone to tell you."

"Shut the fuck up and stop lying; you wasn't gone tell me shit. You just like your lying ass father. This your last time, Byron. You got one more time and your ass outta here; outta my fuckin' house; you hear me! I'm sick and tired of this shit! You wanna think you a man, be a man and bring some groceries in this muthafucka since you in the streets. If you gone be in the streets, at least get some money. Otherwise, you in the fuckin' way!" Ilena stood up and staggered toward Byron. "Now I'ma go to court with you. You better hope they don't lock your ass up, but remember, this is your last damn time. Next time you on your own like Patti LaBelle; you hear me!" Ilena walked past Byron, heading to her room, leaving a stale scent of cigarette smoke and Byron pondering in his thoughts.

S. Allen

Chapter 5

Byron and his mother sat in the crowded corridor of the bustling courthouse on 11th and Hamilton in Calendar 57, waiting to see the honorable Judge Kelly. Nervous and shaking like a leaf in the tree, Byron didn't know what to expect being that this was his first run-in. Intensifying the situation, Ilena hadn't spoken a word to her son on the bus ride to the court building. She was mad at the fact that she had to take a day off work, and the thought of her racist boss docking her paycheck made her indeed pissed.

After sitting in limbo over two hours, Byron's name was finally called for his day in court. "Byron Hobson?" The court deputy yelled looking out in the crowd who were seated, standing and conversing in the chaotic hallway.

Byron and Ilena walked through the heavy doors of the courtroom with Byron approaching the defendant's table to stand before the Honorable Judge Kelly. Judge Kelly, known to others outside the court room as Edith, was an early 50-year-old, pale skin, petite, blonde-haired woman who stood without heels at 5'7", weighing 115 lbs. To be petite, her body was toned from her commitment to workout, swim laps every morning before breakfast in her indoor pool, along with her rigorous appetite for sex, especially her closet endeavor of being intimate with young African Americans. Well, as Byron stood before her, Judge Kelly took her specs from her forehead, placed them on the bridge of her nose, overlooked Byron up and down, assessing the specimen before her very eyes, all the while naughty thoughts emerging causing her to make a mess on herself, wetting her dress, robe and creating a smear on the leather chair she sat in with no panties on. Forcing herself to shake the thoughts and get on, she began, "We are here today presiding in this case, the state of Illinois versus Byron Hobson. It is deemed that Mr. Hobson was apprehended with an illegal firearm— a one 9-millimeter Beretta, serial number V-five, one, six, three, zero, nine, two— is that correct?"

"Yes, ma'am, Mr. Hobson is charged with that felony." The prosecutor, a ruddy-faced, bad breath, built like a sack of mash potatoes, Assistant District Attorney Robert Landrieu confirmed.

"And what does Mr. Hobson plea before this court?" Judge Kelly inquired.

Byron, standing there completely dumbfounded, did not know what to say, until his court-appointed lawyer, Mr. Joseph Lewis III, whispered in his ear, "Not guilty, son. You respond not guilty."

"Not guilty, ma'am," Byron stammered.

"So, the defendant pleads not guilty. The state will call for its first witness at this time, an Officer Michael Calhoun?"

"Your honor, with all due respect, the state is asking for a continuance being that Mr. Calhoun was not able to make this court appearance today. He canceled at the last minute, literally, with me just being informed like five minutes ago," the sack of shit, A.D.A Landrieu stated.

"So, you mean to tell me the arresting Officer is not present? Does the state have any other witnesses?"

"No, ma'am," Landrieu uttered.

"With no witnesses to this allegation there is no case. I will not reschedule this matter due to the irresponsible acts of the Chicago Police Department. My docket is overflowing as it is, and I will not subject myself or this young man to be placed in a game of ring-around-the-rosy. Therefore, I am dropping the charges. Mr. Hobson, consider this your lucky day. My advice to you is to change the crowd of people that you hang with, the places you choose to hang and the activities you are indulging in, that way you won't have to possess a gun. Mr. Hobson, you are eighteen years old, no other abrasions with the judicial system is found in your record, so I declare to you to get your life together and do something positive. Since you seem to have a thing for weaponry, maybe you should enlist into the military— the Army, Marines— that way you can gain full knowledge of dealing with weapons along with learning some intensity and self-worth. But before you leave, I stress to you right now, if I see you in this courtroom again, Mr. Hobson, I will send you to the Department of Corrections so fast you will think that I was driving the bus myself! Do you understand me? This case is dismissed with prejudice due to the lack of witnesses. Good luck,

Mr. Hobson." Judge Kelly stated while also blowing a slight breath of air as Byron turned to walk away.

Later that night, Byron stood on the corner of Avers and Augusta accompanied by Lil' Pooh, his road-dog and right-hand man. He paged Billy Good and told him that all was well, that *he had his money*. Billy Good responded that Junior would swing through and scoop him. Being that he wanted to see him personally, he sent Rico to pick-up his young'n.

As he and Lil' Pooh were kickin' it, his right-hand man asked, "So, you think he gone let you cop some work for yourself or he just gone give you some more Nation work?"

"I don't know, Lil' Pooh. I don't see why not being that he getting all his money in three days. With that, he gotta recognize the potential of our program; feel me! Furthermore, a closed mouth don't get fed, so it's only one way to find out." Byron replied, hoping that his confidence didn't lead him wrong.

"Yeah, you right, Joe. I feel you. the more work, the more money." Lil' Pooh nodded with a smile plastered on his face.

"Where that nigga Funk at?" Byron asked.

"I don't know. I seen him earlier with the nigga Meathead from across the avenue. They rolled through looking high as hell." Lil' Pooh answered.

"Oh yeah? That nigga sure know how to get around, with many friends. You know what I'm sayin', Lord." Byron stated knowing that Funk was untrustworthy and needed two sets of eyes on him at all times.

"You know Funk extra, Lord. You can't add nothing to him and you can't take nothing from him." Lil' Pooh admonished as an attempt to cease the fire that was slow-cooking the beef between Byron and Funk.

Just as Lil' Pooh finished speaking, Rico's S55AMG pulled over to the curb in front of the duo with the sounds of Crucial Conflict bumping through the Alpine surround sound stereo system.

"Aye, check it out, Lord. Let me get up with you later. I'ma go handle this business so we can get back to the money. Hold it down, Lord. Almighty!" Byron stated as he shook up with Lil' Pooh before grabbing the door handle of the whip.

"You already know, Lord. Almighty!" Lil' Pooh retorted as he let his hand rest on the butt of his new Glock 31, .45 caliber equipped with night-sights and laser-beam that was tucked inside his Girbaud jeans as Byron was just hopping in the whip.

"What's good, Lord?" Rico greeted as he slid back into traffic.

"Ain't shit, Lord. Another day, another dollar." Byron responded as he bobbed his head to the tunes.

"So, you mean you got the count right then?" Rico probed in regards to that scrilla.

"Yeah, most definitely! I wouldn't have called the Chief if I didn't have that paper right." Byron retorted.

"Don't get slick, shorty! Don't let them stars go to your head, nigga, you still got a lot of learning to do. I didn't get my status from being a lookout, I got mines from sending cats to the cemetery!" Rico stated just as smooth as the ride of the luxury vehicle they were cruising in.

Byron sat quietly the rest of the ride. He knew not to challenge Rico as Rico was a certified head-bussa. However, he was consumed with his own thoughts of how his name would ring in the near future throughout the streets of the Chi and within the Mafia Organization.

An hour later they arrived in Noperville, Illinois, a quiet suburban area south of Chicago. The neighborhood Billy Good lived in was a gated community stocked with homes starting at the range of $500,000.00. As they rode up the street where the Chief's abode resided, Byron couldn't help but admire the numerous exquisite homes that graced the community of the Chief, as if it was simply fit for a king. Pulling in the driveway of an immaculate designed mansion, Byron immediately recognized the cocaine-white S600 accompanied by a candy-apple red Corvette.

"You got any heat on you, shorty?" Rico inquired as he placed his own hammer, a Glock 22, .40 caliber within his waistline before exiting the ride.

"Nah, fam, all I got is stacks in rubber bands on me." Byron slickly replied.

"Man, get your smart-ass mouth outta my whip." Rico said, yet smiling as well at the comeback of the youngsta.

After Rico rang the doorbell five times in a quick succession, the heavy oakwood door was unbolted and there stood the Chief, live in the flesh, wearing a velour Gucci sweatshirt with some Gucci sneakers. "Come on in, Lord. Welcome to my home. I been expecting y'all." Billy Good asserted.

Byron stepped in the entrance way, shook hands with the boss the Mafia's way, looking around and completely astonished as his eyes were greeted with complete lavishness. In a sense, it was as if he was inside a museum.

"You looking like you see something you like, Lord." Billy Good shot as he proceeded to his well-stocked bar.

"Man, Lord, your shit tight! I wish I could live like this." Byron avowed.

"Keep your loyalty to this Nation, continue with your production and in due time you will live like this. Now, with that, you standing in my crib like you don't owe me some money." Billy Good spoke with a smirk as he poured three shots of Remy Martin XO, handing a shot each to Byron and Rico.

Byron placed his drink down on the bar counter, reached into the front pockets of his denim blue Girbaud jeans and retrieved the stacks of money. $4,500.00 in each pocket, handed it to Billy Good and smiled.

Billy Good received the cash, thumbed through the $100's, $50's and $20's, then asked Byron, "Do I need to count this?"

"No, sir. It's all there, Lord. Every dime. Not one short." Byron asserted feeling warm from the effects of the cognac he downed in one quick motion after handing the money to the Chief.

"You hear that, Rico? Every. Dime. Not. One. *Short!*" Billy Good was cheesing like he was campaigning to be the mascot of the Cheetos Brand.

Rico stood there stroking his goatee, staring Byron up and down, holding in his admiration of the youngsta.

"Calm down, Rico, Byron here good people. Our future." Billy Good declared while pouring another shot into Byron's empty glass, adding, "Matter of fact, let's make a toast. A toast to money, power and to the Mafia's. Almighty!"

"Almighty!" Byron and Rico averred before they all tossed the liquor down their throats, creating a warmness throughout.

After two shots of Remy XO, Byron's nerves were easing and he decided it was now or never when he asked, "Lord, I was wondering when you give me that next demo, can I grab some extra for myself?"

Billy Good slammed his shot glass down, eyed Byron for a moment, then asked, "You got extra money?"

Byron, knowing where things were heading due to the Chief slamming his glass down, swallowed and answered, "Yeah, Lord. I got ten thousand cold cash." He reached in each of his back packets pulling $5,000.00 out of each, placing the stacks on the bar and attentively looking at the Chief.

Billy Good diminished Byron's uneasiness when he began to smile, nodding in the affirmative, admiring the vigor of the young hustla. Turning his attention to Rico, Billy Good instructed him, "Go get Lord a whole thing. A *kilo,*" Billy Good said, eyeing Byron with bloodshot eyes, resembling the devil himself, as Rico walked off to get the work. In that moment, as it was just them two, Billy Good avowed, "Byron, I must say I'm proud of you, but it seems not fitting because it's actually an understatement. From the first time I actually met and spoke with you, it was like I, me, speaking to my younger self. The manner you conduct your function displays the leader within you, however, remember, the more money, the more problems, and the more you gotta watch your back, front and sides. Keep your circle small, always know to never let your right hand know what you left hand is thinking, because everything ain't for everybody, because it's a dog eat dog world! You understand me?"

"Yes, sir," was Byron's response as he absorbed the jewels of the game fed to him by a ring.

Rico returned with a brick in a Louis Vuitton handbag, handed it to Byron, then for a slight moment, allowed the hardened demeanor of his bearing to crack a smile as Byron grabbed the bag as they locked eyes.

Billy Good commenced to relaying the order of business to his young'n. "Now, that's a whole thing. You owe me eighteen thousand dollars for the two quarters. The other half is yours for the ten thousand. Remember what I said about your circle. Handle your business, Lord, and don't let your business handle you, okay? Aight, with that, it's now time that I go tend to my wife, so holla at me when you're done."

"Alright, Lord, I will see you real soon." Byron replied, for surely psyched at the development of the situation.

"That's what I like to hear. Almighty!" Billy Good stated.

"Almighty!" Byron and Rico saluted in return as they headed toward the front door.

Later that night, Byron sat in his basement breaking down the brick into single ounces, while his mother was upstairs asleep because she had to be at work at 5:30AM. After the completion of bagging and weighing each ounce, Byron proceeded by chopping and bagging six ounces for preparation of his own workday which would begin not long after his mother's. While in the midst of the task, Byron reflected upon the words shared by Billy Good in regards to keeping his circle small, planting his hands close to his chest, and how the more money you made, the more problems that seemed to surface.

Byron had managed to achieve copping a half of a thing along with calculating a sum of $30,000 that would be grossed off the Nation work he would issue, he envisioned himself just as the NASA spacecraft dubbed Discovery, because he was most definitely on his way to discover new heights and the sky was the limit. After the workers were paid, $20,000 would be left among him, Lil' Pooh and Funk to split, as well as they had more loot to rake in from the distributing of the half of brick that was all theirs. Thoughts of financial success flooded his mind non-stop as Byron placed the razor atop the slab to cut pieces. Byron's dream was to be the biggest drug dealer the city of Chicago would ever witness.

Once finished and cleaned up, he ascended the stairs to check on his mother, when his thoughts flipped to the statement his mother spat at him— how he wasn't a man and would be just like his father. Byron shook his head in a negative motion, vowing inwardly to never succumb to sucker status. He knew he was nothing like his father; he would never run off and leave her. He loved his mother and they were all each other had. With that thought, Byron retrieved a few $100's from his stash spot in hopes of showing his mother that he was becoming a man. After the day began and all were in position with the show flowing steadily, he would go make groceries fill the fridge and the cupboards, and hopefully the void in his mother's happiness.

As the day began and the traffic flowed, even in the blistering 30 degrees below 0 weather of the Chi, Byron caught the city bus to Dominick's Grocery Store. He had never been grocery shopping by himself. He knew nothing about checking prices, or which brands to get. He solved it with just throwing whatever he wanted in the cart, no concern at all in regards to the cost. While browsing and retrieving a box of CoCo Pebbles in the cereal aisle, somebody accidentally bumped into his cart with theirs, startling him completely.

"Oh, excuse me. I wasn't even looking."

Byron looked up to view just who it was that spoke so soft, yet, was recklessly driving. "It's all good, ma," Byron stated, mesmerized by her natural beauty.

She was a light-skinned younger version of Clair Huxtable from the Cosby Show, standing at just 5'5", body of a track-star, hairdo a bob like Nia Long in Boyz-N-The- Hood, pearly white teeth, and dressed nicely in the winter blizzard wearing a multi-colored, dark blue, pink, sky blue and white Liz Clarborne turtleneck, a pair of denim Guess jeans, on her small feet were a pair of three-quarter dark blue Gucci boots, topped off with a dark blue Chanel Peacoat. An intoxicating scent of Mariah Careys *Diva* perfume wafted toward Byron's nostrils causing him to gulp so hard it appeared as if he had swallowed his tongue; he was so awestruck.

However, he shook the jitters and bounced back stating, "My name is Byron. What's yours, Miss I Can't Drive," all the while smiling, looking her in her eyes, trying to sound cool.

The female laughed at his dry approach before she responded, "My name Carmella, and if your cart wasn't on my way it wouldn't have gotten hit," placing her hand on her thick hip, rolling her neck in a sassy manner, all the while faking much attitude.

"Well, I'm glad that I got hit. By you."

"Is that so, and why is that?"

"Because if you wouldn't have hit my cart, I wouldn't have met my future baby mamma."

"Boy, please. How you know I don't already got a baby daddy?" Carmella, not able to contain herself, started smiling, actually busting herself.

"Because if you did you wouldn't be tryin' to bump into niggas' carts in aisles so you could flirt." He loved the cat and mouse flirting he was having with Carmella.

Carmella let out a small chuckle, then smacked her lips. "Listen to you, now you Dr. Phil, huh?"

Byron had to smile at her witty remark before he spoke. "Listen, Ms. Carmella, on some real shit, I'm liking what's before my eyes. I just want to know if you're single and if so, how could a brother get to know you a lil' better and enjoy the image of your beauty more?"

"Well, since you so blunt, Mr. Byron, yes, I'm single. I'm also liking what I'm seeing, and if you want to get to know me better you gotta play your cards right, playa." Carmella replied, still trying to keep up her front.

Byron and Carmella chatted a few more minutes before Carmella ended up giving Byron her number as they planned on spending some time together real soon to get acquainted. Byron left Dominick's Grocery Store with bags full of groceries, as well as his tank of joy, as he stood in the blizzard waiting on the Kedzie bus. In spite of being out in the cold, Byron was warm and happy, and things were starting to turn around more and more for the better for young Byron, so he thought.

S. Allen

Chapter 6

Byron stood on the block with the Mafia's, watching his block rotate, everything moving smoothly, money coming from all directions because he had made the size of the rocks bigger than he had the last time and the fiends were in a frenzy, loving every hit of it.

"How many packs we done ran through today?" he asked Lil' Pooh who was smoking a Backwood filled with Blueberry Kush.

"I don't know exactly." Lil' Pooh hunched his shoulders.

"Lord, that's your job. To make sure every bag is accounted for. This shit is serious, Lil' Pooh. This is an enterprise, my nigga. Tighten up, Lord."

"Yeah, you right, Lord. I'ma go do inventory right now. One of the workers need another pack anyway." Lil' Pooh said placing the blunt behind his ear as he turned to walk off.

"That's what's up, Joe. Just make sure shit right, and when Funk come through tell 'em don't leave the block. I gotta holla at y'all. I'ma run in the crib for a minute, okay?" Byron stated before proceeding to his house.

"Alight, Lord, that's a bet. we'll be out here." Lil' Pooh assured as he began to continue with his task.

When Byron walked through the front door he was greeted with the smell of fried chicken. After he took off his First Down parka, he walked into the kitchen to see his mother at the stove cooking and singing along with Chaka Khan which she had playing on the stereo before she commanded him, "Go wash your hands and come to the table." Ilena focused on her doing, never turned around as Byron had entered the kitchen, but knew it could be no one else entering her home, as she lifted a piece of chicken out of the grease.

Byron did as he was told and sat at the kitchen table awaiting to devour the meal his mother had prepared. Ilena loaded his plate with two big breast of fried chicken, macaroni and cheese, and three biscuits. It had been a very long time since Byron saw his mother at the stove, and in a good spirit. Ilena placed Byron's plate before him. The heat from the food slapped him in the face, and his stomach did somersaults as it anticipated being filled with the delicious presentation. Ilena fixed her own plate then took her seat across from her son. Byron could tell that his mother was sober and her attitude was peaceful, and all he could do was mouth the words *thank you* under his breath, because he didn't like being at odds with the woman who birthed him.

They commenced eating their meal in complete silence for like five minutes. The only sounds were heard was the scraping of the fork against the plate, and the slight smacking being committed by both. But just as the old saying goes, all good things must come to an end. that's indeed what happened.

Ilena broke the peacefulness when she inquisitively interjected. "I want to thank you for going grocery shopping for us. You bought a lot of stuff I see. Look like you spent about three hundred dollars?" She eyed Byron while she inserted a forkful of macaroni and cheese into her mouth, waiting for a response, yet Byron remained silent. After swallowing the forkful and not receiving any feedback from her son, she continued, "Where you get the money to go grocery shopping?"

Byron continued to devour the last of the mac-and-cheese that was left on his plate, along with the half of biscuit and slab of white meat, really not wanting to disrespect his mother. However, not wanting to squabble either.

"So, you gone answer me when I'm talking to you, Byron?" Ilena's voice raising, eyebrows arching, holding the fork erectly, stabbing into the biscuit on her plate. "Where did you get the money to buy all this food?"

Finally, knowing that it was no way around not addressing the matter with his mother, Byron uttered, "I busted a move, ma, that's all."

"So, you busted a move, huh? What kind of move, Byron?" Ilena questioned, mimicking her son's talk and voice.

Byron, agitated from his mother's interrogation, spoke, "Ma, you said to start helping out around here, right? That's what being a man is, right? Well, ma, I am a man and that's what I'm tryin' to do; help out around here! Why does it matter how I do it?"

Ilena,fed up and not liking the reproach of her son, pushed her plate forward and eyed her son menacingly as she insinuated, "Oh, I get it. This supposed to be your justification for selling drugs, huh? You come and bring in a coupla hundred dollars' worth of groceries and I'm supposed to be happy and kiss your ass like you high and almighty. Well, let me tell you somethin', if you got these groceries with drug money, then you can throw all this shit in the garbage for all I care! I would rather us starve to death than for you to be out there risking your life in them streets. Taking a risk of somebody taking you away from me! You all I have, but no, you don't care. All you care about is yourself. Act like you can't go out and get a job like everybody else and work for your money."

"Mama, don't nobody want to hire me. I have handed in plenty applications, but no one has called me back. I'm not gonna just sit around and starve, mama!" Byron retorted as he stood to empty the remnants of his meal and place the plate in the sink.

"Boy, you're eighteen years old and you the one dropped outta school. You may think that jobs are gonna just come knockin' your door down, but newsflash, they're not. You're sadly mistaken! What you need to do is find you somethin' better than what you're doing. Maybe what that Judge suggested. Enlist into the military. You'll probably learn some skills that will help you in life, because like I told you before, you got one more time to fuck up and you'll be finding yourself somewhere else to lay your head!" Ilena stated sternly.

"Alright, ma, you got that," Byron said as he proceeded to put his Carhartt parka on.

"So, where you goin' now? Back on the block to sell your drugs? Byron, I hope you know I'm serious. One more time and it's over; you got that?" Ilena asserted, standing out of her seat, heading to the trash can to dump her plate of food that she picked over, disgusted with her only child, in a dire need of a Newport and some E&J.

Byron zipped his coat and slid out the door into the grimy streets of the Westside to get up with Lil' Pooh and Funk to handle some Nation business as his mother went to retrieve her half pint to drink her pain away.

Sitting in Lil' Pooh's room, Byron, Lil' Pooh and Funk tended to the task at hand. Byron had given Lil' Pooh and Funk two-half ounces each off the half of brick he had purchased from Billy Good. Funk, admiring the chunk of cocaine resting in his palms then placed his gaze on Byron and asked, "So what's this for?"

"Listen, the packs for the runners as y'all know are already made up and ready for distribution. As of now, we only got three ounces left of Nation work. The work I just gave y'all is off the half of key I copped with our money. We got a half of a brick for our ten grand. Off the two and a half ounces I just gave y'all, y'all should come up with like five thousand, four hundred dollars. Bring back two grand and y'all pocket the rest. I suggest y'all keep a few dollars put up."

"You acting like that's a lot of paper. What a muthafucka able to spend and do since you suggest to put something up, my nigga? Whatever happened to the twenty stacks a brother was supposed to be getting?" Funk menacingly insinuated as he fired up a White Owl filled with strawberry Kush.

"Aye, Lord, you know somethin'? You always got somethin' to complain about. You the head of my security so you gonna eat regardless, as long as you handling your function. You could be a pack runner and not really making shit, so if I was you, I would be content with the position; you feel me!" Byron slung his line of bait out there, tryin' to see what he'll catch.

Funk, blood boiling beyond 250-degrees Fahrenheit, couldn't stomach the way Byron was handling him in front Lil' Pooh, as if he was the Chief, but he knew he couldn't respond like he used to with aggression because of the status Byron now held. So, Funk decided to keep his temper in check and his contempt to himself. With Byron's status, Funk wasn't ready to be violated or even worse— removed from life totally for his disrespect— so he would just have to harbor his feelings. As much as he hated to, Funk retorted, "Yeah, you right, Big Homie. I was just trying to see what was the deal with the cash. It's Almighty though, Joe." Funk hit the blunt once more then passed it to Byron.

"Now, the Chief is feeling how we got the block pumpin'. We bringing in the cash even faster than when Rico had the block. We keep moving like how we moving, it will be no limit to how much work he will give us. We just gotta weather the storm and grind every pebble around this bitch. After the storm, the sun shall shine bright, so just hold on." Byron iterated as he stared Funk in his eyes. Byron wanted his crew to have the morale and motivation to get the money up, and he wanted it to be crystal clear that that was the reason they were in this—for the money.

After Byron finished conducting his business with Lil' Pooh and Funk, he hopped on the Pulaski bus. He had talked with Carmella on the phone earlier and they made plans to meet up downtown at the Navy Pier. He had a few $100's in his pocket and figured he would show Carmella a good time. After conversing with her earlier, Byron learned that Carmella was a senior at Marshall High, and she was an only child just as himself. And like when he attended school, she excelled in her academics. She had plans of attending Illinois State after graduating, which definitely told him that she was a sister with goals and ambition. Byron was in total bliss as he thought about the beautiful Carmella when his thoughts were rudely interrupted with the boarding of three thugs onto the bus at Chicago Avenue.

They were loud and boisterous as they made their way to the back of the bus where he was seated. One of them mean-mugged him then whispered something into his potna's ear, thus causing his potna to place his focus upon Byron with a disrespectful and disdainful look plastered upon his face. Byron being Chicago-born was unfazed because he knew the streets of the city like he knew the color of his skin. Chicago was gangland to the youngstas, and for most young black men in the Chi, the gangster mentality ran through their bloodstreams like venom. Sensing the tension, Byron nonchalantly raised the bottom of his Carhartt, revealing the butt of the Ruger P-89 that rested on his hip. The unarmed thugs, learning that Byron was strapped with the deadly tool, done a very quick assessment of things and decided it was best to exit the bus at the next stop.

Pussies, Byron thought, glad at the same time that they didn't want no smoke because he would've sparked their asses up like a blunt of Kush. Three more buses and two trains later, Byron was walking up to the Navy Pier which sat on the side of the frozen Lake Michigan. Carmella told Byron to meet her at the arcades. Once he entered the Navy Pier, he headed straight to his destination with butterflies fluttering within his stomach at the mere thought of being in close proximity of the beautiful Carmella.

The arcade was huge, and it was packed almost to capacity with a stew of teenagers and others in their early 20's. Afterall, it was a Friday night. Byron walked around, passing the throngs of others, some challenging their mates on the various gaming machines while some were merely chit-chatting. He hadn't been to the Navy Pier in over two years. The call of duty of the Mafia had not permitted him time for such condiments. Byron identified numerous new games that were out now. He couldn't wait to play them. But first thing first, he was on a mission, or rather a date, so once he spotted Carmella after about 10 minutes of roaming through the massive crowd of the arcade, the butterflies ceased and his game face appeared as he walked up on her from the rear, admiring her derriere and her curvaceous shape as she was engrossed into the game of Mortal Kombat.

"Damn, kick, kick, kick," Carmella yelled as she tapped repeatedly on the buttons.

"Look like to me somebody getting they ass whipped." Byron snidely remarked as he approached her.

Carmella was about to turn around and snap on the wisecracker until she saw that it was Byron. She rolled her eyes and smacked her lips, then retorted, "I bet if you get on, I'll whoop your ass." Immediately she turned her attention back to her game, all the while allowing a smile to spread across her luscious lips that were shining like potent leather from her application of MAC strawberry lip gloss.

Byron, digging the cat-and-mouse challenge, simply stated, "What you wanna bet, shorty," as he dug in his pocket to retrieve a quarter.

"Make it light on yourself, playa, and stop calling me shorty!" Carmella stated as she poked her lips.

All Byron was able to say was, "You got that..." allowing a pause to think of what the wager would be. He continued, "I tell you what. If I win, you gotta give me a kiss with those pretty ass lips."

Instantaneously Carmella asserted, "And, if you lose, which you are, you gotta take me to Ryan's Steakhouse. Bet?"

Byron, being game for anything involving her, simply stated, "Bet, lil' mama," as he inserted his quarter into the game system.

He chose Sub Zero and Carmella selected Scorpion, and just like that the battle engaged with great intensity. Both were trying their hardest not to lose the bet, but more so the game for bragging rights. Carmella was no slouch, she was good, but Byron was better due to him and Lil' Pooh always battling it out on Lil' Pooh's Nintendo system.

Byron ended up beating Carmella and she immediately insinuated, "You cheated!"

All he could do was laugh because that was always the remark from the loser, so to rub it in more he merely said, "I didn't cheat, I just whooped your pretty, round ass black and blue!" all while chuckling and showing all thirty two.

"Whatever, boy! Anyway, what's up?" Carmella inquired looking intently into Byron's eyes. As she stared at him she allowed various thoughts to roam through her head, as she indeed found Byron to be attractive in a manly way, yet he possessed a hardened face and without a shadow of a doubt a thuggish swagger, which in turn was a double entendre, thus creating severe moistness in her pelvic area.

Allowing and liking the stare down himself, Byron let a moment of silence remain before he replied, "What you mean what's up? What's up with my kiss?" He beamed, poking his chest out while beating on it.

Carmella simply teased and stated, "Well, if you gotta ask about it, then I guess you don't want it, and I don't owe you, cheater."

Byron, not able to contain the lustful demon within, promptly swooped in like a hawk, grabbed her by her waist, pulled her close and kissed her lips. The strawberry taste was so sweet and intoxicating to the extent he was simply savoring it, but his heat index rose as Carmella inserted her strawberry tasting tongue into his mouth and explored the realms of his game-spitter, causing Byron to achieve an erection that appeared as if he had a model of the Sear's Tower stuck in his Girbaud jeans.

Seeing that they were getting caught up in the moment, Carmella lightly pushed away and said, "Uh-uh, we better chill before you hurt yourself."

But just as Byron displayed an erection, she too had her own. Through the material of her shirt, he was greeted with two protruding knobs, which she noticed him staring and immediately slapped him on the arm and crossed her arms over her chest.

Byron, knowing she was feeling it just as him, asked, "What you mean uh-uh? And I'ma hurt myself? Nah, lil' mama. If anything, the pain and pleasure would be all yours."

"Boy, uh-uh, you too much!" Carmella beamed at Byron's statement.

"Oh yeah? So, I've been told. But, let's get outta here, I'm kinda hungry." Byron declared.

"Where we going?" Carmella inquired.

"I'm taking my future wife to Ryan's Steakhouse, per her request!" Byron responded.

"Your future wife, huh?" Carmella responded with her hand on her hip.

"Yeah, you heard me correctly. Now, let's get outta here, future wifey," Byron stated while grabbing for her hand as if they were walking down the aisle.

Chapter 7

Byron and Carmella sat in the back of the dimly lit Ryan's Steakhouse in Downtown Chicago, each caught-up in one another's bliss and replaying the events which led up to the present. The waiter had brought their food and the two indulged in the best food Chicago had to offer.

Carmella meticulously chewed her food, savoring the zest of her steak Parabola as it danced on her taste buds, looked Byron in the eyes and averred, "Thank you for bringing me here, even though I lost, cheater," she teased but continued, "I been wanting to come here ever since I was a kid. My momma's pimp boyfriend used to always bring her here and she would brag about it to me."

Byron raised his head from his plate of chicken fettuccini, taken aback from the statement and the openness. He asked with concern, "Your momma had a pimp?"

"Yeah, a few years back. His name was Magic. He used to have my momma on the stroll of Chicago Avenue and Pulaski. But he took real good care of my momma and me."

"Whatever happened to Magic?" Byron pried, yet also took notice into her change of demeanor.

"He got murdered by another so-called pimp over a dice game."

"That's fucked up! You and your mom's cool?"

"Yeah, she straight. She needed to be freed from him anyway..." She paused so she could gain control of her emotions, then continued, "He used... to beat her a lot. So, in a way everything turned out for the better. Anyhow, what about your family? Your family doing good?"

"My pops left me and my mom's when I was like five years old. He was out there bad on them drugs. My mom's been fending for us ever since."

"That's messed up. It seems like y'all straight. I mean, you got money to spend at Ryan's Steakhouse on me, so what you do for money?"

Before responding Byron took a forkful of his fettuccini to appease his hunger for the food, and after swallowing he meekly replied, "Carmella, I do whatever I gotta do to survive."

Carmella loving the thug appeal, looked him in his eyes and strikingly leaned over and kissed the fettuccini sauce off his lips, and then teasingly licked her lips and smiled.

Back at Byron's home, Ilena had just finished her bottle of E&J as she sat on the couch staring at the blank TV, lost in the thoughts of her only son out selling drugs. She was completely vexed and couldn't understand why he wanted to throw away his promising life to the bowels of the streets that possessed no love. He was smart, young and healthy, and could get a job like every other regular, working class type, instead of wasting his time hanging with friends in the streets. She wanted him to be different from his environment. She wanted more than the penitentiary or gravesite, either one most likely caused by the so-called friends. The same one that would either testify against him, or shoot him in the back of the head in an alley. The mere thought of that unwantedness caused her nerves to jerk, pressuring her to reach for her pack of Newport longs off the living room table and chain-smoke two, quickly.

"Shit!" Ilena cursed out loud as she just realized she had smoked her last two cigarettes and would have to go out in the freezing night's air. She dreaded the walk to the corner store, but she couldn't do without her Newport's. she needed a fresh pack to soothe her nerves, to help her relax.

Walking into Byron's room to retrieve one of his hoodies to use to protect her form the biting cold, Ilena immediately took offense to how junky his room was and made a mental note to check him about such. The E&J doing its job had her to stagger a bit toward his closet amid the clutter on the floor, and she grabbed a black Nike hoodie off the hanger. Struggling slightly to pull the thick sweatshirt over her head, she was greeted with a loud thud from something landing on the floor. Obviously, in the midst of her struggle, out of the pocket of the hoodie fell a plastic ziploc bag that contained a hard, white substance. She gasped, then a look of curiosity and confusion became plastered upon her face as she bent over to pick up the bag. Examining the contents in her possession, it felt as if her heart had stopped.

Ilena never used drugs or was ever in the company of such, but was no damn fool. She knew she was holding some form of narcotic. Instantly, her emotions entangled with the effects of the brown liquor she had consumed and caused a tear to fall from her eye. She couldn't believe after all the preaching she'd done, Byron would betray her trust and bring drugs inside her home. The anger she harbored from her husband leaving her to raise a child by herself, the minimum wage pay she was receiving for slaving over 40 hours a week, and now her beloved son having drugs in her house was the tipping of the iceberg.

Too much to bear, Ilena's anger reached her apex, causing her to breakdown and sob unwillingly. She knew it would hurt her heart and soul to kick her only child out of her home, relinquishing Byron to the deadly streets of the Westside, but the stress he was inflicting upon her, she couldn't endure. Tonight would be the last night her one and only child would reside in her home. The last straw had been drawn.

"So, did you enjoy yourself, Ms. Carmella?" Byron asked as they snuggled on the back of the bus, headed down California Avenue. They finished their dinner at Ryan's and walked around the streets of downtown Chicago, hand in hand, conversing and sight-seeing. Oblivious to the harsh weather, even stopping at a small doughnut shop for hot-chocolate and eclairs, Byron and Carmella shared mutual feelings– the enjoyment of each other's company.

"Of course, I enjoyed myself!" Carmella avowed, basking in the comfort of her knight. She proceeded by insinuating, "I think I can get usesd to going out for steak dinners, fine dining, then strolling around in below zero weather with my man!"

"Oh, so now I'm your man, huh? Shorty, don't say shit you don't mean."

"I don't say things unless I mean it, and I'm not gonna tell you no more about calling me shorty." Carmella replied with much fake attitude.

Knowing she was fronting, Byron allowed with pleasure as he turned on his Casanova and simply stated, "Well, show me you ain't no shorty then," before he leaned over and kissed her soft lips, then doing his rendition of Mint Condition's *Pretty Brown Eyes*.

Carmella beamed at his charisma, but also assured him, "I will show you, Mr. Byron, in due time. Let's just take it slow," while striving to contain herself from his swift move of passion.

The California bus stopped at Sacramento which was Carmella's stop.

"You sure you don't want me to walk you home?"

"Baby, I'm cool. I stay right there on the corner in the two-tone brown house. You would have to wait in the cold for another twenty minutes."

They embraced and kissed again before she walked toward the door to exit.

"Call me when you get home, Byron," she said as she waved bye to him.

Byron intently watched as she exited, love-struck like he had just been hit with 5 arrows from Cupid. He liked everything about Carmella, and he couldn't wait til he saw her again, which would be real soon.

Byron got off the bus on Augsta and began his trek toward his house. His thoughts were consumed with nothing but Carmella. The softness of her lips, her smell, her body, as well as her intellect and her ambition. His thoughts of his future wife were broken as he eyed the police cruiser heading his way. He instinctively reached for the butt of his Ruger. Back in the trenches automatically called for Gangsta Mode, making a vow to himself after that night of being assaulted by that detective. He declared that he would *never* let handcuffs touch, let alone lock, onto his wrists ever again. If they had plans on stopping him, it would be disrupted with his own. It was dark and quiet. He would bang-out with the pigs, get away and make it to safety.

As the cruiser got nearer, he gripped the burner tighter. The pale, pock-face officer slowed down a bit and looked in Byron's direction. Byron's palms were sweating, butterflies fluttering. Then, as if in the military, it was at ease solider. The cop kept going down Augusta. Exhaling a deep breath and allowing his nerves to relax, Byron picked his pace up to make it inside before any other encounter, glad he didn't have to handle his function on the pig.

Turning on Avers and Augsta he saw that his block was dead quiet. No activity whatsoever. The windchill was so cold even the crackheads and jack-boys decided to stay in. The prostitutes that normally roamed the hood had found shelter for the night. It was late when he walked up the steps to his house. Noticing the lights on in the front room, Byron wondered why his mother was still up.

As he turned the key in the lock mechanism and entered, he was greeted with his mother sitting on the couch. Closing the door and locking it, he approached her. As he got near, he noticed that her eyes were red and appeared swollen. Looking more intently, he couldn't believe what rested on her lap. The last ounce of work. Instantly, it was as if he had contracted salmonella. His stomach begun to bubble and seemed like his bowels were about to just release as if he had diarrhea. The questions began to bombard his mind. *Why was his mother holding his drugs, the mafia's drugs? When did she get them? How did it happen? And, why would she go snooping in his room?* From the look on his mother's face, he knew it was over. It would be no amending this wrong, in no form or fashion.

Without facing her son, Ilena swallowed hard and stated, "I don't want to know why you brought these drugs into our home. I don't care who drugs they are. I have done nothing but try and provide for you. Working all them damn hours so you can have a roof over your head. I have provided for you by my-fucking-self since you were five years old. But you wanna live your life how you want. You wanna be a man, you think, and be a drug dealer, gangbanger? You are eighteen years old and you can do as you please. But one thing for sure, you will not do it in my house."

Byron stayed facing the floor, embarrassed, ashamed and perplexed all at the same time.

"Byron, I have done all I can for you. You will not lay your head in my home another night." The tears streamed down Ilena's cheeks. "How could you do this? How could you do this to me, to us?" Ilena screamed as if she was possessed with some Satanic power. She rose off the couch, ran toward Byron and began striking him with the plastic bag filled with drugs.

All he could do was take it like a man. In a weak attempt, he tried to console his mother. Didn't work not one bit, only heightened her anger.

"Muthafucka, I hate you! You stupid muthafucka!" She stormed off en route to the bathroom. Before registering what was taking place, it was too late.

Byron reached the bathroom door only to see his mother dumping the last of the crack into the toilet as it was flushing. "Momma, *no*! No, momma!" was all he was able to muster.

"Now get your shit and get out!"

Byron was lost for words. He went to his room and packed two garbage bags full of clothes. He looked at his room one last time. It had been his domain since a baby and now it was no longer. He closed the door, walked downstairs and was greeted with his mother at the front door. She stood there rigidly with the tears steadily falling. She opened the door, and as Byron exited, she slammed it behind him.

He pulled his hoodie over his head, and tossed the bags over his shoulders. He began to make his way to his only option and thought— Lil' Pooh's house. While walking, his thoughts were strictly on how he was going to explain to Billy Good the situation.

Chapter 8

"How we gonna open up the block in the morning, Lord? We only got six hours until the workers gonna be in the alley waiting." Lil' Pooh was nervous as hell.

The situation they were facing was total havoc. Byron's mother had flushed everything. Not just their work, but the Nation's also. They had no crack to distribute to the workers which would nonetheless cause an uproar amongst the fiends. Not to mention the fracas that would be created by the workers. Running to report to Billy Good, Byron sat in complete silence. Trying to come up with something, only to keep arriving to a brick wall. He had seen guys get severely punished for less. That thought alone had him intimidated. To state to Billy Good that his mother found the stash and flushed it would not be acceptable.

"How much work do you got left?" Byron asked Lil' Pooh.

"I got about an ounce left of that demo you gave me."

"Did you page Funk like I told you?"

"Yeah, Lord, he ain't hit back. He told me earlier that he was fresh outta work. He had said that he was trying to get up with you. I told him you was with Carmella."

"Man, we owe the Chief eighteen stacks. I only got a lil' under half. Joe, this shit is crazy."

"Lord, you just gonna have to holla at Lord. Tell him what the situation is. When the workers come for they packs, tell 'em everything on hold 'til further notice."

"Fam, I gotta call Lord now. This shit can't wait 'til morning."

Lil' Pooh gave Byron the house phone. Byron reluctantly dialed the number the Chief provided him for emergencies only. This situation was indeed fitting as an emergency. Ten minutes after paging the Chief, Billy Good returned the call.

Byron answered the phone apprehensively. "Hello."

"Who the fuck is this calling me at two in the morning?"

"It's me, Byron, Lord."

"So, what's up, shorty? This better be urgent."

Byron explained the situation in great detail. Billy Good simply listened in complete silence. Resolutely the Chief done so, then rudely hung up the phone. Byron just looked at the phone in astonishment. His hearing was kidnapped with the sound of the dial tone.

"What he say, Lord?" Lil' Pooh inquired.

"He hung up."

Both young gangstas knew that something major was about to go down. For the major fuck-up, at approximately 5:30 in the morning, they saw Rico's Benz pull into the alley. They looked on for a moment from Lil' Pooh's window. Rico stepped out in a cocaine white quarter length mink. He was handing out packs to the workers who were already out waiting when he arrived.

Byron needed his right-hand man with him. "We might as well go see what's up."

They walked out the house, heading to the alley. As they were approaching, simultaneously, they both became aware how Funk stood at the side of Rico, grinning like the cat that caught the canary.

"What's up, Lord?" Byron acknowledged the underboss.

"Ain't shit up. Billy Good wanna holla at you, ASAP. Go ahead and get in the car." Rico said as he issued out the last pack to one of the workers.

Byron glared at Funk and noticed that Funk had his hand under his arm inside his coat. His facial expression was enemy-like. Byron, not feeling Funk's demeanor challenged, "You good, nigga?"

Funk, quickly accepting the challenge, retorted, "I will be, nigga." Then spat on the ground and mugged Byron.

"Man, both of y'all shut the fuck up and get in the car. Lil' Pooh, you stay here and run the block. We'll be back in a minute."

Lil' Pooh nodded in agreement as he went to go handle his function. With grave concern for his guy, he watched Rico get back in the Benz and pull off.

Rico glided the Benz through the early morning hustle and bustle of the westside traffic. Funk occupied the backseat on the passenger's side. Byron rode shotgun, all the while sneakily gripping the .40 that was on his waist. He had a bad feeling, especially with Funk being in the picture, sitting behind him. He didn't know if he was gonna come out of this alive, so he silently prayed for his safety and well-being. Rico pulled in front of an abandoned building on Franklin Street and killed the engine.

"The old man wanna holla at you, Lord. He in the building. Come on."

All three of the hoodlums emerged from the foreign car. Rico led them into a three-story building. Inside, rats scurried away in fear of the approaching men. Walking up a flight of stairs entering a room, eight Mafia members were standing in there accompanying the Chief, Billy Good. The look on his face told a story of an individual who didn't play about his money and drugs. Byron didn't just sense the tension, he was now able to see the thickness of it as if he could slice it like a three-tier cake.

"So, what's up, Lord? I see we done got our self a situation, am I correct?"

"Yeah, Lord. My ma went in my closet and found the work and flushed it like I told you on the phone."

A few of the Mafia's laughed in humor

"So, you expect me to believe that? You being a member with status, let your momma flush our shit down the toilet? And, we just supposed to take that loss?"

Byron had $6,000 of Billy Good's guap in his pockets. As he attempted to retrieve such, that was just as fast as automatic weapons were pointed at him. Billy Good's henchmen were on deck and ready to deal. Only, they weren't dealing Aces, Kings, or Queens, rather, they were into hollow points. Byron, spooked from their reaction, froze up.

Billy Good asked, "What you got there, shorty?"

From the sight of Rico's Ruger 4-5 trained to his head, along with the numerous others aimed in his direction, Byron stuttered, "I-I-I got six thousand of your money, Lord, that's all." Visibly he was shaken accompanying his stammer.

"Funk, get that off him and pat him down." Billy Good commanded.

Funk smiled and with great pleasure obliged. He retrieved the loot from Byron, then aggressively patted him down. He relinquished Byron of the Springfield Armory .40 ACP that he was packing. "Won't be needing this, bitch ass nigga." Funk sneered. Funk handed the wad of cash to Billy Good and tucked the small compact .40 in his front pocket.

Billy Good peered through the wad of bills. "Six grand, huh? Where is my other twelve thousand, Byron?" He placed the wad in his pocket.

"Lord, just give me a lil' minute. I'ma have your money."

"You didn't even have nothing to issue to the workers. How you gonna get my money? What you gonna do, ask your new lil' girlfriend Carmella?"

Byron just glanced in the direction of Funk with pure hatred.

"You see, if you would've been handling Nation business, you wouldn't be in this situation. Instead, you decided to go tricking off on a bitch, now look at the mess you're in."

Funk glared back at Byron with a smile as if a sign of triumph.

"Now, I know and believe you are gonna get me my money. Because if you don't, you are gonna be a prime candidate for the Burr Oaks Cemetery. But, trust and believe, you gonna get some motivation here today. For breaching security and losing that work, you got five minutes head to toe."

Two Mafia's immediately grabbed him. One put him in a full nelson, the other grabbed his legs. That was done so he couldn't resist or move. Funk, Meathead and Trell were commanded to carry out the violation.

Rico looked at the face of his diamond studded Ceilex Rolex to time the beating and nonchalantly said, "Begin."

Funk, slobbering at such a chance, punctually punched Byron in his eye. He continued to land blow after blow until he was out of breath. Blood spilled on the cluttered concrete as they took turns beating Byron's mind, body and spirit. Spitting out blood, Byron couldn't help but feel betrayed and treated as an enemy to his organization. The guys continued to issue the hellacious punishment upon him, almost pushing him to a comatose state.

At the end of the five minutes, Byron's face was

unrecognizable. Anyone that may have known him, wouldn't at this moment. Rico commanded the Mafia's to shake up with Byron the Mafia way and show him some love. Albeit, they had just given him a dose of tough love. In Byron's mind, there was no love in this evil organization. People had their own motives. The laws and policies taught meant nothing.

After the physical violation, Rico pulled up in front of Byron's house. Funk and Meathead opened the back door to let him out. The cold air stung his swollen face as he staggered up the sidewalk. After climbing the steps to his mother's house, Byron weakly knocked on the door. His mother opened the door and let out a piercing scream. All Byron could do was fall inside his mother's home and lay there.

Seeing the wounds and the condition of her son's face and body caused Ilena to race to the phone to call the paramedics. In a hysterical tone she said, "I need an ambulance at ten, forty-eight Avers. *Please* hurry; I think my son is dying!" She went on to answer the dispatcher and assess the blood that soaked her son's clothing.

"An ambulance is on the way, ma'am. Stay on the line with me, okay?" The dispatcher responded.

An hour later, Byron laid in a bed in Saint Bernard's Hospital. His eyes were closed shut. The right side of his jaw was broken in three places. He suffered a minor concussion. And it was all from the violation handed down from Billy Good. Byron couldn't see from his eyes due to the pain, but he could hear his mother sobbing at his bedside. She held his hand tight, as if her life depended on it. He couldn't believe that the Mafia's had carried him that way after all he had done for the Nation since he was young. Funk turned on him the first time the opportunity presented itself. Thinking about revenge on Funk caused his pains to subside. He attempted to sit up, but it wouldn't happen at that moment. The pain from the broken rib caused him to think twice and simply laid back.

"Byron, stop moving around, son. Just sit back and rest, sweetheart." Ilena softly spoke as she stroked his hand. Byron had not heard that tender side of his mother's voice since he was five

S. Allen

years old. "Baby, I am so sorry for getting you into this mess. I wish you would just listen to me and stop hanging with those guys. They don't mean you no good, baby. Lil' Pooh told me what's going on. I can't believe I'm the reason you are laying in this hospital bed. Son, you are young and you have your entire life ahead of you. I do not want you to throw it away in these streets, you hear me?" Ilena wiped a tear from her eye. "Byron, when you get well, I am gonna send you away from these wicked streets. Son, I think it would be best if you enlist in the military like that Judge said. It will teach you discipline and some skills to better yourself. Byron, it would make me so happy if you changed your life for the better. Get away from these streets. It's no love in them! Son, will you do that for me?"

Byron thought about all the stress his mother endured. His father abandoning them. The pain and suffering he was causing, running with the Mafia's. He wanted nothing more in life than to make his mother proud. Maybe Judge Kelly and his mother was right. Maybe the military could change his life for the better. After being betrayed by the Mafia's, he now knew that there was no love and loyalty in the streets. The only thing that was for sure in the streets of the Chi was prison and death. With that conclusion, he wanted no parts of either.

Precisely, Byron made a life-changing decision. He would leave his old life behind, even his newfound love Carmella. He wanted a better life and future, therefore he would enlist in the United States Army. Feeling his mother's pain deeply, to ensure her a change, his swollen lips formed a weak smile and he squeezed her hand tightly.

"Thank you, *Jesus*! Thank you!" Ilena kissed her son's cheek in celebration of Byron and a better future.

Chapter 9
Part II

It had been two years since Byron laid in that hospital bed, promising his mother he would enlist in the military. It had been a long time coming, but the self-discipline instilled in him made him elevate. Earning the title of Sniper in the First Marine Division in Camp Pendleton, California was a testament of him taking a hold of life and advancing to the next level. The ten-week course was hellbent. Many cadets did not make it through the course. Only 25% of them completed. That was sort of the norm, and Byron made certain to be in that percentage. The course was split into two phases. They would learn everything from urban warfare to stalking enemies, as well as the traditional sniper skills. The final six-weeks were dedicated to mastering the art of shooting the different types and calibers of weapons. Byron also had to pass a psychological exam to ensure that he was mentally prepared and ready for the repercussions of the duty that he would uphold.

He had always maintained physical fitness. So, the 9-mile treks with 20-pound backpacks were not so strenuous on him. In oppose, others fell off one by one. While in Sniper School, Byron learned the art of stalking his prey with a M107 long-range sniper rifle equipped with a night vision scope. He could hit a target dead on. His vision and aim was totally in sync and superb. Any target within 800 meters was successfully completed with ease. Utilizing the modified M4 assault rifle with 7.62 Nato rounds, he was a beast. But, the tool for the trade he admired the most was the art of being undetectable. To release lead from a fitted suppressor, putting an enemy target down without a sound being heard, was music to his ears. The only sound and sight would be of the body hitting the ground.

Byron completed the ten-week course at the top of his class. Upon his graduation, he earned the Military Occupational Specialty of 0317. Just as important, he earned the right to be called a hunter of Gunmen; certifying the degree of his skills.

As a trooper of the 101st Battalion, he was assigned to a five-man platoon which consisted of five other snipers.

Craig, whose nickname was Juice, graduated from the Third Marine Division in Kaneohe Bay in Hawaii. Juice hailed from Kansas City and was Byron's closest comrade. They were the only 2 African-Americans in the Caucasian Division. Juice was a good man and one hell of a spotter at target practice. They worked together the most, creating a well-working duo. Then you had Mike Solbert. Mike graduated with honors from the Second Marine Division in Camp Lejuene, in North Carolina. He was a pale-faced, sandy-colored hair joker. He spent most of his time cracking jokes. However, he was a fierce animal with the heavy, single-shot bolt-action .50 caliber sniper rifle.

Not the one for jokes, you had Willie Paddon. He in turn felt like all problems in the world could be solved with a Bolt-action .300 Winchester Magnum. On his worst day, he would spit a wad of chewing tobacco out of his mouth and zero in on a target 1000 meters away. Exactly 3,300 feet, at any windchill, a bottle of Jack Daniels, it was hell to tell the captain.

Last but not least, you had Reggie Banks. A freckled-face carrot-top who also graduated from the First Marine Division in Camp Pendleton, California. Byron and Reggie bumped heads in Sniper School on a few occasions. In Byron's mind, Reggie was simply another racist redneck. Being that Byron excelled in his duties, it wasn't liked by all, and Reggie was the leader of the pack. From the studies of book work, to the cracking shots of the rifle, Reggie could not get in Byron's business. Hailing from a small hick-town in Wisconsin named Appleton. Population was only 1,800, with maybe two or three Blacks residing in the entire town. With such disparity, Reggie most definitely didn't like the writing on the wall— a Black man was superior to him. In his mind he felt no way, no how, thinking that coming from a military background would somehow supply him with an edge. His father had been a Green Beret in the Marines, and he wanted badly to surpass his father's career. That's what motivated him to enter into Sniper School. He had envisioned himself being the best Sniper the United States would ever produce. Nonetheless, that vision was distorted by none other, Byron Hobson, the 21-year-old Black guy who he despised. Byron made things impossible, thus creating a severe level of animosity. Racial remarks were dispersed from Reggie's lips every time he was in the vicinity of Byron's hearing. Byron would check Reggie, but the issues never escalated to physicalness. They tried their damnedest to stay clear of one another, unless unpreventable due to military business.

It was in Australia when Byron's life dramatically changed. It was his first deployment. At twenty-one years of age, he spent all of his years in the Battalion Sniper Platoon after graduating from the First Marine Division Sniper School. Learning what it meant to be a certified sniper of HOG, he was well equipped with the knowledge and was a natural born team leader. His platoon of the 101st Battalion spent it's time patrolling and shooting on a sniper range outside of Darwin. After the exhausting training, they were allotted some leisure time to roam the town of Darwin. Like anyone else in the world, they loved to enjoy some freedom and relaxation.

Byron spent his time at a nearby casino. Always having a thing for the dice, that was exactly where you could locate him. His roll was precise and sharp, affording him the confidence to bet on every point the dice landed on. Utilizing this hustla's trade he grasped in the mean streets of the Chi, Byron would walk away after every endeavor a couple of thousand dollars heavier.

Well, one day after such, he and his platoon met at a local bar named Sal's. Being that Byron had a continuous hot-hand on the dice, he elected to show the guys a nice time, blowing some of his newfound fortune, compliments of the casino.

Inside the smoke-filled, crowded bar, Byron ordered a cold pitcher of Bud Light before heading to the restroom to relieve himself. As he did, he recognized the World Trade Center attack on the television that sat high in the corner of the bar. "What movie is this?" Byron asked a local, not knowing that he was watching actual footage.

"It's not a movie, pal. You guys shouldn't be here. This is some serious shit." The local replied, then took a long swig from his Budweiser long-neck.

Byron stopped and watched a little longer, astonished at what he suddenly realized was the situation. Soon the entire crowd of patrons was glued to the tube. Looks of shock and pure horror were plastered on many faces as the planes collided into the buildings. Shortly after, Shore Patrol stormed the bar and announced that all soldiers report back to the ship.

On the ship, Byron's Commander enlightened them about the terror attacks. The next day, September 12, 2001, the ships wafted from the ports of Australia, with Byron and his platoon set out on a mission. They would be entering the concrete jungle of Afghanistan. Precise destination, Kabul, the capital of the country. By the time he and the crew arrived, they were full of anxiety and rage, ready to dive head-first into some action.

His platoon's camaraderie was hard to duplicate. The assistant team leader was none other than Juice. Byron trusted in Juice's ability to help lead in the mission at hand. He packed his M107 long-range rifle, while Juice carried the heavy .50 caliber. Juice, like Byron, was always physically fit. So, to the 6'3", 230 pounds, cornbread eater from Kansas City, Kansas, carrying the artillery was merely a day of working on his Grandfather's farm.

Willie, never on nonsense, was elected to operate the radio. His communication skills were over average and he was very observant. That's exactly what they needed. Any slip-up, and it would be game over for them.

The mission they were set out to perform was securing a road in West Kabul. The chances of them engaging in enemy conflict would be high, just as their nerves would be. Anticipation had him jerky and edgy. As a trained Sniper, he wanted to use all he was taught, so he had to calm himself because that was instructed in school. It took a few days to finally come through. Afterall, what he was experiencing was normal, being that he was going into combat for the first time.

On November 24, 2001, he and his team were prepared to handle their functions, all in the name of the United States of America. The anticipation of encountering the enemy kept Byron awoke on the night of the mission. Him and Juice rode in silence in a Light-Armored Vehicle.

Juice broke the silence by asking, "So you scared, B?" checking the magazines to the .50 caliber, making certain that when the time arrived they would be ready.

"Scared of what? This the shit we trained for, soldier. When it's time to boogie, we'll dance, but it's a chance that we might not even see no action out here." Byron replied.

The weather was cold, but not like in the Chi. As they traveled down the dark, rocky road, they pulled up behind another Military Vehicle. Two Marines hopped out to run barbed wire across the pavement, attaching chemical lights to ward off traffic.

Byron and Juice stepped from the vehicle with their weapons to supply security for the other Marines as they commenced their task. The two Marines who ran the wire would be the ones to pull passengers from their vehicles. Byron and Juice would supply them security from behind, covering their six.

A few hundred meters from the road, Byron and Juice set up their shooting position. Byron rested his rifle on his backpack which was atop the hood of the LAV. The PVS night-vision scope provided perfect sight. Him and Juice discussed the distance from the barbwire.

"Don't you think we a lil' too far out, Sergeant?" quibbled Juice.

"Not at all. I got a good view from here. This night vision shit is official." Byron retorted as he scanned the perimeter through his scope.

Juice heard something from his earphone and got excited. "Sergeant, we got a convoy heading our way. What you think gonna happen when the vehicle hit that wire?" Juice questioned, but keeping his focus on the road, looking through the infrared binoculars to confirm the activity.

"If all is well, they'll stop and comply with the directions administered by the Marines. If not, somebody getting dropped." Byron declared, injecting a Nato round into the chamber of the rifle.

As the convoy approached, all the vehicles stopped at a distance except one truck. It continued to speed toward the barbed wire. The headlights of the truck lit up Byron's scope. The champagne colored

Ford F-150 drove straight over the wire, which became mangled under the truck, causing it to halt to a complete stop. A few seconds passed before a man of Middle Eastern descent emerged from the right side. He stood 5'11", appeared to weight about 210 pounds, a thick moustache, bald head, with a long scar that ran from the top of his left earlobe down the left side of his jawline. He examined the damage of the vehicle, noticing the Marines approaching on the road from the rear. In a quick succession, he immediately climbed back into the truck.

Byron grew tense. Sweat poured from the side of his face as he placed his right index finger into the trigger-well, allowing his finger to move slightly before the trigger mechanism in the motion of come-here sideways. He noticed the two Marines yelling at two men who were covered in blankets in the bed of the F-150.

"Slight breeze to the left, two miles per hour." Juice stated, as he was now looking through the mounted scope, spotting for Byron.

"I got the driver and the clowns in the bed." Byron averred, finger still jerking, ready to apply the slight pressure. The anticipation was getting the best of him.

Suddenly the men in the bed of the truck jumped to their feet, wielding Romanian style automatic AK-47'S with 100-round drums.

"Fire! Fire!" Juice exclaimed, looking through his spotting scope.

Byron was already proceeding with the motion before Juice could even declare such. Having scoped and planned his course of action, the crosshairs of his scope was already on one of the gunmen's forehead. The recoil from the high-powered rifle slammed the butt of the gun smack-dead on Byron's right shoulder. The purple-tip Nato round splitted the first gunman's head like a cantaloupe being struck with a machete, splattering his brain tissue upon his comrade. Byron quickly scoped his comrade, pulled his trigger once more. The large slug penetrated the man's upper chest, causing the man to tumble over the bed of the truck onto the dirt road.

"Sergeant, enemy still intact. I repeat, enemy still alive. Two to the right."

Byron ejected the spent shell-casing. Injecting a fresh one, setting his crosshairs on the wounded man's forehead, he squeezed the trigger once more, painting the passenger side of the truck with the man's last thoughts.

The Marines didn't even have time to react. Had it not been for Byron's quick trigger finger, they both would have been had-beens strolling up the stairway of heaven.

The driver immediately got out of the truck with his hands raised skyward. Speaking hysterically with his deep native accent in broken English, begged, "Please, please, don't shoot."

The Marines handcuffed him, led him to their Humvee and placed him on the floor of the rear seat.

After investigation of the F-150, the Marines found two LED bombs. Byron and Juice had saved a few lives.

"That was some damn good shooting, Sergeant."

"That was some precise spotting, potna." Byron replied to his second-in-command as he stood up from his position, wiping the perspiration from his forehead onto his right pants leg of his desert-patterned fatigues.

Juice commenced to picking up the shell casings, then walked toward Byron and handed them to him.

"What's these for?" Byron asked, taking the three 7.62 shell casings in his palms. Shaking them in his hands as if they were three dies and he was about to roll four, five, six.

"They are mementos of your first kills."

Byron stared at the casings for a long moment. He had enlisted into the military to better his life. So far, the bettering was solely his aim and reaction timing. He had just killed two men in the matter of five seconds. The thing that worried him the most was his lack of remorse. It was just the beginning of the war on terror and he was about to get knee deep in the game of bloodthirst.

Chapter 10

Back in Chicago, Ilena concentrated on the task at hand. She held a silver teaspoon in her right hand and a red Bic lighter in her left. The flame from the lighter was being held slightly below the oval bowl of the utensil. The substance in the spoon began to boil, thus causing her to put the lighter down. She had spent her last $10.00 on the substance that was packaged in a square piece of aluminum foil. The powdery substance with just a tad bit of water and heat was now her magic potion and liquid solution. She took a piece of cotton swab, rolled up a tiny ball, dropped it in the spoon and grabbed her tool, taking the syringe and drawing up the liquid. In anticipation of her medicine, Ilena passed gas, then inserted the needle into her left arm and injected the addictive potion into her veins. The intense rush that flowed through her blood stream brought about a sense of calmness as she rocked, enjoying the motion of her ride.

Chicago had now been flooded with this new cheap drug that would take users for a lifelong ride straight through the gates of hell. The Chi had now reintroduced its residents to mother heroin.

Since Byron had been in the Marines, Ilena fell into a deeper depression when her boss at the Sears Roebuck Company fired her for being five minutes late to work. Falling back on her bills, having no way to pay the rent, she began to prostitute. An old friend of hers enticed and encouraged her. Little did Ilena know, Ralph was still harboring bitterness within of losing her to Byron's father. So, in his twisted mind, this was his revenge.

It hurt like hell to Ilena's soul, selling her body for sexual encounters. Yet, she had to make ends meet until she found another job. Things got worse when Ralph offered her some heroin for the first time. After the first experiment of drugs, more so the most potent and addictive, Ilena was hooked, lined and sintered. She began chasing the drug like she was chasing the multi-million-dollar lottery. Only thing, she was actually chasing the high. Trying to obtain that feeling she experienced when she first tried the venom. It was nothing to trade her body for the drug. Some of the drug dealers on Avers and Augusta would readily exchange a bag or two for a rendezvous with Byron's mother, especially none other than Funk.

Times had definitely changed on Avers and Augusta. Instead of crack cocaine flooding the strip, heroin had taken complete control. The Mafia's still ran the drug market, but different people were in position. Billy Good no longer controlled the area. The United States Government put an end to his criminal enterprise. With a 360 month sentence, residing in Beaumont, Texas as USP Beaumont, Billy Good was now out of the way.

Rico, his most trusted henchman, was found murdered on the southside. As they say, what goes around, comes around. His body had been riddled with bullet holes, and no suspects to the day had been apprehended. Not like Chicago Police Department actually gave a care.

Funk and his new crew now were in control of the Mafia's and the functions of the organization. Funk had finally made it to baller-status, what he always felt was rightfully his position. He patrolled the neighborhood, flaunting his money-green Cadillac Escalade that rolled on $10,000 chrome and money-green 28-inch Davin rims, showboating his success in the faces of his subordinates.

Ilena hated the fact that she was strung out on smack or drugs period. At times, she wished her son was home to help her out. Give her the motivation to do better in life. Instead, he was in another country, fighting the so-called war on terror. A war she persuaded him to join ignorantly. As she sat, pondering, she now felt as if that was a terrible, terrible mistake.

Byron's best-friend, Lil' Pooh, used to come by and lend a hand. Helping her out around the house, making sure she ate and to see to it that bills were taken care of. But it had been months since she last seen or heard from him. Ilena knew that Lil' Pooh sold drugs for Funk. Sometimes, when jonesing real bad, she would attempt to get something from him. To no avail, Lil' Pooh would *never* supply her with such. However, he would consistently bring bags of groceries to keep something in the fridge.

Letter after letter would arrive from Byron as he was overseas.

A Shooter's Ambition

Always asking about her well-being. Ilena would continually lie to him. Not having the nerve to tell her son just how low she had fallen. It had been almost two years since she was employed. She definitely wouldn't dare tell her only child that she was strung out on heroin. Ever since Byron left her house, it was no longer a home, and her life changed dramatically.

All of that rummaged through her head as she nodded from the effect of the drug. In a state of lethargy, Ilena sat on her sofa with a speckle of blood oozing from the open wound where she had just punctured herself with the needle containing dog food. Not a care in the world to her. Her house, filthy, just as she was. From not bathing, she possessed a foul smell that reeked from her pores beyond imagination. The kitchen had large roaches in different squads roaming around as if they were different organizations. Ilena had completely lost her will to live and in the process lost her soul. She knew her steady travel of the road she was on would eventually lead to her ultimate demise. A tear streaked from her left eye. She made a silent prayer to GOD in attempt to rebuke the devil, the temptations and the stronghold that it had on her life.

Ilena wasn't the only one who suffered from Byron's adolescent ways. His right-hand man, Lil' Pooh, sat on the curb on Kedzie Street. His hands clutched a $1.00 bottle of wine. His clothes had seen better days. His hygiene was not up to par, as his dreadlocks smelled of mustiness. He was now known to the streets as a wine-head. Funk had used Lil' Pooh as a worker, all because of the bitterness he harbored. When Lil' Pooh started to make a name for himself in the Nation, Funk dismantled such. Funk restricted Lil' Pooh from hustling on Avers and Augusta, or anywhere. When Lil' Pooh tried to hustle on a different block, Funk sent members of the Mafia's to rob and pistol-whip him into unconsciousness. Funk let it be known, if Lil' Pooh wasn't working for him, he wasn't allowed to hustle period. Lil' Pooh knew he couldn't go to war. He knew he would be gunned down in the cold streets like a dog. So, after his recovery from the brutal attack, he resorted to drinking heavily. Nothing in life mattered anymore, except the bottle of Night Train that he purchased every day.

Lil' Pooh always thought about how his main-man Byron was handling himself in that war. He had heard about the terror attacks in New York. How so many soldiers were deployed to Afghanistan, only to be shipped back in pine-boxes if they were permitted. He didn't know if Byron was participating in the ground war, so he prayed for his homie's safety. It had been almost three years since last seeing his potna. At this present moment, it was most definitely the time of day he longed for Byron's presence, as he sat alone in this cruel, cold world.

Chapter 11

"In Afghanistan, the enemy, the Taliban and Al-Queda fighters, they're not scared of us. They're just as excited about killing an American as we are about killing them. But, I can assure you one thing that they do fear, and that's the unknown."

Byron thought about the words of the US Special Operations Sniper Commander who had given his squad this mission. After that night of Byron's first kills, he had grown to acquire a blood thirst like none other. He anticipated the engagement with the Taliban, as he patiently waited for his prey. Byron and his four-man team were posted in the Spīn Ghor Mountains of northwestern Afghanistan. From their position, Byron kept an eye out for enemy movement. He was not hunting for deer, he was hunting for human prey. Taliban, Al-Qaeda or any other faction.

Byron was given the opportunity to choose his four-man team from the likes of his platoon. Without a doubt, Juice would be the designated spotter. Nine out of ten, Byron would be the shooter, therefore he had to have his most trusted comrade at his side. Willie would be the forward observer, carrying the SAW— Suppressed Automatic Weapon. Mike, the composed communicator, would be the communication operator. His task would be notifying the Apache helicopters for cover-fire, if the situation got out of hand.

Byron tried his best to always leave Reggie out of the missions. The last mission completed, Byron had earned honors amongst his peers, as well as his superiors. But, not with Reggie. Reggie was vexed. He felt that Byron shouldn't have took the fatal shots due to the closeness of the fellow Marines. Others felt different. Had it not been for Sergeant Hobson's quick reactions, it would have been at least two dead Marines with the terroristic Taliban being able to claim the fame of such act.

The winding valley that platoon was in allowed Coalition Forces to ship supplies from Pakistan, but it also allowed enemy fighters an advantage. The enemy could orchestrate attacks on Byron's base and slip back across the border.

The attacks happened every Wednesday morning at 0900 hours.

Byron's outpost took fire from multiple RPG'S handheld rockets. In a few incidents, a few Marines were injured but no fatalities.

Unfortunately for the enemy, their pattern of attacks supplied Byron and his platoon their own vantage point. They devised a plan, fixing their own positions of fire.

The planning took a few days. In procession to carry out their tactic, Byron, Juice and Willie moved from the base. It was after midnight and the climate in the mountains was close to arctic. They hitched a ride with a Patrol Unit until they were about seven kilometers from the target area that gave the enemy an advantage. In days to come, what was once an advantage would become a disadvantage, leading ultimately to the enemy fighters' deaths.

For more than two days the four-man team laid on the mountainside. Byron and Juice were fifty yards above Willie who had the 1,000 round SAW ready to get active. Their fatigues matched sparse brush and rocks of the mountains. Byron's painted M110 blended well with the blond-colored dirt.

After scanning the map of the area, Byron chose the apex of the area. From that position they had a perfect view of the canyon below them. The enemy shooters would open fire with the RPG'S within a few hundred yards from them. When they did, they would be in for a rude awakening. Byron and his team would be ready to pounce on them like a jaguar on a gazelle.

On Wednesday morning at 0900 hours, the soldiers scoured the valley for their enemies. Found none, but stuck to their game plan.

At 0915 hours, Byron began to feel exhausted and tired from lying in wait. Anxiety getting the best of him. "I think our intel was bogus." Byron asserted in a hushed tone. Laying under some broken tree branches, his location and M110 rifle totally undetectable.

Juice laid by his side peering through the scope. "One thing for sure and two things for certain, it's cold as a hoe heart out here, partner. If the information was bogus, they gonna definitely hear about this shit."

The two snipers had been in position for two days and two nights. No food or water. But Byron was trained by the best in his Sniper School and this was what he was trained for.

0930 rolled in and simultaneously Juice spotted something. "Get on point, Sergeant. The mice have come out to play. Here we go."

Before Juice could even finish his statement, Byron had his scope to his right eye, viewing the three men who were strolling with caution from the other side of the valley.

Juice quickly informed Byron of the range to the targets. It was 600 meters— 2,000 feet— and counting. They knew right away that these were their subjects. From the possession of the Russian AR-47's, to their Puma gym shoes. Complete giveaways. The shoes were a match to the other enemy fighters they had encountered and targeted before.

"This is Red-Fox One, up top. Are you seeing what I'm seeing?" Byron queried into his mouthpiece, notifying Willie with the SAW.

"This is Omega, down low. Yes, I see the three wondering through Disneyland. What's the command, Sergeant?"

"Command is to hold your position. Over?" Byron then contacted Mike. Told him to notify the Apache personnel. He remained affixed to his scope. Ready to engage the inevitable. The shots would be a bit difficult, due to the wind that swept over the mountain behind them and met with a crosswind from left to right at 500 meters away. To add insult to injury, Byron would be aiming downhill. The closest target was more than 600 meters away.

"Sergeant, we have all enemy targets in sight. I say we take the shots." Juice averred, noticing their enemies looking like sitting ducks.

Byron thought about the situation. He would rather wait for the Apache to come and give them cover, but that would be wasted time. The men had RPG's and plans of causing harm with the deadly weapons. "This is Red-Fox, up top. Enemy in sight and I'm taking the shots." Byron informed the rest of the team. He inhaled, then exhaled a long, deep breath for composure. Not even waiting for a reply from his team, lined his crosshairs of his scope leveled with one of the enemy's center chest and squeezed the trigger.

Foooftth!

Traveling at 2,571 feet per-second the slug tore through the man's rib cage, instantly dropping him. The man's friend stared at him, confused, looking at his partner's intestines running off the side of his hip. The smell of his comrade's blood permeated his nose. Almost in motion of puking from the sight of death was short lived. Byron trained his night-vision scope upon the terrified partner's facial expression. The dark green and brown war paint that he wore blended him well in the bushes. Byron lowered his aim of his crosshairs upon the man's throat.

"Are you sighted Sergeant?" Juice asked Byron as he sighted the same target.

"We're fitted like a glove, partner. On five I'm taking the shot."

"One, two." It was one shot, one kill.

Byron sneered a mask of death, as the thought of taking another life aroused him.

"Three, four."

The sound of the Apache helicopters was close, and Byron would be damned if that RPG came to life at the hands of the man.

"Five!" Juice yelled.

Byron applied pressure on the trigger. The weapon kicked, causing him to lose sight through the scope temporarily. A spark came from the barrel of the M110. The enemy fighter never felt a thing, as his motion to puke was never borne. The bullet went through and above his collarbone, knocking him down to his knees as if he was attempting to make his last salat. Grabbing at his throat, blood spurted limitless from the gaping hole as he began to fade to black.

"Will you believe that that cat is still alive?"

Without saying a word, Byron placed his scope on the man's head and squeezed. As his head exploded from the impact of the bullet, Byron retorted, "Well, that was number nine's finale."

Just then the Apaches arrived, gunning down the remaining Taliban soldiers who had been hiding. Later a Patrol arrived, inspected the bodies and collected intelligence from them.

In the end, Byron's platoon and the other soldiers didn't receive any more indirect fire from the Taliban. That murderous night in the mountains would make the Islamic fighters think twice about stepping on grounds occupied by the Marines from the Great Ole US of A.

A week later, Byron stood on the base of the Naval ship, US Magerio, overlooking the ocean, consumed with thoughts of back home. The weather was fair. The smell of the ocean was relaxing, but his gut instinct was something wasn't right. He hadn't heard from his mother in almost two months. He tried contacting her via telephone, only to learn that the number was disconnected. Something she said in her last letter didn't sit right with him. He thought about his mother's words. "Baby, please pray for me, and just know that I care for you and never meant to hurt you." *What did she mean by stating to pray for her?* She had never expressed herself with such degree of emotion. A year left of deployment, then he would be back in the Chi. He couldn't wait to hug his beloved mother. Yet, the time seemed to move in slow motion. Byron's thoughts of home were abruptly invaded.

"Sergeant Hobson, Juice told me I might find you out here."

Byron about-faced the voice. Standing face to face with Reggie, the two saluted one another.

"How is it going, Marine? I didn't disturb you, did I ?" Reggie queried, then stood beside him overlooking the murky water.

Byron grinned before he spoke. "No, sir. I was just sitting here getting my thoughts together. What's up?"

"I just wanted to commend you on a job well done on that mountain. They said you did some real good shooting, *boy!*" Reggie emphasized boy.

Byron struggled to keep his composure before he spoke. "Well, you know, Marine, when you're one of the best snipers the US Marines has ever produced, it seems to just come naturally."

Reggie let out a chuckle. "You don't really think you the best, do you? I hear you was some kind of gang-banger back in Chicago. In my book, you no better than the cow-herders we out killing now, boy."

Byron's grip on humbleness was becoming unfastened. "I think you need to watch who you call boy, *cracker!*" The two Marines faced off.

"Boy, I don't think you could fuck with a drawn picture of me. I'll stump your ass so far in the ground you might see one of your nigger ancestors."

Before thinking about what he was doing, Byron swung a right hook, connecting the base of Reggie's left side jaw, catching Reggie with his mouth agape. The impact of the blow shattered Reggie's jawbone, causing him to stumble backwards. Reggie's adrenaline edged him to rush Byron and the two rumbled and tussled until Major HeKley intervened.

"Hey, hey, you two Marines break it up! Sergeant Hobson, I'm giving you a direct order to stand down. Stand down now, Sergeant!"

Byron let go of Reggie and saluted Major HeKley.

"Sergeant Hobson, you are to report to the brinks in o-two hundred hours, is that understood?"

"Yes, sir." Replied Byron. As he proceeded to walk off, he stared Reggie directly in the eyes and avowed, "This ain't over, *cracker*!"

Reggie just cowardly stood there holding his jaw, hoping to keep it from landing on the deck.

Later that evening, Byron walked in Major HeKley's office. Upon entering, he noticed Major HeKley along with US Special Operations Commander Rick Sanchez. Both men held serious facial expressions.

Byron saluted his superiors as they saluted him back.

"Sergeant, have a seat." Major HeKley suggested, blowing smoke from a thick Cuban cigar that rested between his fat lips.

Byron took a seat, awaiting his reprimanding.

"Sergeant Hobson, you want to tell us what that situation was about?"

"Permission to speak freely, sir?"

"Permission granted."

"Sir, I have a lot on my mind and that Marine kept testing my patience."

"Sergeant Hobson, this is the United States Marine Corps. In this here, we have no room for emotions. I suggest that whatever animosity you have with Sergeant Banks, you guys put it to rest. We have a serious war going on. A war on terror and it is our job to end it. You are one of our best shooters, damnit. It would be a waste of your talent and our countries time if you were court-marshalled for insubordination, is that understood, Sergeant?"

Byron took his chastising from his superior in stride. He knew that the time would come when he would be able to get his free rein with Reggie. When he did, he would capitalize on the moment and punish Reggie not only for the disrespect he shovel toward him, but also for the pain and suffering of the past endured by his ancestors. "Yes, sir," was Byron's reply.

Commander Sanchez interjected, "Sergeant Hobson, I have heard a lot about you. I hear you have the skills and determination to succeed in this field. That is a major asset in this combat on terror. But to defeat an enemy, Sergeant, you have to first know your enemy. What do you know about the enemy, Sergeant?" At 63 years old, Commander Sanchez had seen it all. From the guerilla fought warfare in Vietnam, to the bloody lands of Uganda, Africa. As a mercenary soldier, Commander Sanchez had mastered the art of sniping. His intellectual wisdom was impeccable.

Byron sat silently. In reality he didn't know the enemy at all. He had killed six men and didn't have a clue why.

The commander clasped his hands behind his back and walked from behind the desk. The silence of Byron confirmed his contention. "Like I thought, Sergeant. The Taliban are recognized as students. These men implement a strict interpretation of Islamic law, and brutally enforce them as they believe. The Sunni Islamist's are the bulk of the group. But Pakistanis and others have joined the ranks. They have dominated Afghanistan for hundreds of years, Sergeant, and they have a lot of influence. The tribal alliances cross geological boundaries into Pakistan, giving them a haven to retreat and rest."

Byron focused in on what the Commander was relaying.

"You see, Sergeant Hobson, as of now, the Taliban has regulated to an insurgency. Their influences over civilians in the

Afghan Military is powerful beyond reason. Their control covers most of the south and east. But, attacks have spread throughout other regions of the country as well. Like the enemies in Iraq, Taliban fighters hit and run. They employ the use of roadside bombs as well as indirect fire as you have experienced. Most of the ground they choose to fight on are from caves and mountainsides. But there are also groups living in and operating from their hometowns and villages."

Major HeKley thumped a thick blog of ashes into the teal green ceramic ashtray that sat atop the table next to him. "That's not even the tip of the iceberg, Hobson," Major HeKley averred.

"Then you have the enemy, Al-Queda. They were created by Osama Bin-Laden who is now Public enemy number one! This piece of shit and his organization are the ones who caused the September eleventh attacks. They fight to drive non-Islamic agencies and their influences, particularly the United States, from Muslim nations with the purpose of installing fundamentalist Islamic rule, Sergeant. These Islamic extremists are dangerous and detrimental to our country and they must be stopped."

Commander Sanchez intervened, "Sergeant Hobson, I want you to take a look at this video." Sanchez grabbed the remote to the 32-inch plasma screen that rested on the far-left side wall and pressed play, bringing the screen to life.

Immediately, Byron was entranced with an image of a man kneeling, his face covered with a pillowcase, three men with black ski masks holding AK-47's posted behind the bound man. Byron couldn't see who the bound man was. All of a sudden, a masked man appeared on screen, read something from a book in the Arabic language. After the completion of his reading, he produced a large hunting knife that displayed sharp, jagged ridges, uncovered the bound man's head and commenced to saw his neck. Blood squirted everywhere. The man's eyes bulged from the horror. As the masked man continued to saw with a knife, he spoke something aloud in Arabic, spittle flying from his mouth as he raged on. After about four minutes, the masked man raised his left arm. In the grasp of his left hand was the severed head of an American.

Byron felt the vomit rush from his bowels as he puked all over himself. He had never seen this level of violence. To him that was some sickening shit.

"What you had for lunch, Sergeant? Chilli?" Major HeKley joked.

Commander Sanchez stood silent as he turned the disturbing video off. "Sergeant Hobson, that was a United States Navy Seal Sergeant Major Thomas Langston. He was caught in the Korengal Valley. They posted this video on YouTube about a week ago. So, you see, we are not dealing with just anything average or normal. We are dealing with complete savages."

Byron caught his breath, wiped the vomit from the corners of his mouth with the back of his hand. "So what now, Commander?" Byron managed to ask, still possessing the gruesome murder scene in his vision bank.

"Byron, you have the most qualified sniper team. The Hundred and First Battalion. We need you and your team to lead Operations Whaler."

Major HeKley handed Byron a Manilla folder enclosed with the contents of the mission. "In that packet you will find all the information you need on Bashan-Abbudah. He is the first of command for the Taliban in the Korengal Valley."

Byron opened up the folder. First page of the intel was a photo of Bashan-Abbudah.

"We need this warlord taken down. We would rather have him alive for interrogation, but we are willing to accept his deceased corpse. Your team will provide cover for the Marines in Korengal Valley. They will flush the terrorists out. Your team's duty will be to pick them off. It's going to take some good shooting, Sergeant. Just keep in mind, these terrorists have a stronghold on this area. This is exactly where their organization abducted one of our Navy Seals and savagely murdered him as you've witnessed. It's up to you and your Battalion, Byron. Let's take this son of a bitch down, and bring our boys back."

Byron stood up, and saluted his superiors in agreement to the mission at hand. He left the office en route to inform his squad of their mission. He was the leader of his platoon, but for good reason, he was scared to death.

Chapter 12

Looking at his Military Swiss Army watch, Byron noticed that it was exactly 0700 hours. He and the 101st Battalion rode in the Apache in complete silence. All six men waited patiently, all in their own thoughts about the mission they were heading into. War paint covered their faces, as well as the slight mask of fear they all possessed. The only thing that could be heard was the loading of magazines and checking of weapons. Outside of that, the hovering of the blades of the Apache was drowning.

Byron carried a M-16 with sixteen fully loaded magazines. Juice possessed a M40A3, a spotting scope, and binoculars. Mike carried a M4 with two radios and a medical kit. Reggie would control the powerful .50 caliber Bushmaster rifle, while Willie clutched his .300 Winchester Magnum equipped with a RVS night-vision scope mounted atop it.

New to the squad, possessing a M14 and explosives was Rodney Smith.

Byron pulled a map of Korengal Valley from his Military Vest pocket. "Now listen up, soldiers," Byron began to address his platoon and go over the objectives of the mission. "We're gonna be landing at the rendezvous in thirty minutes. Abbudah's men will be in the lower part of the Valley. We will make our way in the direction of Abbudah's base from the south. Let the Marines come from the east. I was informed that at least eighty of Abbudah's men are in the proximity. It's a strong chance we will be engaged."

"Sarge, you mean to tell us it's us against eighty? What kind of odds is that? Why would they send just six of us?" Rodney asked. He was as nervous as a prostitute in Sunday school. This was his first deployment.

"Soldier, the numbers mean nothing to us. We are snipers, and this is the job that's been handed down from up top."

Everyone felt some twinge of fear. The odds they were up against was troubling. But now was not the time to show it. It was time for precise execution, and they were required to be exactly that.

As the Apache was nearing the drop off point at the top of

Korengal Valley Mountain, all six snipers were in a serious mood. It was wartime. Kill or be killed. Arriving at the drop off point, all six soldiers deported the chopper, lowering themselves on the rope that hung from the cabin one by one. They all wanted payback for Sergeant Langston. Animosity and malice ran deep within, and it was the fuel that pumped through their bloodstreams.

Once they all landed, they proceeded on their trek to the top of the mountain. Reaching their destination, they rested at the edge of a large grass field. They were all fully camouflaged in green, matching the vegetation of trees and the grass on the ground. Their boots blended with the dirt and rocks.

Stopping at an area where a lot of trees were, Byron figured it should suit them from being detected. They had been on the move the entire night. This would be a good place for the squad to catch some much-needed rest. "Aye, check it out, soldiers. We gonna post-up right here for the night. We move in o-three hundred hours. Is that clear?"

The region they were heading for was Abbudah's safe haven. The exact domain where the decapitation of Sergeant Major Langton occurred.

The platoon unloaded their backpacks and caught some rest while Byron stood guard. Byron, not wanting to sleep, and taking full responsibility for the successful completion of the mission, popped a No-Doze pill to stay awake. If not for the pill, his anxiety and nervousness wouldn't allow him a wink of slumber. He needed and wanted to be on point. That's why he elected himself to stand guard with his M-16. He was determined to assure their safety.

The next morning, Byron and his team were on the move when they ran into a goat herder. What really piqued their interest in him was the fact the he had no goats. Reggie immediately pat searched the man for communication devices or any weapons. The man came up clean. Byron cleared him and the goat herder walked off in the opposite direction.

Juice instinctively studied the man for a long time, up until he was no longer in view.

Byron asked, "What's up with you, Juice?" Noticing the

immediate change of his attitude and behavior.

"I don't know, Sarge. Something just don't seem right. It's something up with the goat herder. Can't put my finger on it though."

"Just stay on point, soldier. We're all good." Byron stated, attempting to lighten their situation. After all, they were en route toward Abbudah's base.

It wasn't even five minutes. The crack of a rifle sounded off from across the field.

"Everybody, down!" Byron raised the M-16 clicking the safety to fire and returned fire in the direction of the gunfire that polluted the air. Bullets whizzed by his head and arm.

The Taliban militants had been in the high grass area. Spotting Byron and his team first they promptly decided to let their AK's spit venom at their enemies.

"It's an ambush! I repeat, it's an ambush, damnit!" Reggie yelled into his earphone as he tried to find a spot to lay fire with the .50 caliber.

"How many we looking at?" Willie had his .300 Magnum pointed, swaying from left to right. Obscuring his view was the high grass he laid in.

"It's like a billion of these muthafuckas. They like roaches in the projects!" Byron yelled as he continued to apply return fire upon Abbudah's men.

Rodney ran over to Byron while Byron was inserting another 30-round magazine into the M-16. It was vividly visible that he was shaken by the events that was unraveling before his eyes.

"Sir, sir, what do we do?" Rodney asked, yelling over the rapid, thunderous gunshots.

"Hand me a grenade, and give me some cover fire."

Rodney handed Byron two grenades, cocked his rifle and said, "Aight, sir. I got you."

Byron could see from a distance the top of a few Taliban fighters' heads. "Now, on three, I need you to let that sucker spark, okay?"

Rodney was scared to death, but as Byron began with the count of 1, it was as if he became transfixed.

"One, two, three!" Byron stood and ran toward the crowd of Taliban.

Rodney jumped up and let the M24 loose. "Muthafuckas, yeah! Muthafucka, this what you want!" He was shooting wildly like a deranged man.

Byron threw the two pineapple grenades in the directions of the enemy fighters. *BA-BOOM! BA-BOOM!* The explosion of the two devices landed on target. Some lost limbs, others were showered with shrapnel.

Rodney, possessed and totally out of his wits, was continually pulling the trigger, not being in the right frame of mind. A 7.62 by 39 millimeter slug hit him in his stomach, severing his spinal cord in half, while he possessed an empty rifle.

Byron saw the hit, but it was too late. Rushing toward Rodney, bullets whizzed past his head, like the Grim Reaper was chasing him. When he made it to him, Rodney just laid in the grass. Crimson fluid oozed from the wound, gagging from the thick blood that engorged in his throat.

"Rodney? Rodney, hold on, soldier. We gonna get you up outta here. Just hang in there."

Rodney grabbed Byron's vest tight. Holding with a death grip, his eyes rolled to the back of his head. Byron saw the transformation of living to mortality as he just stared at the white irises that were occupying Rodney's lifeless eye-sockets. Yet, he tried to remain optimistic. Byron grabbed his walkie-talkie. "Mike, this is Sergeant Hobson, I got a man down! I repeat, man down! We need medical assistance! Now!"

Mike came back over the two-way, "Sarge, I'm pinned down by enemy fire. In a minute, I'm gonna need some fucking medical assistance my-fucking-self."

Byron turned to Rodney. Rodney's eyes just stared into space. Hoping against the worst, at that moment was indelible. It was game over for Rodney's life on earth.

Byron closed Rodney's eyes, and said a silent prayer for the fallen soldier. The imminent sound of gunfire seeming to get closer and closer. He knew if he stayed in that position, he would certainly be joining his comrade. That was a no-go. Byron grabbed the remainder of the grenades off of Rodney, cocked his rifle and commenced action of survival.

The Taliban didn't let up, as they continuously fired on the snipers. Byron's adrenaline pumping kept him shooting his gun and moving steadily. An enemy fighter came across the grass field not noticing Byron. His mistake, which would be his last one. Byron squeezed a shot that gave the man a complete face lift, as the slug from the rifle did exactly that. Lifted the man's face off. After seeing the demise of his comrade, Byron vowed, before he goes, he would unleash a barrage of havoc upon the enemies. It was kill or be killed.

In the midst of the action, two slugs tore into Byron's back, stumbling him, yet he remained on his feet, thankful to have the heavy armor vest on. The slugs had slammed into his backpack, applying the feelings as if someone had taken a hammer and hit him with it. His breath was knocked out of him, but life still remained. That was most important. He quickly unlatched the pack from his back to assess the damage. The SAPI plate in his backpack held strong. The bullet was nowhere near able to penetrate his flesh. It was a blessing. One he quickly thanked God for.

He reattached the gear and proceeded toward Abbudah's compound. He needed a good firing position. One where he would be able to have a fair chance at survival. Replaying the images of the murdered Navy Seal, all the strength and motivation to succeed was supplied by the horror scene.

Noticing a tree a small distance across the field, Byron raced toward it ignoring the bullets that were flying in his direction, throwing grenades at enemy soldiers. Byron made it, took cover behind the thick bark, and commenced picking them off one by one with his M-16.

Juice's voice came over the airwaves of the radio. "Aye, yo, Sarge, you still in the fight?" Hot shell casings ejecting from his M40A3 sniper rifle, spilling the blood of Islamic Terrorists.

"Yeah, I'm still in the game. I don't know for how long. Get those damn Apache's down here now! I don't know how long we can hold these muthafuckas off," Byron said as he gunned another fighter down in cold blood.

"That's a bet, Sergeant."

A number of dead bodies and a few minutes later, Mike came over the radio. "Howdy, cowboys and cowgirls. Apache coming to come take us home. It's a small camp up ahead. Some kind of base for Abbudah's men. All we have to do is seize it. Our ride will be here in about thirty minutes. See y'all at the house. Yee-haw!" Mike shouted, squeezing the trigger of his M4.

Byron let off a flurry of automatic gunfire, aimed at his enemies, as he proceeded toward the camp. He mercilessly chopped down anybody that stood in his path. The smell of gun smoke and death engross the battlefield. He heard sound of the Apache rescue team from the heavens above.

"This is Hitterman from up top. Coming to assist Operation Whaler. I suggest you boys get low." The words spoken from the pilot was like music to every one's ears.

The Apache roared over them while the heat guided missiles dispersed from the chopper. The explosions were like a scene from a Rambo movie. Taliban fighters tried to escape with their lives intact. To no avail, running from the base into the scopes of the 101st Battalion. They never knew what hit them. Large caliber rounds sent them into eternal darkness. The military chopper guided its missiles into the camp, destroying the compound and everything in it. Bashan Abbudah's main base in Korengal Valley had just been demolished by the United States Military.

Byron and his squad searched the premise of Bashan Abbudah's compound. To their liking, the Taliban General had been killed in the bombing. Byron snatched the military stripes from Abbudah's shirt and pocketed them.

After the investigation of the premise, and the gathering of intel, Byron and the 101st Battalion loaded the Apache heading back home. Everybody sat silently in the chopper. The death of Rodney weighed heavily on everyone's mind. As well as the close call that was sprung upon them, was nothing short of light. It was a deadly, murderous mission for them. But that was what they signed up for.

Byron had just found a new respect for the enemy. One thing he would never forget in his life— the time he was in the Korengal Valley.

S. Allen

Chapter 13

Biggs — AKA William Sullivan— sat in his immaculate condo in Oak Park on Chicago's westside. It had been a long profitable week as he ran the 100's and 50's through the money counting machine that sat on his living room table. A cigar hung from his lips while he wrapped a rubber band around a thick stack of bills, totaling $10,000.

Ever since he moved to Chicago from Milwaukee, Wisconsin his dreams to be a successful drug dealer began to flourish. At 53 years old Biggs had seen it all in the grimy streets of Milwaukee, from money to murder. Born and raised on the Northside of Milwaukee in a neighborhood known as the H.O.P.— a poverty-stricken neighborhood where drug dealers and gangs attained most of the population. Mr Biggs lived in a household most people would call dysfunctional, due to the fact that his father sold crack cocaine, the same substance his mother was addicted to. With so much negativity surrounding him, he found home in the bloody streets of the Mill. Mr Biggs got his name because at the age of 14 he weighed 250 pounds, and as a youngster the currency he obtained from selling drugs swelled his pockets to capacity, so the streets named him Mr Biggs.

Mr. Biggs' life took a dramatic change when he witnessed his father get murdered by the hands of a rival drug dealer. The horrific tragedy brought out the violent side of Mr. Biggs. In return, he released his pain on the streets of Milwaukee. He and his young crew from H.O.P. took the murder of his father personal. Mr. Biggs gained alliance with other small drug crews throughout the city, and they all came to the round table to discuss the serious business off murder. They made a pact to eliminate all the competition in the drug trade. Finesse and murder would be their recipe for success.

The summer of '83 was hot while local known drug dealers were mysteriously coming up missing. Later, they would be found with their heads busted open to the white meat, all at Mr. Biggs' command.

The word on the streets was to be careful if you were selling drugs in the city because Mr. Biggs was getting niggas snatched up, earning him and his crew the moniker *The Body Snatchers*, and with the fear he instilled in the streets, Biggs no longer went by Biggs. The streets of Milwaukee had crowned him Mr. Biggs.

Mr. Biggs' empire came crumbling when an informant for the feds penetrated his organization, which led him to doing 15 years in Lewisburg Penitentiary in Pennsylvania. The charge, conspiracy to commit murder. Mr. Biggs was approached by a local drug boss who wanted a supposed to be government witness killed. The compensation, $100,000. Mr. Biggs and The Body Snatchers took the murder contract. The intended target was a Alea Lopez from the southside of the city. Mr. Biggs sent two of his goons to handle the demonstration and was met by the FBI. Since the feds had him on wiretap, there was no chance of him taking the case to trial and winning an acquittal. Therefore, he accepted a plea deal and landed at the FCI in Lewisburg, Pennsylvania.

Times had definitely changed in the city in the last 15 years. Mr. Biggs found out after his release that the streets were under new management. The new generation. While in the fed, Mr. Biggs had befriended a Mexican immigrant by the name of Roger Castilino. Castilino was the leader of the Sinola Cartel and was incarcerated for running 100 kilograms of cocaine into the United States. Roger was just what Mr. Biggs was looking for in the federal system, someone who could supply him with a lot of drugs. With his plug he was back on the streets of Milwaukee. To Mr. Biggs, Milwaukee was too small for what he was trying to accomplish. He couldn't play the game how he wanted. Knowing that he had an aunt in Chicago he set his sights on the motherland. In the fed, he had been around a lot of dudes from the Chi and all they talked about was the money they accumulated through drugs. Mr. Biggs packed his bags and headed to the deadliest city in the United States. Chicago, Illinois.

For the first month Mr. Biggs laid low at his aunt's apartment located on the Westside of the city on Homan and Ohio. He would watch the traffic on the corners as the dope fiends came to get served their drug of choice. The traffic was almost endless, and at that point

Mr. Biggs made up his mind, that he wanted a piece of the action. After using the number Castilino had given him he met up with a Mexican on 26ᵗʰ and Coliternia, and was passed a kilo of pure heroin.

Mr. Biggs took the heroin and broke it down into grams and quarter grams and approached the dealers on the corner of Homan and Ohio with a business proposition they couldn't refuse. An opportunity to make some money, and a lot of it. At a time when grams where going for $150, Mr. Biggs would give it to them for the low, at $65 a gram. Enough room where the dealers could see a substantial profit. The more money they brought back the more work he gave.

After seeing how the dope money was in Chicago Mr. Biggs sent for a few of The Body Snatchers to aid him in building his empire. The three he sent for were legends in Milwaukee with the murder game. Body Bag, 8-track and Killa Fred. Chicago was known for murder and mayhem so when the word got out about some out of towners getting some money, a local by the name of Ty Banks tried to test the water by not paying Mr. Biggs for $1,500 worth of heroin. Mr. Biggs knew that his gangster was being tested and had to make an example. A deadly one. Ty Banks was kidnapped, tortured and hung from a light pole on Chicago Avenue in the middle of the Westside with his testicals stuffed in his mouth and the words *Body Snatchers* carved in his chest. The Murder of Ty Banks was never solved and the streets of the Chi now knew that Mr. Biggs and The Body Snatchers were about that life. Homan and Ohio was moving like a racehorse as Castilino flooded Mr. Biggs with the purest of dope. After one summer all the local free lancers on Homan and Ohio found home with The Body Snatchers and every one of them willing to kill in the name of Mr. Biggs.

With a mob of killas at his beckoning and call, Mr. Biggs started setting his sights on other drug turfs on the Westside. With the plug he had he could supply the city. If Mr. Biggs saw a turf he wanted in on, he sent his cronies to take it over. It was a spot on Polk and Lawndale that Mr Biggs found out was doing no less than a $100,000 a day in sales of heroin. The young hustler that ran the block was named Toto. Mr Biggs contacted Toto and asked to meet up with him for a business proposition. The youngster told him they could meet at the Red Lobster at the Brickyard Mall.

When Mr Biggs and Killa Fred walked in the restaurant, Toto and a few of his homies were at their booth looking at their Facebook pages on their phones. At the sight of the youngsters, Mr. Biggs knew they were not about the street life that they portrayed nor were they aware of the dangerous situation they were involved in.

"What's up, youngster? I'm glad you found time to meet up with me." Mr. Biggs greeted, as he slid in the booth across from Toto while Killa Fred remained standing.

"How you get my number?" Toto asked not even looking up from his phone.

"Let's just say a mutual acquaintance wanted to see you make some real money."

"What make you think I'm not already making some real money?" Toto looked up with a smirk on his face.

"Because if you was making some real money you wouldn't be in that box Chevy. You would be in some grown man shit like a Benz or a Loc. That's what grown money look like." Mr Biggs said rubbing his goatee. He continued. "You probably paying one-fifty for a brick that's cut up. You may be making a twenty thousand-dollar profit if you lucky, and after you finish tricking on hoes and cloths you back broke. Basically you working for free." Mr Biggs said in a calm but serious tone.

One of Toto's men screwed up his face and slid his hand in his True Religion hoodie. Killa Fred peeped his demeanor and already had a firm grip on the 357 Python that rested in the confines of his Pelle-Pelle leather jacket, ready to pop the young nigga's top if need be.

Toto let out a slight chuckle and laid his phone on the table. "What gang you run with?" Toto asked pertaining to gang affiliation.

"The Body Snatchers, nigga." Mr Biggs sneered.

"So, what? You here to try an extort me, old-school?" Toto

heard about The Body Snatchers and how they were around laying the press game down. "I don't see that Body Snatchers shit; I think you better ask about me." Toto said hitting his chest for emphasis.

One of Toto's homies got nervous at the sound of Body Snatchers as sweat lined his forehead. Killa Fred tightened the grip on the revolver.

"Alright, youngster, you said what it is. I was just trying to give you room to eat out here, that's all." Mr BiggsBiggs said in a fake apologetic tone.

"Well, I'm already eating, fat boy. So why don't you and your mens go try that intimidation shit somewhere else 'cause we ain't going."

"Alright, soldier, that's what's up." Mr Biggs stood up from the booth and gave Killa Fred a wink and a smile.

At that point a look of death plastered across Killa Fred's face as he squeezed the chrome trigger on the large hand cannon. The gun barked venom while the hollow point splattered Toto's brains. Killa Fred pulled the smoky gun from his jacket and pointed it at one of Toto's men and squeezed the trigger twice, catching him in the throat. Blood spurted from his wounds as he tried to hold onto his lifeline. His attempts were futile as he slumped over face-down in his shrimp scampi.

The crowd in the restaurant was ecstatic as they ran away from the horrific violent crime they had just witnessed. The other bodyguard that accompanied Toto sat in silence, shocked as his boss's brain tissue dripped from his young face. Killa Fred pointed the evil weapon in his direction.

"Now, I want you to go back to your hood and let them know, Polk and Laundale is under new management. Mr Biggs is now in control of that area, and if you serve drugs, you do it for me and only me, is that understood?" Mr Biggs said as the screams from the petrified parties filled the restaurant.

The shook youngster that was soaked in warm blood nodded.

"That's what I like to hear. I'm looking for a lieutenant to run the block. If you trying to get this money, give me a call." Mr Biggs pulled his contact card from his shirt pocket and threw it on the table. It landed in a pool of dark blood.

"Come on Big homie. Let's get up outta here." Killa Fred said as he tucked the murder weapon in his pants.

The two fled the restaurant in a Cadillac Escalade just as some of Chicago's finest and ambulance invaded the parking lot of Red Lobster.

That was 1 kilo and two years ago. Now Mr Biggs and The Body Snatchers had taken over most of the westside. Either by choice or force, except for the most lucrative of all. Avers and Augusta, the strong hold for the Mafia's. He knew that Avers and Augusta was led by a wild nigga that went by the name of Funk, and the Mafia's were loyal to him by any means. Mr Biggs knew that it would take calculated finesse to take over the block. He was blessed by the game god to run into Funk at a bar called the 007 on the far westside.

He had gotten word that the loudmouth, flamboyant character before him was indeed Funk from Avers and Augusta. The low grade jewelry shined off his neck in the dimly lit bar. Mr Biggs watched as Funk was spitting game to a curvaceous, thick female who seemed to be intoxicated by what Funk was saying. Mr Biggs grabbed his bottle of Remy XO and made his way to the bar where Funk was. He tapped the thick big booty chick on the shoulder. "Excuse me, beautiful. Can I have a word with your man real quick?"

The female looked Mr Biggs up and down, seeing the clear diamonds in his ear and the expensive Prada jacket on him. She knew that the big man was of some importance. She looked at Funk for approval.

Funk also gave Mr Biggs a once over before he pulled a small knot out of his pocket and gave it to the female. "Shorty, go grab me another shot of Grey Goose."

The female smacked her lips with much attitude, with her hands on her hips and went to get Funk's drink.

"That's a nice lil' piece of ass you got there, youngster." Mr Biggs said and took a drink from his bottle.

"Yeah, she alright. What's up, though? Who is you and what

you wanna holler at me about?" Funk asked getting straight to the business.

"My name Mr Biggs and I came to offer you a job, shorty. I hear you got Avers and Augusta on smash, then I also heard the dope ain't hittin' on shit."

The thick girl came back and gave Funk his drink and walked off, straight out the front door. Funke downed his drink. "You know you just cost me some pussy right?" Funk said now becoming irritated with his time being wasted.

"Shorty, you fuck with me, pussy will be endless."

"Oh yeah? So, go ahead and talk, I'll talk back." Funk said now interested in what the old timer was about to speak.

"I hear your block is doing numbers, but I'm trying to get them numbers up."

"How you gone do that?" Funk questioned.

Mr Biggs looked at Funk through bloodshot eyes as if he was searching his soul. "By giving you giving you the best dope in the city, that's how. I'll front you a key a week for a hundred thousand."

At the mention of keys, Funk's eyes bucked like he had just hit the lottery. "So, you just gone pull up on me like this without knowing me from nowhere and front me a brick?"

"That's what I said. That's your turf so you run it how you see fit. Just make sure I get mines off the top and everything will be all well."

Funk did some mental math in his head and saw a huge profit. With a whole kilo he could stretch it to maximize his bankroll and really come up. This would be the chance to see some major paper and climb up in the dope game like he always wanted. "Alright, big homie, I'm with that lick. When my first demonstration gone come through?"

Mr Biggs went in his pocket and produced his contact information and passed it to Funk. "Call me tomorrow at two-thirty." Mr Biggs stood up and killed the rest of the Remy XO. After letting the smooth alcohol invade his bloodstream he left the bar, leaving Funk in the bar with a smile and his dick rock hard from the thoughts of riches.

From that point, Funk and Mr Biggs had been getting money. Funk was bringing in 100 geez faithfully and today was no different.

Mr Biggs had just finished counting the money from the week's profits and put the last $10,000 bundle in the Sentry safe that was embedded in the floor of his closet. The dope game had bought him millions in just a few years and he reigned supreme on the vicious Westside of Chicago. In his eyes the sky was the limit and his desire was to ball into he fell. He closed the safe feeling like the true king of the streets.

Chapter 14
Funk

"Man, I'm telling you, if this hoe ass nigga don't have that money right, I'ma do something to his ass. This clown act like he don't understand morals and principal. This shit ain't personal, it's business; feel me?"

Meathead nodded in agreement as he slid the Buick Lacrosse through the mid-day traffic. Funk and Meathead had been riding around, picking up money for Mr Biggs on a few of his drug blocks. It was still early and they had three more blocks to pick up from. The individual they were speaking on was a worker from Avers and Augusta who went by the name of Monkey-Lord. Monkey-Lord had been ducking Funk for a couple of weeks. He owed Funk for two packs of heroin, totaling $1,000, and Funk was agitated, and the situation was coming to a boiling point.

In the last two years Funk had taken complete control over Avers and Augusta and was now the operating Chief for the Mafias. Dealing with Mr Biggs, he was able to keep the block pumping with dope, and in return his swagger and status elevated in the streets. The position Funk was in didn't come easy, but in his case it came almost as easy as it could come.

One night while Funk was on the block serving solo, he fell for the okey-doke and served a undercover cop two dime bags of heroin. He was arrested and taken down to the precinct where he sat with a $4,000 cash bond, due to the bundle of drugs found in his coat. Just when Funk thought things couldn't get any worst it did. Detective Calhoun came to his cell with another cop.

"Larry Banks, what's up, playa?" Detective Calhoun said showing his stained teeth from years of coffee and tobacco use. The detective resembled a run-down Clint Eastwood. The last time Funk saw the cop was in the raid he was caught in with Byron and Lil' Pooh, and at the sight of Calhoun he knew he was in some deep shit. "Now, I'ma get right to the point, Banks. You got caught slipping with quite a bit of dope. With that much in your possession it's a good chance the fed might want to touch this. But the good thing about this is that I personally know you are not the boss and you're just working for Billy Good, am I correct?" Funk remained silent. "I'm offering you a chance to save yourself, son, because I seriously doubt you are built for the United States penitentiary. They say on average, with the amount of dope we confiscated off you, you'll be looking at a sentencing guideline of ten to twenty years. Banks, all we want is Billy Good." Detective took a pack of cigarettes from his vest pocket and lit one of the cancer sticks.

"So, you want me to snitch? The Mafia's find out I ratted, I'll be dead by the weekend." Funk said knowing he was caught between a rock and a hard place.

Detective Calhoun blew out a thick ring of smoke before he spoke. "Nobody saw you get arrested. You were the only one on the block. You give a location to some drugs and guns, and where the Oldman lays his head, and you are free to walk. How you survive is on you. If I was you I would invest in a hole to dig myself in so I can hide. But I tell you this, you drug-dealing son of a bitch. The feds pick up your case, you are guaranteed to see the penitentiary, with a lot of time to get your mind right. The choice is completely up to you."

Funk thought about the situation he was faced with. He couldn't do County time let alone federal time in somebody's penitentiary. The police confiscated his money so he couldn't bond out, and he was damned if he contacted Billy Good to get him out of the jam. He was already in violation for hustling on the block when it was supposed to be closed and shut down. If he stayed in the precinct, if what Calhoun said was true, the feds were going to be on his ass. He had to get out of jail and quick. It was at that time Funk would make the decision that would change his life.

"So, all I gotta do is give you some stash spots and where old head at, huh?"

"That's all, Banks, and all your troubles are over. No charges, no nothing. You walk right out the front door with no strings attached."

"Alright, cop. Bet." Funk retorted with a wicked grin.

Officer Calhoun flicked his cigarette butt on the ground and squashed it with his foot. "Officer, cuff this inmate and bring him up to the interrogation room please."

Later that night, BillyGood was in a pleasant sleep with his beautiful wife Debra at his side, until he heard a *BOOOM!* At the sound of the thunderous noise Billy Good awoke, startled and shaken. Thinking that his life was endangered he reached under his pillow for his chrome 357 Dessert Eagle.

"Baby, what's going on?" Debra asked, frightened from the loud crashing noise that came from downstairs.

Billy Good heard the footsteps racing up the stairs as he cocked the hammer off the large weapon, ready and willing to send the those who invaded his home to early graves.

The bedroom door was kicked in. "DEA! DEA! Put the gun down now! Let me see some hands!"

Billy Good knew they weren't home invaders the moment he saw the AR-15's and bold yellow letters that read DEA across their jackets. Billy Good let the revolver fall from his hands. They rushed him with force, cuffed him and Debra, and led them to an awaiting unmarked Crown Victoria.

After the feds searched the home of Billy Good they ended up confiscating 2.3-million in cold cash, 13 kilograms of pure heroin and 6 firearms that he had no right carry. Billy Good was indicted with the drugs, along with a king pin charge that would definitely land him in a maximum-security prison. A warrant was placed on his henchmen, Ricardo Davison, AKA Rico, and as soon as he heard of Billy Good's arrest, he took off.

Rico had been on the run for two months now knowing the feds had a hard on for him. They connected him to 10 gang-related shootings. Rico knew at this point it was do or die, kill or be killed, as he constantly saw his face on the WAN news. Rico was laying low on the southside with a female by the name of Sherieka. He was a nervous wreck while he chained smoked blunt after blunt, with an assortment of automatics laid at his feet as he anticipated and envisioned a shootout with the Chicago Police Department. Rico's money was low. The feds hit all the stash spots and took the dope.

He knew it was an informant in the clutches of his circle but couldn't pinpoint who. Billy Good had been governing the Mafia's for so long it could have been anybody who penetrated the organization. Rico couldn't focus right now on who the rat was, he had to focus on eluding the cops. He knew he had to make a play for some finances and soon. So, when Funk called him with a lick, he jumped on it with the quickness. Funk told Rico he had a lick for 10 kilos of cocaine.

"So, how you know this nigga got that much work?" Rico asked as he rode shotgun in Funk's Ford Taurus. His 45 ARP rested on his lap.

"I know he good for it. This my mans' uncle. I told him I could pay for five and he said he could front me five with that." Funk replied.

"He be strapped?"

"Man, it don't matter, 'cause we gone kill him anyway. You know how it go; it's about who get the drop first." Funk said and made a left on Bosworth on the city's Northside.

"That ain't what I'm talking about. You get the same time for ten bodies as you get for one." Rico said while he checked the magazine to the 45.

Funk pulled up behind a blue conversion can and killed the lights.

Rico looked around, scanning the dark street. "Where he at?" He gripped his tool, as he stood ready to get it cracking.

"He should be pulling up in a minute. We got here a lil' early," Funk said, looking at the clock on the dashboard as he slid his hand to his waistline. The two gangsters sat in complete silence while a car turned down the street. Funk's heartbeat began to beat faster. "That should be him right here." Funk said nodding his head toward the vehicle creeping up the block.

Rico turned his head in the direction of the car. At the same time, Funk pulled the Glock 17 from off his waist. That one millisecond was all it took and Rico's future in the underworld was over. He turned back around and met the nose of Funk's Glock. "What the fu—" was all he could manage to get out before Funk squeezed the trigger.

The bullet caught Rico in the forehead. Blood plastered the passenger side window along with brain tissue and skull fragments from Rico's cranium. *BOC! BOC!* The gunshots echoed in the confines of the car as Funk shot him twice more in the head, sealing his death. Rico passed to the afterlife, head slumped on the dashboard. After relieving Rico of his weapon he exited the vehicle and jumped in the car that turned down the block. Rico's murder was never solved.

With Billy Good in federal Prison for 30 years and Rico in the cemetery, Funk stepped up to the plate to gain control of the Mafias. The majority chose to follow Funk and welcome his leadership as the minorities began to pop up all over the city it on the WGN with their heads knocked off. Challenging Funk's authority was detrimental as Lil' Pooh would soon find out.

Funk had never really liked Lil' Pooh or Byron. He would envy Lil' Pooh as he wished to be in his shoes. He hated Byron with a passion. He felt Byron wasn't capable of holding the position he held. In his heart he felt Byron wasn't devoted to the Mafia's, he was a mama's boy who wanted to be part of the lifestyle to be cool, not as a means of survival in the concrete jungle as he. After Byron enlisted in the Marines, Lil' Pooh started to distance his self from the gang. He would come on the block after it was shut down and cash in. Lil' Pooh had his own operation going on and that was something Funk couldn't endure. He sent Meathead and a few other Mafia's to rob and pistol-whip Lil' Pooh. Lil' Pooh bowed down to Funk's dictatorship.

"I'm hungry as a hostage. Pull up right here real quick so we can grab something to eat, Joe." Funk said referring to the pizza spot on Chicago Avenue called Pete's.

Meathead parked the vehicle in front of the restaurant and the two thugs got out the whip. Noticing the crowd of youngsters posted in front of the establishment Funk double checked where his Smith & Wesson rested inside his Coogie jeans. At the site of Funk and Meathead the crew gave head nods, acknowledging the new boss of the Mafia's.

Monkey-Lord was in Pete's awaiting a deep-dish cheese pizza

when he heard a very familiar voice that made him freeze like a popsicle.

"Damn, Lord, where you been hiding? You know we been looking all over the city for your punk ass. And I know one thing for sure, you better have that Nation money." Funk said with a sneer, his gun now visible and out of his pants.

Monkey-Lord turned around and farted at the sight of Funk and the huge canon in his hand. "Man, Lord, I was gone call you in a minute when I got finished with the pack. I got three hundred on me now." Monkey-Lord was shaking like a hoe in a church while he pulled out the crumbled-up money.

Funk looked Monkey-Lord over as his handed tightened on his weapon. "Muthafucka, it look like you already finished the pack. You got on all new shit. A hundred and fifty dollar Jordan's on your feet and you don't have my money?" Funk raised the gun toward Monkey-Lord. A customer screamed while others made a dash for the door.

"Lord, just give me a few hours and trust and believe I'ma have that bread. On Mafia," Monkey-Lord pleaded.

"Alright, fam. That's what's up. Only thing is you gone have to get it while you on crutches." Funk lowered the gun to MonkeylordLord's leg and pulled the trigger.

POP! Monkey-Lord dropped to the floor holding his leg in peer agony while blood poured from his wound.

"You got to until nine. If you don't have my money or my drugs, the next one gone be in your head." Funk threatened and tucked the smoking gun under his white t-shirt. "Let's get up outta here." Funk said as him and Meathead left the pizza joint and Monkey-Lord in pure pain.

"Damn, Funk, did you have to shoot 'em?" Meathead asked as he pulled off into traffic.

Funk looked at Meathead like he was the scum of the earth before he said. "I ain't taking no losses on nothing. Niggas come up short, they getting crushed. *Anybody* can get it; ain't nobody exempt." Funk mugged Meathead. "Now, take me to Mr Biggs's spot so we can drop this cash off, and stop asking so many questions."

S. Allen

Chapter 15
Byron

Cha-kah! Cha-kah! Cha-kah! Byron ejected a spent shell casing and injected a fresh 7.62 round into his rifle. He was 600 yards away from his target as he set his sights inside of his scope. After taking a deep breath he placed his finger on the trigger mechanism. His nerves were still shocked from the engagement he had in Korengal Valley. Byron squeezed trigger. *Cha-kah!* The rifle's butt kicked hard inside of Byron's right shoulder.

Juice had been spotting for Byron and looked through his binoculars at the target Byron had been firing at. "Man, homie, it look like you about ten inches off the mark."

Byron laid his rifle down in frustration.

"Aye, Byron, what's up with you? You normally hit that with your eyes closed. Sergeant, you got something on your mind?" Juice asked. He had been noticing a certain change in Byron's behavior since they came from the last mission.

"Juice, I'm starting to feel this military GI-Joe shit ain't for me."

"What you mean by that? The way you perform on the battlefield, I can't tell."

Byron rubbed his baldhead. He had been under a lot of stress since he had gotten a letter from Lil' Pooh, running down what was taking place in the hood. The Mafia's and Funk were shitting on everybody, especially his mother. Byron couldn't believe his moms was on drugs. The revelation explained her behavior for the last two years of his deployment. It angered him that Funk would violate him in such way and Byron wanted Funk's head on a platter. But the fact was he was stuck thousands of miles away from home and wasn't in a position to do anything about the things that caused his heart to ache; he was in another country fighting a war on terror.

"Juice, we over here fighting a war and the real war is at home. The enemies we need to be killing is right in Chicago. Our very own."

"Why you say that?" Juice replied not knowing where his mans was going with all the extra shit.

"I can't get what happened to Rodney out of my head. Rodney died in my arms and I could do nothing about it. He was protecting me, Juice, and I couldn't save him."

"Bro, I feel what you saying, but this war ain't no game. This is war, and in war there is casualties. You gotta remember, Byron, you didn't get drafted, you enlisted so you signed up for the job. You gotta put your feelings to the side and continue to handle the business, because if you don't you gone lose your life on the battlefield, and that's what's real."

Byron picked up one of the brass shell casings off the ground and twirled it at his fingertips. He looked at it and tried to figure how something so small could cause so much death and destruction. Enemies were everywhere— on the battlefield of Afghanistan to the blood-soaked streets of the Chi. In his mind death was inescapable. The thought of his loving mother strung out on drugs and Funk supplying her enraged him. Byron walked over to a table where they had their arsenal set up and picked up a Browning 50 caliber sniper rifle and two metal boxes of shells and went back to where Juice was standing.

"Give me a spot." Byron said as he laid on the ground with the rifle. A tripod rested under the heavy weapon. After loading the rifle's deadly chamber Byron took sight behind the scope and zeroed in on the target.

Juice looked in the binoculars. "We at six hundred yards, enemy is armed and dangerous with what looks to be a female hostage. Head shot five centimeters to the left of the sustained area."

Looking through the scope he saw the board target that resembled a Taliban fighter with a female hostage. Wicked thoughts filled his mind frame as he cocked the bolt-action on the rifle. After putting the crosshairs on the head of the target, Byron began to control his breathing and rested his finger on the trigger. Calming himself he applied a firm, steady squeeze to the trigger mechanism. The hard recoil from the powerful gun jerked ion his shoulder. The gunpowder aroused him as he ejected the spent shell and replaced it with a fresh one.

"Eight hundred yards out, enemy insurgent behind a black

A Shooter's Ambition

SUV! He seems to be heavily armed!" Juice yelled from behind his binoculars.

Byron zeroed in. The thought of his mother helplessly strung out on heroin caused a tear to fall from his eye. Again, he applied pressure to the trigger, causing the rifle to bark. Reload, shoot, reload, shoot. Byron continued to work the 50 cal until one of the heavy shells hit a gas tank of the SUV, and exploded into a large ball of fire. His gun was now empty, the barrel of the weapon as hot as fish grease.

Juice looked at Byron, astonished. "Damn, Sarge, you was on that fifty-cal like a demon. All targets eliminated."

Byron stood up and knocked the dust off of his pants. His demeanor stone, his eyes bloodshot.

Later that night, Byron was sitting at his desk writing Lil' Pooh back. He missed Lil' Pooh and hated the fact he was in the situation he was in, so he felt it was his duty to give his comrade some words of encouragement.

Dear Lil' Pooh,

What's good, homie? I just received your letter and I'm taking this time to hit you back. First and foremost, your information saddened me to the core. I can't believe my moms out there on that shit. She only writes me every once in a while. I didn't know how to take this shit, bruh. Funk bogus as hell. That nigga has disrespected me, my family and the Mafia's, and his actions will not go unpunished. I will spend the rest of my life pursuing it. I promise. Lil' Pooh, you gotta get yourself together, stand up and get out of that slump you are in. We desire to be successful, all you gotta do is believe in yourself. I grew up looking up to you. I know you are a hustla and ambition runs through your blood. You are smarter than that nigga Funk. Move around from that lame. I don't know if I'm going to make it home, Lil' Pooh. This shit is wicked, and death is constantly around me. God's will I will be back in Chicago next year if not sooner. Trust and believe things will change for the better. Please, Lil' Pooh, look out for my momma and tell her that I love her. Remember my words, Lil' Pooh. Just get yourself right, mind, body and soul. I love you bro.

Byron

Byron had just sealed the envelope when there was a knock at the door. "Come in." Byron said standing up from the desk.

US Special Operations Commander Sanchez entered. Byron saluted his superior. "At ease Marine." Sanchez saluted him back. "I thought I might find you here."

Byron and Commander Sanchez respectfully shook hands. "What brings you here, sir?"

"Well, to be honest, something big has come in from the big wigs in Washington, DC." Commander Sanchez laid a brown manila envelope on Byron's desk along with a video tape. "We just received information on an individual from within the ranks of Al-Qaeda who is believed to be operating in the town of Ah-Amiriyah outside of Fallujah. His name is Amad Aliqued." Byron opened up the envelope to see the information for his mission. "We have reason to believe this terrorist is planning to assassinate our president."

Byron looked through Amad's credentials. "Al-Qaeda militant, graduated from a college in Sudan, responsible for six major bombings in the last three years, was trained in a camp with Al-Qaeda, Special Military background. Explosive devices, counter spying, and assault sniping. This dude has an impressive resume." Byron said in a sarcastic yet serious manner.

"Sergeant, this is a very serious manner. If this individual makes it to the ground of United States soil, with all the protection in the world, our president will not be safe."

"So, I guess you want me to capture this scum?"

Commander Sanchez shook his head. "Sergeant, this is a top secret mission. A lot of people within the power circle know about this. We don't want him killed, Marine, we want him eliminated at all cost. A man of his caliber will never allow himself to be detained. Sergeant, this is the only way."

Byron looked at Amad's photo. The turban that covered his head was black and grey. His beard was full and the AK-47 that was slung over his right shoulder was gold. The magazine inserted in the weapon Byron guessed held no less than 100 rounds. But it was the eyes that caught Byron's attention. The eyes where the key to a man's soul and looking into the depth of his eyes Byron knew Amad didn't have a soul.

Commander popped the video tape in the VCR and turned on the television. "This is actual footage of some of our Marines who were killed by Amad's rifle. All footage is from the body cameras on our soldiers. I suggest you study these tapes and learn from their mistakes, because if you don't, there is no way you are going to leave Al-Amiriah alive." Commander Sanchez started to make his way to the door.

"How much time do we have?" Byron asked stopping commander Sanchez in his tracks.

"Time is not a friend of ours. I strongly suggest you and your men get a move on and handle this business. You have exactly twenty-four hours to complete this mission. Enjoy the rest of your day." Commander Sanchez exited the room leaving Byron staring at the television.

From what he could see, the Marine was in the confines of a base looking through a scope. He figured he had his target in his sight but waited too long to squeeze the trigger.

First mistake. Too much fucking time, Byron thought. Through his scope the Marine saw his target, Amad, pointing his rifle in his direction and then a bright flash. In less than a millisecond the Marine's head exploded from the 3.08 bullet that penetrated his brain through his eye socket. Byron rewound the video twice. He couldn't believe the shooting accuracy that Amad possessed. Byron watched two more Marines get crushed by Amad's rifle. They were American snipers like him, but now laid in caskets because of Amad's ambition. Byron knew when the time would come, he would have to perform righteously if he ever wanted to see his mother again.

Six hours later...

Byron and his platoon had just landed at the drop off spot two miles west of the town of Ah-Amiriah. The weather was beyond hot as the heat index soared above 100-degrees. Byron had chosen his team from the 101st battalion. Juice, Craig, and Mike Solbert would join him in bringing Amad his swift and violent death. Known that Byron's shooting was superior to his team it was understood that it would be Byron to fire the kill shot. Juice would work with Reggie to locate Amad while Mike and Craig would give them suppressed back up when Byron engaged the enemy.

CIA intelligence informed that Amad was in the town of Ah-Amiriah. The ancient mosque that was located in the middle of town was a known hang out for the strong militant Taliban. It was also heavily guarded by the extremist.

The plan was to locate and kill Amad on sight. One shot, one kill. Man down, and back to the drop site.

Once inside the congested town of Ah-Amiriah, Mike Solbert navigated the military Humvee through the crowded streets. Ah-Queda were known to open fire on Americans with AK-47's, so the platoon had to move with caution and be on point through the deadly hostile environment. The team was headed to an area of town not far from the midsize mosque for surveillance.

"Seems like the entire city is out. You men keep your eyes open for anything suspicious or out of place." Byron said placing a full magazine of 3.08 caliber ammunition into the belly of his rifle.

"Yeah, they got all the goat herders out today. Somebody's definitely going to feel the wrath of this fifty-cal." Reggie replied spitting a wad of chewing tobacco out the window.

Byron turned in his seat agitated, and faced Reggie. "Y'all already know what the mission is. We are here for Amad and Amad only. If anybody gets in the way of our orders that was given from up top, then we do what we have to do. But the objective is to eliminate Amad and Amad only; are we understood, marine?" Byron directed his statement to Reggie.

Reggie stared at Byron with pure disgust. He couldn't stomach taking orders from Byron and was beginning to wear his emotions on his sleeve. And plus, he still hadn't gotten over Byron breaking his jaw. Reggie gave a fake smile and mockingly, replied, "Yes, sir."

Byron pulled out the map of the town and spread it across his lap. "We should be about five minutes away from the surveillance site. Hopefully we can spot this clown and drop 'em." Byron said with confidence.

Stuck in the middle of traffic, a blue, rusted two-door car pulled on the side of the Humvee. The driver seemed to look a tad bit nervous as he kept his head forward. To Byron the passenger of the vehicle looked extremely familiar. Looking closer and more intensely, Byron couldn't believe his luck. He was looking at the target right in the face. Amad. Once the traffic started to move Byron ordered Mike to follow the van.

"Are you sure, Sergeant? We supposed to be in route to the surveillance site."

"Mike, just follow the got-damn van." Byron commanded.

"See what happens when you give a boy a grown man kind of authority." Reggie said with a smirk.

Byron ignored Reggie's sly remark for the moment as Mike stayed close to the van, trailing it but not to be noticed. "It's something about those men in the van." Byron retorted.

The traffic was at a standstill and it was at that point everything went in slow motion. The doors to the van slid open and four masked men hopped out pointing AK-47' s at the Humvee.

"Get down, now!" Byron yelled as the thunderous cracks from the rifles erupted and pandemonium broke out.

Shells from the machine guns ricocheted off the armor-proof Humvee as the men fired on the Marines with 100-round drums attached to their weapons. Reggie was the first to leap from the Humvee and take cover behind a parked car.

Mike Solbert slid from the driver's seat firing his 911. "Byron, Juice get outta there!" Mike yelled, letting the 45 rip.

The four men continued to spray the Humvee, hot shell casings covering the ground and gun-smoke polluting the air. The passengers of the van leaped out and ran in the opposite direction of the drama that was taking place in broad day light.

A sniper rifle slung over his shoulder, Mike sent four hollow points sailing his way but missed. "Sergeant, it's Amad! I have a visual." Mike emptied his magazine and replaced it with a fresh one.

Byron slid out the Humvee through the passenger side and came up busting the 3.08. The sound of the rifle sounded like bombs being dropped as a slug tore into one of the gunmen's mid-section, splitting him in half. Juice also joined the shootout spitting rounds with his M-16, catching one of the terrorist in the face, giving him a facelift. Byron fled from the gunfight in pursuit of Amad.

"Reggie give us some cover. Fire got-damnit," Juice franticly yelled as they took heavy automatic fire from the Afghans. Reggie was frozen behind an unoccupied car clutching the 50 caliber Beav. Sweat poured from his face as bullets whizzed by his head, penetrating everything around him. His nerves were shot so he jumped at each gunshot. He was scared shitless in the presence of battle and to him the safest place in the world was behind that car.

Mike took cover at the Humvee. His enemies were relentless and focused on his position while spraying unlimited bullets. Mike saw his life flash before his eyes as a slug tore through his right shoulder. Like wolves smelling blood, the terrorists moved in to finish off their prey. That was until Juice sprang from his cover pulling the trigger to the M-16. One of the masked men took one to the back while spinning around busting the AK-47. Juice was hit twice in the chest.

Byron hid by the corner of a building as he watched Amad run into a rundown complex. Looking through the scope of his 3.08, he heard Mike's voice crack over the radio.

"Man down. I repeat man down."

Byron's heart skipped a beat at the thought of one of his men sprawled out in the street in a puddle of blood. A whistle rang through the air and a piece of concrete exploded next to his head.

"This muthafucker just tried to end me." Byron seethed as he got low. The predator was now becoming the prey.

Looking through his scope, Byron saw Amad running full speed on the roof of the building. Pulling the bolt action back and injecting a round into the Winchester, Byron focused steadily on Amad. Amad paused and knelt down in attempt to take another shot at his adversary. He had truly underestimated The United States of America. Byron would have never thought the kill would be this easy as he put the cross hairs on Amad's head and pulled the trigger. Byron watched as a pinkish mist sprayed from his head and his body hit the ground.

Apache Helicopters could be heard from the skies about Ah-Amiriah as Byron walked back to the Humvee with his rifle slung over his shoulder. Four of the terrorists lie dead in the middle of the street while Reggie and Mike stood over one of their own. Instantly, he knew who the fallen soldier was, and took off running toward him.

"NOOOO." Byron yelled and fell to his knees beside Juice as he lie in the puddle of blood. The 7.62 rounds fired from the Russian AK's had penetrated his bulletproof vest. Juice coughed up blood as he tried to speak. The scene before him reminded him of Rodney.

"Hang in there homie. Help is on the way." Byron said holding Juice's head in his lap.

Juice smiled a bloody smile. "That scary muthafucker didn't even bust his gun. Reggie froze up like a popsicle." Juice joked. Byron stared at Reggie with pure hatred.

"Don't trip, you good. Just be still and stop moving." Byron glared at Reggie in evil attempt.

"Byron you a real nigga. Make sure you take care of your moms and be a good son. Remember, you control your own destiny."

At that moment, Juice's eyes rolled to the back of his head as he passed to the afterlife. Byron closed Juice's eyes with his blood stained hands as he stood up, pulling his 40 caliber XDM pistol from his leg holster and aimed it at Reggie.

"Byron, what are you doing, Sergeant? Put the gun down, he not even worth it." Mike pleaded with Byron.

"Yeah boy, why don't you listen to Mike and put the gun down? Unless you wanna spend your life behind bars." Reggie said, putting his hands up in surrender.

Byron continued to aim the gun in Reggie's direction, ready to put Reggie out of his misery.

"Byron come on, mon. Put the fucking gun down."

"Yeah nigger, you think you gone shoot me and get away with it? This a white man's world and you're just a nigger on the frontline."

Byron raised the gun above his head and hit the magazine release button. The 20 round clip fell to his feet as Byron rushed Reggie, raining hate filled blows to his face and head.

"Bitch..Ass. Mutha.Fucka, I told you."

Whap! Whap!

Byron held Reggie's red hair in his hands as he continued to pistol whip him. Blood soaked Reggie's face as he started to lose consciousness. Byron was in a murderous rage until a few Marines, who had pulled up on the scene, rushed and disarmed him.

"That's for Juice." Byron spit on a badly bloodied Reggie who looked comatose.

Chapter 16

It was one of the coldest nights ever in the city of Chicago. The chill was unbearable as Lil' Pooh walked down Kedzie Avenue. He hadn't eaten all day and his stomach was in his back. The chills from not having alcohol was driving him insane. Lil' Pooh had to get the shakes off so he headed to the Five Star Liquor Store on Kedzie and Ohio. Lil' Pooh walked with his hands stuffed in the pockets of his thin Nike jacket. The heavy wind blew through him like he was made of paper. He was freezing and didn't have a dollar to his name, but the 38 Special in his front pocket would have to do. Desperate times called for desperate measures. The thought of robbing the liquor store had Lil' Pooh a bit nervous, but it was either rob the store or die in the frozen streets of the Westside. His conclusion was a no-brainer as he entered the store owned by Mr. Alam.

Mr. Alam and his family had come to Chicago from Pakistan in the 1970's to pursue the American dream. The westside of Chicago wasn't particularly a safe haven to run a small business, and in some way, it reminded him of the war torn streets of Pakistan. The westside of the Chi was pure poverty as abandoned building laced the neighborhoods. It was now the 90's and the city's gang culture had gripped the attention of the youth that had come from broken homes and use their social problems to release anger and violence to the streets. Thus, turning the streets into a battlefield.

Mr. Alam made legitimate money from his store that he used to provide for his family and send his son and daughter to college. So, the murder and mayhem surrounding his establishment didn't bother him. Nor did the gang members that posted up in front of his store to sale their drugs.

Mr. Alam was putting a bottle of Remy Martin on the shelf when his bell rung indicating somebody had just entered his store. Turning around to see, he saw a young black man with a hood covering his head. Mr. Alam was a little suspicious at first about the hooded individual, but put it aside.

It's freezing outside, he should have a hood on. Mr Alam reasoned with his self and continued to stack his shelves but kept the man in his peripheral vision.

When Lil' Pooh entered the store, the warmth from the inside greeted him. He had been in the store a thousand times and in a way, felt bad about the cruddy act he was about to perform. The sight of the fifths of Vodka made him quickly put those thoughts aside. Keeping his hood on, Lil' Pooh walked in the aisle and grabbed a fifth of Dimitri gin and proceeded to the counter.

After placing the bottle on the counter, Mr. Alam came over to ring up the items. At the sight of the familiar face, Mr. Alam felt more relaxed and spoke as he rang up the items.

"Very, very cold night. They say its below zero. Way too cold for my blood." Mr. Alam said putting Lil' Pooh's items in the brown paper bag. Lil' Pooh stood silent with a stone face while his hand gripped the handle of the 38 in his pants.

"That will be 26 dollars and 15 cents, my friend." Lil' Pooh looked around quickly, then pulled the gun from his pants and pointed it in Mr. Alam's face.

"Open the muthfucking register and hurry up. This a robbery, don't make it no ambulance pick up." Lil' Pooh snarled.

"Okay my friend, please don't shoot. I'll give you all the money I have." Mr. Alam proceeded to open up the register but thought about reaching for the 357 that rested in clear view under the counter. Lil' Pooh's nervousness was evident as his hand shook holding the gun. Mr. Alam grabbed a couple hundred dollars from the confines of the register and handed them to Lil' Pooh. It hurt his heart to let this hoodlum take food from off his table and out of the mouths of his family. The thought made him reach for the 357.

Lil' Pooh saw the move and reacted with action and squeezed the trigger. The loud pop from the handgun echoed through the small store as the hollow point round found home in Mr. Alam's head. Brain tissue plastered the wall behind him as his body hit the floor. Lil' Pooh couldn't believe he had just shot somebody. Looking over the counter, he saw Mr. Alam face down, blood thickly covering the tile floor. Grabbing the rest of the money from the open register and the bag of liquor, Lil' Pooh fled the horrific scene and into the wicked streets of the Westside. with his first body.

***

"Hurry up and get this work bagged up so we can get it out on the block. Shorty and them said they outta packs so they had to shut the block down. That's unacceptable. Keep this shit pumping." Funk said as he stood in the kitchen overseeing his workers cut and bag up heroin.

They were in a trap spot a block away from Avers and Augusta. Avers and Augusta was doing numbers on the dope. Most of the fiends in Chicago came to Avers and Augusta to cope work because the heroin was more potent. The few deaths that were caused seem to only draw the block more customers. Funk's workers worked tirelessly as they cut the drugs using Dorm pills. The dope that Mr Biggs was giving Funk and the Mafia's was talking an 8 meaning that it could be cut 8 times. For every one gram, it could be mixed with Dorm, turning one gram into 8 with ease. Funk's profits were impeccable. All his life he wanted to be in the position of a Boss and now his dreams had become his reality. The more dope he got from Mr Biggs, the more money swelled his pockets.

Funk already had a serious demeanor. Now with the money he was making, he was just out right cocky. Being the Chief of the Mafia's and controlling the open drug market had him feeling invincible. While Funk observed the workers conducting his business, a few of his flunkies entertained themselves playing Nintendo on a big screen TV. Meathead and Cockroach was in an intense game of NBA Jams when there was a knock on the door.

"Who the fuck is that?" Funk yelled from the kitchen.

Meathead paused the game, picked up the 40 Caliber handgun that rested on the floor in front of him, and went to answer the door. Looking through the peephole, he noticed it was a fiend coming to cope some work.

"It's Byron's mama." Meathead said over his shoulder. At the sound of that, Funk felt a familiar feeling in his groins. The thought of Ilena's lips around his manhood caused his dick to stiffen.

"What you waiting on, let her in." Funk commanded.

Ilena stood on the other side of the door in the blistering cold, ashamed like she always was when she came to buy drugs from Funk and the Mafia's, with no money. She knew she would have to perform some type of sexual favor in order to get what she came to get, and the thought of it all almost made her puke. But she knew if she didn't get the dope, she would become gravely ill.

Ilena heard the bolt action of the lock mechanism on the other side being unlocked, and then it was opened. She was now standing face to face with Meathead. A sly grin was plastered across his dry lips.

"Where is Funk at? I need to see Funk."

Funk walked in the living room smiling from ear to ear.

"Meathead, y'all go in the kitchen and secure that demonstration." Meathead locked the door back and proceeded to the kitchen to oversee the workers. On the way past Ilena, he made it his business to grab her butt. Ilena tensed up at his perverted touch.

"What up, ma? What can I do for you?" Funk said cutting right to the chase as he took a seat on the couch.

"Well, I was wondering could you front me two dimes until next week when I get my unemployment check on the first?" Ilena nervously asked. Funk put his hands in his pants and let it rest on his erection..

"The first is about a week away. I need my money now. I mean right now." Funk coldly spat.

"Come on Funk, you know I got you. I don't have no money right now and I'm getting sick."

"Sick? Bitch I'm sick of you coming to me with no money, That's what I'm sick of." Funk replied heartless as ever.

"Funk, please I'm begging you. You know I'm good for it." A tear begin to form in Ilena's eye. She dreaded not getting the dope that would serve as her medication.

"Ma, you know what you gotta do if you ain't got no money."

"Please Funk, just let me give you the money next week." Ilena pleaded. Ilena's pleas fell on deaf ears as she watched him pull his penis from his Coogi jeans. Ilena once again had to put her pride to the side as she fell to her knees. She began to sob as she started to put her mouth on Funk's erection. She gave him a blow job until Funk pushed her head from his dick.

"Nah, I got something else I want you to do for a nigga. I want some of that fat ass you got."

"Funk come on, just let me do this for you." Ilena said trying to put Funk's tool back in her mouth.

"Bitch, what I say? Now bring your ass in this backroom." Funk said menacing while he stood up and made his way toward the back. Ilena followed him into the bedroom, where he violently had anal sex with her. 30 minutes later, Ilena laid in the bed almost unconscious while blood leaked from her anus. Funk got up and pulled his jeans and then threw Ilena two dime bags of heroin.

"Now, get your shit and get up outta here. We even on the work." Funk walked out the room. Ilena in weak attempt, got up and got dressed. She couldn't wait to get home so she could get high.

After retrieving a spoon and a syringe from her purse, she couldn't wait to get high. She had to get high, and high right now. So after fixing the potent drug, she injected it into her greedy vein. The pain she had just endured from Funk became a distant memory as she nodded off into a feeling of pure ecstasy.

Chapter 17

It was almost 8 months later after Byron had pistol-whipped Reggie in the war-stricken streets of Ah-Amarriyah. The mission that was handed down to kill the war general, Amad Ablique had been a huge success for Byron and the U.S Military. The activities that followed had put him in a bad predicament and as he would find out, would be the cause of his demise.

A day after the assault on Sergent Reggie, Byron was detained. He had been informed that his inability to make the correct choices had faulted. In letting his emotions cloud his judgment, he endangered not only his self, but his platoon as well. The result in his decision to take matters in his own hands resulted in immediate relief from his leadership position and expulsion from his sniper platoon. He was a sniper, who had received meritorious promotions and awards, and was one of the deadliest snipers the United States had ever produced, but all that was insignificint now.

Everything he had worked so hard for was now taken away.

Byron was scheduled to stand trial under an Article 32 hearing, similar to a civilian preliminary hearing, to determine if he could face the most serious of court marshal, The General Court-Marshal. He was faced with one count of assault with a deadly weapon with a minimum of 15 years. A mix of emotions ran through his mind. He felt that he had let his country down, but at the same time, he felt no regret for the pain he inflicted on Reggie. He knew that had it not been for Mike Solbert, instead of an assault charge, he would be fighting a body.

Byron was detained in a small cell in a military prison waiting to be transferred to Camp Pendelton, California to face trial for the charges brought forth on him. He would either face hard prison, or be discharged from the military by Dishonorable Discharge. Byron thought about his future and it's possibilities as he did his last set of pushups. He was tired of all the bloodshed that was involved in carrying out his orders handed down by his superiors, to put an end to the war on terror.

Being so close to death, in so many incidents he couldn't count.

The thought of being discharged and going back to Chicago gave him a sense of motivation.

He hadn't seen or heard from his mother in years and he was in desperate need to see her. And on the flipside, he wasn't ready to sit in a cell in a federal military prison for 20 years either. Going back to Chicago didn't seem bad at all. Maybe things wasn't so bad.

The next week, Byron walked inside of a small courtroom in California in his Charlie uniform. The atmosphere was serious as was his charges, and he was now waiting to face his dilemma. A lot of the Marines were backing Byron and there for his support. America's military knew that Byron was the best when it came to the scope, and they genuinely wanted him to be found innocent of his charges. It was because Byron and the duties he performed that the United States of America would have justice for the losses due to terrorism in the U.S.A.

But after the testimony from Mike Solbert, they all knew what the outcome would be. Mike Solbert felt guilty for taking a stand on him. He looked at Byron as a friend and comrade, but Byron's actions left him with no choice. There was no way he could muster up a lie for Byron. Especially when fellow Marines pulled up to assist the platoon, only to see Byron pistol whipping one of their own. Even with Commander Sanchez testifying on Byron's behalf, letting the commission know the talents Byron possessed. He was the best sniper in the history of the military and had completed some of the most deadliest missions since his deployment in the military.

Even though the Judge Advocate General knew this to be true, and respected Byron and his sacrifices, his actions could not go unpunished, and he would have to pay for his bad decision making.

"Mr. Hobson, we the people for the United States of America find you guilty on the one count of indictment for the Assault on Sergeant Reggie Banks. It is recommended from the United States of America that you be discharged from the Marine Corps."

Byron put his head down. The Marines had made him into a cold blooded killer, an assassin with a rifle. In some way, he felt betrayed by the military for cutting him loose. After all the work he had put in, it seemed to mean nothing. He had experienced the war on the battle fields, now he was experiencing another kind of war. The political side where the United States handled their own.

"Court is now ajourned." The Judge Advocate General said before he slammed the gavel. When Byron was walking out of the courtroom, he was approached by Mike Solbert.

"Excuse me, Sergent Hobson. Can I have a quick word with you?"

"No need to call me Sergent anymore, Mike." Byron said shaking Mikes hand.

"Sir, if it means anything to you, I didn't want to testify." Byron stopped Mike before he went any further.

"Mike, no need to apologize. You did what any Marine was supposed to do and I respect you for that. As a man and a soldier. Listen Mike, I got some things going on back home in Chicago, so I'm kind of glad things worked out the way that they did. You a good dude. Keep doing what you do to make America a safer place."

"Sergeant Hobson, it was a honor to meet you and serve under your leadership."

"The pleasure was all mines." Byron replied and saluted Mike Solbert. More words didn't have to be explained. The two Marines even though from two different walks of life had formed a special bond. A bond formed through blood, sweat and tears.

Walking down the halls of Camp Pendleton, the same place that had trained Byron to be a monster with a scope, he ran into Special Commander Sanchez.

"Sergent Hobson." Commander Sanchez greeted, saluting Byron.

"Mon, why do everybody keep calling me Sergent like they didn't get the memo?" Byron said sarcastically.

"You know if you used your brain as much as you talk shit you might be on to something." Commander Sanchez joked.

"But anyhow, on a more serious note, just know you will always be a Marine in my eyes, Hobson. Regardless of what they said in that courtroom, you the best got damn sniper to ever fire a rifle. If it was up to me, you wouldn't be going nowhere. Our country needs more men like you and not like that sorry piece of shit, Banks."

"What's up with him anyway? Why didn't he testify?" Byron inquired

"Your guess is as good as mine, Hobson. Maybe he can't talk due to a fractured jaw. Who knows? The commission also knew about him hiding behind that vehicle not firing his weapon. Juice would probably still be alive and you wouldn't be getting court marshaled.

Byron stood in silence listening to Commander Sanchez.

"Let me ask you something, Hobson. What are you going to do when you get back to Chicago?"

Byron hadn't even thought about how he was going to make a living once he got back home. All he knew was that he needed to get to his mother. Byron thought long and hard before he answered.

"You know Commander, I really don't know."

"Well, I tell you this, Marine. Just know that shit out there in the real world is not going to give you anything on a silver platter just because you served this country. Hell, most people out there in society can give a damn about this so called War on Terror or the lives lost in it presence. People these days only care about themselves and not their fellow Americans. That's why you will always be a Marine in my eyes, Sergent Hobson because you not like those people. You have sacrificed your mind, body and soul for the United States of America." Commander Sanchez reached in his vest pocket and pulled out his contact information and handed it to Byron.

"If ever in life you need anything or my assistance, please don't hesitate to call. I do mean anything, Marine."

Byron took the card and put it in his pocket. Commander Sanchez had become a mentor to Byron and somewhat a father figure. He was going to miss Commander Sanchez as well as his wisdom he had given. Byron embraced Commander Sanchez as a father figure.

"Always remember Byron, in the jungle always be the predator and never become the prey. You take care of yourself soldier."

And just like that Commander Sanchez was gone. Byron was about to leave his military life behind. For the past three years, he had killed like a vicious animal, stalking and eliminating his prey. He had come to the military a wayward, misguided teenager, but the Marines had turned him to something different. In a few days, Byron would be back in his hometown, Chicago, Illinois. A city plagued with murder and violence. He was sent to the military to become a man and to better his life but they would send him back a cold-blooded beast.

S. Allen

Chapter 18

Byron's plane touched down at O'Hare Airport at 6:45 on a Friday. The long flight had him exhausted and he wanted nothing more but to get some much-needed rest. Nobody knew that Byron had returned to Chicago, and he hoped and prayed that his mother would accept him back into her household.

With nothing more than a couple thousand dollars to his name, he knew he would have to find some steady income and fast. Walking through the terminal of the airport, Byron got a few flirtatious stares from a few women. His freshly shaven head shined like it had a gloss on it as his 5'11" frame, under his tight white t-shirt, looked as if he was fresh outta somebody's fitness center. His dessert sand camouflage pants and his black boots gave him a thuggish swagger as he came through the terminal. His green military duffle bag containing his belongings slung over his right shoulder.

Walking to the nearest payphone, Byron inserted a quarter and dialed his mother's phone number.

"This number is disconnected, please try your number again." The operator said.

Byron looked at the phone confused. He was going to have to go by his mother's house and hope like hell she was there. Once outside the airport, Byron saw a Jamaican standing on the side of a yellow taxi cab and approached him.

"You driving?" Byron asked the man with lens dread locks.

"Ya mon, where you need a ride to Rasta boy?" The Jamaican replied, his accent strong.

"West side. 1048 N. Avers."

"Get in, me take you."

The Jamaican opened the trunk to the cab so Byron could put his bags in. Then, Byron jumped in the backseat.

When Byron got in the cab, he was greeted with a smell that he knew so well. The smell of Marijuana. The Jamaican pulled onto the Dan Ryan Expressway and turned the music down which was playing Reggae.

"You come back from duty, Mebay?" He asked looking at Byron through his rearview mirror. Byron was caught up staring out the window at the scenery. He couldn't believe he was back home.

"Yeah, how you know?"

"You look like warrior. I know warrior when I see one."

"How you know that?"

"I warrior in my country. My AK bleed many bamba clots. Me real with the rifle, Mebey." The Jamaican retorted.

"So, how you go from being a warrior to driving a cab in the United States?" Byron asked now intrigued by the Jamaican cab driver.

"Me killing machine for my Government, Don Dadda in gorrilla warfare. My people tricked me. I think I shed blood for me country against enemies who wish to kill me people but politicians have their own priority's for they self. Not for our people. My family was at risk from bamba clot Rastas'. I take my family and flee to America for a better life. You understand, Mebey?"

"Yeah, I feel you Joe." Byron responded knowing exactly how the Jamaican felt. He was going through the same thing, feeling betrayed after all the sacrifices he made for his country.

"Why you back from duty, Rasta boy?"

"I got kicked out." Byron said with a half-smile.

"You not mind me smoke me spliff?" The Jamaican said holding up a joint longer than a high school hallway.

"Go ahead." Byron said. After putting the joint to his big dry lips, the Jamaican lit the weed and inhaled the potent smoke. He held it in his lungs then attempted to pass it to Byron.

Byron looked at the joint for a minute.

"Smoke mobry. It relax your mind." The Jamaican said still extending the joint to Byron. The dread was right. He was a little tense and needed to calm his nerves. After grabbing the weed, he took a light pull. It had been years since Byron had smoked so the cannabis didn't agree with his lungs. Byron began to cough.

"That's good gunja, from the motherland, meboy." The Jamaican informed while he laughed at Byron, who was continuing to have a coughing fit. After hitting the weed one more time, he passed it back to the Jamaican. The Jamaican took a pull and turned up the radio. Immediately, the THC erupted into Byron's bloodstream as he started to feel a relaxing sensation taking over his body.

Byron stared out the window as the streets of Chicago passed by him in slow motion. He hadn't been home in so long and the city looked so different. The Jamaican sang along with the radio that was playing a song from Damian Marley.

Out in the streets, they call it Murda.

He bobbed his head to the track and exited off the Dan Ryan Expressway on to Independence Street.

Byron was starting to get nervous. He was now only minutes away from his mother's home. To Byron, the westside looked worst then he last remembered it. On every corner were packs of men, posted like wolves. He could tell by their clothes and jewelry that they wore, they were drug-dealers, and cold-blooded gangsters. Sitting at a stop light on Chicago Avenue, Byron watched as a blue Chevy Caprice pulled up on the side of them with the music beating. The candy coated paint looked as if you were to touch it, your hand would become wet. The 24 inch rims where so shiny, Byron saw his reflection in the rims. When the light turned green, the driver who looked to be no older than 15 threw up a gang sign and recklessly pulled off.

Byron just shook his head; he knew that he was back home. A few minutes later, the Jamaican was turning down Avers and Augusta. Byron noticed the crowd of young hoodlums standing on the corner. They all sported black and gold clothing, solidifying their alliance to their nation, The Mafia's. At the sight of the new generation of thugs, Byron started to think about Funk, and what he had heard from Lil' Pooh about him leading the nation. He started gritting his teeth as his hate for Funk began to rise.

"1048 N. Avers, Rasta boy." The Jamaican said as he pulled up in front of Byron's mother's house.

"How much I owe you man?" Byron asked pulling a wad of bills from his pocket.

"60 dollars, Mebey." Byron gave the Jamaican a 100 dollar bill.

"Keep the change, Joe." The Jamaican looked at the bill before excepting it.

"Listen Mebey, my name is Benji. You ever need my service, I got you."

"Appreciate that, Joe." Benji wrote his number on a small sheet of paper and handed it to Byron.

"Promise me one ting."

"What's that?" Byron asked with a perplexed look.

"You stay safe, Chicago murda, murda. Watch yo self."

"You got that, meboy?" Byron said before he gave the Jamaican some dap.

After Byron retrieved his bag from the trunk, he looked around at the traffic that was on the block. It was a hot summer evening and the hood was in full swing. Byron watched as drug dealers flagged down cars and raced toward them to get the serve. He noticed that it was no security set up, no runners, no structure what'soever. It seemed as if everybody was just free lancing and going for self. Byron shook his head in disgust while he walked up the steps to his mother's home.

After knocking on the door twice, he heard a female voice come from behind it.

"Who is it?" He heard his mother say.

"Its me, ma. Your son, Byron." Byron heard the door being unlocked.

"Who the hell playing at my door?" Ilena said while opening the door. When she got a view of the individual on the other side, her mouth dropped.

"Byron, is that you?" Ilena said in a voice that only she could hear. Byron looked at his mother's diminished frame and a tear fell from his eye. The woman standing before him was almost unrecognizable.

"It's me, ma."

"Oh my God, Byron!" Ilena yelled and wrapped her needle tracked arm around her son's neck. Her tears fell like the Nile river. Byron squeezed his mother so hard he almost snapped her in half. Ilena pushed herself away so she could get a visual of her first and only born. She examined him from head to toe trying to see if Byron was well and still had all of his body parts.

"I'm all good, mama." Byron said reassuring her that he was all in one piece.

"Thank God, thank you Jesus. Come in boy."

Byron walked through the front door and looked around. His mother's home was nothing like he remembered it. The house was filthy and roaches plastered the wall. There was no TV or furniture. The inside of his mother's house looked like an abandoned building. Byron turned to face his mother, who had her head down in pure shame.

"Ma, what happened?" Byron let his duffle bag fall to the floor.

"Byron, your mother is very sick. I need help baby." Ilena cried.

Byron had already found out through Lil' Pooh about his mother's troubles and her being strung out on dope, but never in a million years would he thought it was this degree.

"It's okay. We gone get you some help. Your son home now and it's going to be some changes."

"Byron, I lost my job and everything just went downhill. I try to stop baby but when I do I get real sick. Sometimes, I just want to die." Ilena couldn't control her emotions and she let it all out in the embrace of her only son. Byron just held her and let her get it all out.

"Mama, everything is going to be alright. I'm home now and I got you."

Chapter 19

A few days later, Byron sat on his mother's front porch. He had been busy all day cleaning the house and even had the opportunity to go out grocery shopping. While out and about, he filled out some job applications in hopes of seeking some kind of employment. It felt good to be back in the Chi. It was just another day on Avers and Augusta and the drug pushers were doing the same shit, trying to make a dollar outta 15 cents. Different kinds of flossy whips came through the block flouting their dope money. While half naked women roomed the streets in search of a baller to support their chickenhead lifestyles. Byron was hoping he would run into Lil' Pooh. He had asked his mom where he could find his childhood friend, but she told him she didn't know. When she saw Lil' Pooh, he would just pop up.

A group of females were walking past when one said something to Byron. "Damn boy, where you come from with your fine ass, looking like Tay Diggs?"

The chick was light skinned and thick in all the right places. Her Apple Bottom boy shorts hugged her ass righteously and the rest of her outfit left little to the imagination.

Byron thought about getting the girl's phone number. It had been a while since he had sex and he was very tempted. Not to mention she was definitely attractive.

"Girl, you better get that nigga number. You see he a hustler over here serving Ilena dope fiend ass." A dark-skinned chick rocking a full body cat suit said. Byron instantly took offense to the comment.

"Watch who you calling dope fiend shorty." Byron sneered.

"Who you think you talking to?" The girl said and reached in her Danie and Bulk handbag where her 9mm Keltic resided.

"Girl, chill out." Lightskin laughed.

"He kinda cute. Give him a pass."

"Nigga better recognize where he at. This a Mafia world." The girl spit in Byron direction in disrespect. The chicks continued to walk down the block.

Byron hadn't been home 24 hours, and had already ran into some drama. Things had definitely changed around the way. *And the westside was for real.* Byron thought to his self.

Later that night, Byron and his mother sat at the kitchen table eating a dinner that Byron had prepared. He wasn't much of a chef, but he had managed to fry some ham and cheese sandwiches, along with some French fries.

Ilena picked over her food, barely even touching it.

"What's wrong, Ma? You don't like my cooking." He said in a playful tone as he took a huge bite from his sandwich.

"It's not that baby. It's just that your mama don't have an appetite right now." Ilena said scratching her arm.

It was 9:00 at night and she hadn't had a fix since earlier that morning. It was hard to get high with Byron around, but she definitely had a monkey on her back. Trying to take her mind off getting high, she changed the conversation.

"Byron, you know I thought of you every day since you left our home. I would watch the news and see all the chaos going on over there. I cursed myself for sending you over there. I didn't want to come home and get a phone call from somebody telling me to come identify your body." Ilena eyes began to water.

"At times, I feel like sending you over there was the worst mistake of my life. When you left, a piece of my heart left. They say you never know what you have until its gone. The tears had begun to fall from her eyes.

"Ma, I missed you while I was over there. I wrote and tried to contact you. When you didn't write back, I got worried. I had to find out through Lil' Pooh about what you were going through. I wanted to leave ma, right then and there, but I couldn't."

"I was just so weak, son. I didn't want to write you and stress you out while you were over there. I felt if I hid it, by the time you came home I would have myself together but."

"I already knew mama." Byron said cutting her off.

"The most important thing is that we are together." Byron stood up to hug his mother.

"Thank you son, I really appreciate you and I'm so happy you are home. I love you."

"I love you too, mama." While Byron and Ilena were having a mother and son moment, there was a knock at the door.

"You expecting any company? Byron asked as he made his way to the door.

"Nobody." Ilena nervously replied. Byron opened the door and couldn't believe who stood before him. His vision became blood red at the sight of Funk on the other side of the door.

"What do you want?" Byron asked through clenched teeth.

Funk was surprised to see Byron standing before him.

"Damn, at ease soldier. Wonder why nobody tell me GI Joe was back home. If I would of known, I would come bearing gifts." Funk said with a thick diamond chain hanging from his neck. His cocaine white Benz truck parked at the curb.

"Like I said, what do you want?"

"I'm looking for your momma. She owe me some bread and I'm here to collect."

"Whatever she owe you, I'll pay it. And I'm letting you know right now, Funk. Don't ever come over here again. And don't sale my mama nothing else."

"So, you come back home from war on some gangsta shit, huh? Trying to dictate. Well, just in case you didn't get the memo, soldier, I'm Supreme Chief in this area and ain't no nigga gon' dictate my hustle." Funk looked back at his truck and motioned for his goons.

Meathead and Lil' Bud got out of the luxury SUV.

"Aye Joe, look who back on land." Funk said.

At the sight of Byron, Meathead pulled his 40 from his waist. Lil' Bud followed suit, pulling his compact .45. Both men stepped on the porch with Funk.

"What's good, Chief?" Meathead sneered, mugging Byron.

"Na, Lord, Byron one of the guys.Ain't that right Byron?"

At the sight of the guys, Byron tensed up.

"Now listen, this Mafia shit under new management. I run this. I remember how you used to try and carry a nigga back in the day, and for real I should have fam rock your ass. But we over here hustling and it wouldn't be wise to cause heat to my block. So I'ma give you an ultimatum, either you get with the program and get to this paper, or you can get what Lil' Pooh got. eradicated. The choice is up to you."

"I'll never work for you, and like I said, stay away from my mama." Byron said standing his ground.

"Alright GI Joe, that's your choice, but take these words of advice. This a new world order and the Mafia's at the top. Its wicked out here. You just came from Iraq. well this is Chi-Raq. Don't get caught up." Funk threatened.

"Whatever, fam." Byron retorted. Funk's threats fell on deaf ears. If Funk didn't want to take heed to what Byron was speaking, then when the time came, Byron would stand on his words.

"Come on Joe, let's get up outta here before I change my mind and have y'all leave a stain on this porch."

Funk and the Mafia's left off the porch and jumped in the Benz truck and pulled away from the curb. Krucial Konflict blasted through the subwoofers. Byron was left standing in the doorway. He wanted nothing more at the time than to get his hands on a pistol. He knew the situation with Funk was far from over. Funk had just threatened him with violence, and that was something he couldn't stomach. In due time, he would get the chance to check all the gangsta shit Funk was bumping out his gums.

Ilena had heard the entire conversation between Funk and Byron. In fact, she knew it was a strong possibility it was Funk at the door. Funk would pop up at her house uninvited to get his rocks off, and in return, she would get some dope. After hearing Byron close the front door, she met him in the living room.

"Who was that at the front door?" Ilena asked faking ignorance.

"Ma, that was Funk. I told him to never show his face around here again. I also told him to stop giving you drugs. Now I'm telling you. Stay away from him. He is nothing but trouble. You have to be strong if you want to get better." Byron said and headed to his bedroom leaving his mother standing there pondering his words. When Ilena heard the door slam, she knew that her son was pissed off to the highest degree. She wished that Byron and Funk hadn't collided like that. Sweat began to pour from her forehead as her bowels began to loosen up.

Being sick from heroin was like the worst case of the Flu times five. She knew if she didn't get a fix before the night was over she wouldn't make it. Her heart and mind was telling her to be strong and fight through it, but her body was telling her something different. Ilena loved her son to death, but he would never understand the physical hold the drug had on her. Ilena grabbed her house keys and snuck out the house into the hot Chicago heat. She needed to get well, and the only person who could prescribe her medication was her on call physician.Funk.

S. Allen

Chapter 20

Byron headed to the corner store on Thomas and Avers. His mother had asked him to buy her a pack of Newport 100's. Ever since Byron had told her about his small stash, that was quickly diminishing, she would constantly hit him up for cigarettes. Whenever she needed anything, Byron would get it for her, never giving her cash, knowing she would end up buying drugs with the money. Today was no different.

It had been a few days since Byron had the confrontation with Funk. He had seen Funk come through the block a few times, and once Funk made a gun gesture with his hand, aiming at Byron. Byron just mugged Funk as he rode by and made a left on Augusta. He knew he needed some protection, and fast.

While walking down the street, he saw a scrawny dog come out of the alley. The dog started to follow Byron. At first, he was a little nervous because the dog had a menacing appearance. The dog was under fed to the point where his ribs were visible, and his right eye seem to be missing. Byron knew through experience that a lot of young dudes fought their dogs for large amounts of cash. When their dog lost the fight, they were either shot in the head or left to starve in the streets. The strange looking dog seemed to follow Byron all the way to the store. He was thinking the dog was going to attack him. He hurried up and entered the store.

Byron walked in the store owned by an older black man name Mr. Tillman. After grabbing a bag of Doritos and a chocolate Nestle Quick, Byron proceeded to the counter to pay for his items. "Will that be all young man?" Mr. Tillman asked while he started to ring up Byron's things.

"Let me get a pack of Newport 100's with that." Byron said pulling out his wallet. Mr. Tillman looked at Byron over the rims of his glasses. Suspiciously.

"You got some ID, youngster?" Mr. Tillman was set on not selling Tobacco products to minors, and made sure to ID all who looked too young to purchase cigarettes. The only I.D Byron had with his age on it was his old Military ID. Byron took it from his wallet and passed it to Mr. Tillman.

"You served in the military, huh?" Mr. Tillman asked staring at Byron's identification card.

"Yes, sir." Byron replied. Seeing that Byron was at legal age, Mr. Tillman handed his I.D back to and continued to ring up his items.

"I served a few years myself. I was in the jungles of Vietnam. I was Communication Commander. That will be 7.00." Byron passed Mr. Tillman a $10-bill.

"What was your staff title and duties, soldier?" Mr. Tillman gave Byron his change.

"I was a leader of the 101st Battalion platoon and H.O.G."

"Hunter of Gunmen." Mr. Tillman replied with a proud smile.

"That's quite impressive. It's always good to be in the presence of one of our best. You back from deployment?"

"No, sir. Dishonorable Discharge." Byron said shamefully.

"Oh, I see. Well you know things happen right?"

"Yes, sir."

"Whatever the case, you put your life on the line for our country and that I will always respect."

"Thank you, sir." Was Byron's only reply.

"No, thank you, young man." Byron grabbed his items and left the store only to see the same mangy Pitbull sitting outside. Seeing Byron, he immediately sat up.

What the hell? Byron thought to his self. The dog looked to sad so Byron decided to pat the dogs head. In return, the dog licked Byron's hand. At that moment, he was no longer afraid of the dog.

Byron had made it all the way back to his block with the pit trailing behind him. "What you following me for, huh? I ain't got nothing for you." Byron said to the dog like he could comprehend what he was saying.

After Byron went in the house to give his mother the cigarettes she requested, he figured he would sit on the front porch and eat his Doritos. When he stepped outside, the dog was sitting on the steps and opening the bag of chips. The dog started to bark.

"Oh I see. You followed me so you can get some of my chips."

Byron dumped some chips out in front of the dog. The pitbull savagely devoured the Doritos.

"Damn, hungry ass nigga." Byron gave him some more. The dog ate the chips like they were the best on the planet.

"Go ahead and eat boy. It looks like you been missing a few meals." Byron opened his chocolate milk and poured some in front of the dog, and on cue, he started lopping at the milk. Byron rubbed the dogs thin back while it rested beside his leg.

While snacking on his chips, an all slender dope fiend by the name of Marvin approached the porch.

"What's up, youngblood. Where Ilena?" He asked scratching his scabbed-up arms.

"She ain't here, and if I was you, I wouldn't come back around this house again." Byron threatened, ice dripping from his voice. The dog sensed Byron's mood and demeanor change, sat up and started growling. His sharp fangs now visible as his ears pointed to the sky.

"Who the hell died and made you king of the hood? You better ask about Mackin' Marvin boy." The dope fiend replied and threw a weak combo to the air, looking like a smoked out Sugar Ray Leonard.

"Like I said. Stay. Away. From my moms!" Byron yelled. At the sound of Byron's loud voice, the pit bull sprung out at Marvin and locked his jaws on his calf.

"Ahhhhh! Ahhhhh! Get this damn dog! Helllp!" Marvin yelled.

The dog tugged at Marvin's leg viciously. Blood was pouring from the wounds caused by the dog's fangs. Byron watched, astonished as Marvin experienced pure horror from the small but yet strong dog.

"Come here, boy!" called Byron. The dog obediently obeyed and let the death grip go from Marvin's leg, but not before snatching some of his veins and nerves from his calf.

Marvin limped off in pure agony leaving a bloody trail of crimson on the sidewalk. The dog walked back and resumed his position next to Byron, licking the fresh blood from off his mouth.

"Holy shit, Joe, you a killah, huh?"

The dog looked at Byron and barked.

"You small as hell, but you strong. You like Mighty Mouse around this bitch." Then, it hit Byron like a ton of bricks. "You know what? That's what we gone call you. We gone call you Mighty." Byron got up and walked inside his mother's house with his new friend in pursuit.

Chapter 21

Inside a rundown hotel, Lil' Pooh just opened a bottle of Night Train wine. It was 9:00 in the morning and he had to get the shakes off. After killing Mr. Alam in the liquor store last winter, Lil' Pooh started to change dramatically. No longer was he the humble hustler that everybody knew him to be.

Getting away with a body gave him a since of invincibility. The violent rage that rested with in Lil' Pooh was unleashed on the streets of the westside. When Lil' Pooh wanted for something, no more would he sit on the curb and beg for change. His 38-revolver was sure to feed his needs.

After Lil' Pooh took a long swig from the bottle of cheap wine, he sat back and begin to strategize. His money was low and he knew before the end of the night he was going to need to hit a lick.

The night before last while Lil' Pooh was walking down Chicago Avenue, he was approached by a young drug dealer who went by the name of Fontane. Fontane had mistaken Pooh for a dope fiend and offered to sale him some drugs. To Lil' Pooh, Fontane looked to be no more than 15 years old, but the sack of drugs he pulled outlet Lil' Pooh know he was on some grown man shit. From Lil' Pooh hustler instincts, he knew the young dealer had at least $5,000 worth of heroin in his possession.

What kind of dumb ass walks around with that much work on him? Lil' Pooh thought. It was at that point, he came up with a plan to rob Fontane.

The drug spot on Avers and Spoulding was pure poverty. Most of the homes on the block where abandoned with very little police presence. The created a safe haven for dope fiends and the hustlers that sold to them. A criminal organization known as the New Breeds ran the neighborhood with an iron fist. Being in that area, Lil' Pooh knew he had to be extra careful if he wanted to complete his mission. If he failed, it could possibly cost him his life.

Taking another drink from the bottle, he twisted the cap back on and placed it on the table. Lil' Pooh had some running around to do. Today would be his big day. His problems would soon be over and he could get back on his feet. Grabbing his .38, he placed it on his waist. The thought of coming up put a smile on his face, as he headed out the door to go get active.

Mr Biggs was in his lavish estate in the North Suburb of Harvey, Illinois. Surrounding him where his trusted lieutenants, 8 Track, Body Bag and Killa Fred.

Mr Biggs had just ended an important phone call with his drug supplier, Roger Castilino.

"You see thats why soft muthafuckas shouldn't be in the position of power. When shit gets real in the field you go harder, not tuck your tail like some punk prostitute bitch." Mr Biggs vented placing his cell phone on the Oakwood desk. He was intensely aggravated that his plug and his cartel were in a blood fued with another Mexican cartel. The situation was intense and Castilno put a hold on distribution until further notice, which was slowing Mr Biggs money up. Mr Biggs was on a 100 key contract with Castilino, and without his monthly shipment he was getting low on product.

"This wetback still taking the further notice crap. I've spent millions with him and now he just going to freeze the play?"

"Why don't you tell him we can come and get our own work?" Killa Fred suggested.

"These chico's got a funny way of handling business, Killa. They always wanna be in control."

"Killa, right. If we come get our own dope, we can save them some trouble, and we won't have to pay that transportation fee on the bricks." Body Bag intervened, letting his voice be heard.

Body Bag was the youngest of the Body Snatcher crew. Born and raised in the grime of Milwaukee, Body Bag caught his first body at the age of twelve. He had murdered his biological father in cold blood for abusing his mother. After serving a few years in juvenile prison, he was released back to the streets, only to find home with Mr Biggs and the Body Snatchers. Helping Mr Biggs climb the ranks of the Milwaukee drug trade. Leaving his fair share of toe tags and the streets named him Body Bag.

Mr Biggs thought about what Body Bag had just suggested and

it made sense. They were paying 50,000 per Kilo with a $1,000 transportation fee on each key. If they would go to Mexico and retrieve their own work they would be saving $100,000 of a 100 kilo shipment. Mr Biggs stood from the table with his big frame towering over his subordinates. The dope game had been good to him. Money flowed like water and he would be damned if he got his water cut off.

"Listen, I'm a propose to Castilino that he don't have to take the risk of delivering the work to us. We will go get our own bricks."

"And what if he not feeling what we talking about?" 8 Track asked while he rolled a blunt of purple haze.

"If he still playing games then I guess we gone have to show him while they call us the Body Snatchers. We'll lay and wait the predators that we are, and when the time is right feast on our prey." Mr Biggs said.

"That's what I'm talking about. Let's get to it." Thoughts of drama and murder seem to excite him.

"Now Big, I got the word on the street that a few blocks seem to have a problem with math, or a problem with following orders."

"What blocks?" 8 Track asked, lighting the blunt.

"Polk and Lawndale, and Kedzie and Springfield." An example has to be made. I want the niggas that oversee these blocks hit."

"Who got those blocks?" Body Bag asked. Mr Biggs handed Killa Fred the death list with two named on them.

"Antwen and Mario." Killa Fred read, with a look of murder in his eyes.

"We got this boss." 8 Track said passing the potent weed to Body Bag.

"What about them suckas on Avers and Augusta?" Killa Fred inquired.

"In due time, Killa. In due time."

"One more question, Chief?"

"What's that, Body Bag?"

"How do you want this situation handled?"

Mr Biggs thought about it for a minute. He wanted to send a message for those that didn't know. "Make it loud and messy, loud and messy." Mr Biggs directed.

The three goons got up and left the mansion, ready to carry out the orders given. To go and lay the murder game down.

"Come on lil' homie. All I got is fourteen dollars. Let me get a twenty and next time I come through I'ma have your bread." The dope fiend pleaded. He knew from previous experience that the young hustler didn't take shorts, but he was in desperate need of the poison he had, so he figured he would try his hand.

It was late night on a Friday, Fontane only had two twenties left from his sack, and a pocket full of dead presidents. Not to mention, he had met a thick lil' freak earlier that day and was constantly blowing up his phone. Being in the good mood, he was in he decided to let the fiend slide with the short money.

"Look nigga, don't make it a habit coming on this block with short paper. Next time I'ma take it as a sign of disrespect and put them baits on your ass." Fontane reached in his Prada cargo shorts and retrieved the two bags of dope and handed them to the fiend. The fiend stuffed the narcotics in his pants pocket.

"You got that homie, you don't have to worry, I got you." The dope fiend said and walked off happier than a sissy with a bag of dicks. Fontane added the small bills to his big stack of finances, almost totaling 8 geez. Today had been profitable, he knew he was on his way to being a hood star like his older brother. Stuffing the big wad of bills in his shorts, Fontane figured he would walk over to Chicago Avenue and Ridgeway to cop some bags of sour diesel. Then, out of nowhere a man rushed him pointing a gun in his face.

"Kiss the pavement nigga, or your first thought going be your last." The man hissed. Fontane did as he was told and laid face down on the concrete. The individual with long dreads proceeded to search Fontane. After finding what he was looking for, he cocked the hammer on the revolver and squeezed the trigger. The bullet hit Fontane in the back. An old lady looking out the window witnessed the violent crime and let out a piercing scream, before grabbing her phone and dialing 911.

Lil' Pooh took off running down the street as a few people come out if their homes after hearing the loud gun-shot. Fontane laid on the street bleeding profusely. Sirens could be heard getting close to the scene of the shooting, but they would never make it in time. 16 year old Fontane Adams would be DOA, dead on arrival.

Lil' Pooh sat in his hotel room thumbing through the cash he took from Fontane. He couldn't believe his luck. He never would of thought Fontane was holding that much money on him. Tomorrow, he was going to get back in the game and cop some work. He got on his feet.

He didn't need Funk or the Mafia's, He was about to get his own drugs and guns, so he could move solo like he was taught to do. In due time, the streets would respect his gangsta. Thoughts of success caused Lil' Pooh to want to celebrate. On the way home from killing Fontane, he stopped at a liquor store and grabbed a bottle of 1,800 Tequila and walked to the hoe stroll to get a prostitute for the night. The dark-skinned Bombshell now stood before Lil' Pooh in the nude. Lil' Pooh took a drink from the bottle to get his mind right. because tonight, it was going down.

Chapter 22

A few weeks later, Byron was walking back from Mr. Tillman's store. He liked going to the store because of the intellectual conversations he would have with the old-timer. Byron found out that Mr. Tillman had a prosthetic leg caused by an enemy grenade when he was serving in the Vietnam war. Knowing that he was once a soldier for our country, Byron found a new respect for Mr. Tillman. Knowing that they both faced the same tribulations in experiencing close to death situations, they had something in common.

Byron rolled down the street with Mighty on his leash. The dog had come to be Byron's closest companion. He had nursed the Pitbull back to health. In Byron's eyes, Mighty was his soul protector. Anybody coming to close to him, the dog would attack and Byron loved it. Mighty was a goon.

Not even home a month, the pressures of being broke was being felt. He was down to his last 300 dollars. With no source of income, Byron would watch as the dope dealers on his block got to the money. He was a hustler by nature and the lure of the game was right in his face. The thought about getting back to hustling constantly crossed his mind. Byron knew that it would be close to impossible to get money on Avers and Augusta. If he was to get back in the game, a run in with Funk and his cronies would be unavoidable as Funk over saw and ran the block. Byron was in no way in an any position to go to war with Funk. Funk had money, dope and the Mafia's. The only thing Byron could hope for was that one of the jobs he applied for called him back soon.

Cuz in my city its kill or be killed, K-I-L-L oh I will K-I-L-L. Lil' Pooh bobbed his head to the rap song that blasted through the speakers inside his new Ford Taurus. His music pounded the concrete from the 2 15-inch speakers in the trunk.

After Lil' Pooh robbed Fontane, he had got on his feet. Lil' Pooh reached out to an old friend he had met in Cook County Jail 6 months ago. The veteran Gangster Disciple went by the name of Carlos and ran the Notorious Robert Taylor projects and all the dope coming out of it. Lil' Pooh met up with Carlos on the city's southside, and after a blunt of Purple Kush and some brief communication, Lil' Pooh gave Carlos $2,500 for an ounce of heroin. He knew the dope game like the back of his hand and was positive, beyond all doubt, he could triple his money. After going on Western Street, he went to the lot to cop the cherry red Ford Taurus that was in mint condition. Walking in the Evergreen Plaza Mall, Lil' Pooh grabbed some new clothes off the rack and a few pair of Air Jordan's. He was officially back in the game.

Lil' Pooh was sitting at a red light on Thomas and Avers with the music blasting. He figured he would roll through the hood to show the Mafia's he was at his best, and they're hate was his motivation, especially Funk. Lil' Pooh looked to his right and saw a man walking a Pitbull. The guy had his back to him, but his walk and structure was very familiar. The light turned green and Lil' Pooh pulled off driving past the individual, glancing in the man's direction. Lil' Pooh couldn't believe his eyes.

Byron was scratching on a lottery ticket hoping like hell he would win some money when all of a sudden a vehicle pulled up beside him with the music beating. Byron turned to see who it was pulling up on him, praying that it wasn't Funk and his flunkies. Mighty's ears went up instantly as he started barking. Byron put a strong hold on Mighty's leash as the driver stepped out of the whip. Byron's heart almost stopped. It had been a long time but he could recognize Lil' Pooh's smile from anywhere.

"Goddamn, man, you back on deck and couldn't even reach out to your main man, huh?" Lil' Pooh said walking up to Byron but stopped in his tracks at the sight of the menacing dog.

"Sit boy." Byron commanded, and then tied Mighty's chain to a fence. Mighty obediently fell in line.

"Where you get that crazy looking dog from?" Lil' Pooh asked scared to death.

"This crazy looking dog will kill something, ain't that right Mighty?"

Byron replied patting his dog on the head. "But forget all that. What's good bro?" Byron reached out and embraced Lil' Pooh.

Stepping back, Lil' Pooh started patting at Byron's arms.

"You straight, ain't you? Not missing no limbs or nothing?"

"Naw, bro, everything is all well." Byron replied.

"When you get back home?"

"About a month ago. I been looking all over for you. I asked mama where I could find you and she said she didn't know and that you would just pop up. What are you a Jack in the box?" Byron joked.

"Man you know things been a lil' rough for me since you left so I kind of stayed away. I had to go through my trials and tribulations, feel me?"

"Yeah, I'm already hip. I got your letter. Did you get the one I sent you?"

"Yup, and you can see I followed suit."

"I see." Byron said admiring Lil' Pooh's new ride.

"But fuck all that, you home now and that's the only thing that matters. Hop in so we can bend a block, I gotta give you the low down on what's been going on in the streets." Byron untied Mighty and started walking towards Lil' Pooh's car.

"Hold on Byron, you good but that crazy ass dog ain't." Lil' Pooh said serious as Cancer. Byron chuckled before he said.

"He good, Lil' Pooh. He saw us embrace. He know you good people."

"Alright Byron, that dog get to tripping. Lil' Pooh gone get to shooting."

"You got that, bro." Byron said as him and Mighty got in the car.

An hour later, Byron and Lil' Pooh were sitting at the lakefront eating hot dogs and fries. Lil' Pooh had told Byron everything, about how Funk had set up Billy Good with the feds and how the streets was saying he was responsible for Rico's death. He also told him about how Mr Biggs and his clique of murderers had come from Milwaukee, Wisconsin and took over the westside. Byron just shook his head in disbelief.

"So, you sitting here telling me that Funk is a rat?"

"Yep, Mickey mouse in the flesh. Cold blooded snitch!" Lil'

Pooh said taking a bite from his hot dog before giving Mighty the rest.

"So, with all of this going down, how did you manage to get back on your feet?" Byron queried. Lil' Pooh put his head down.

"Byron, I was out here bad. I had nothing or nobody. I was on the verge of dying in these cold streets. It was kill or be killed. I had to take charge of my life." Lil' Pooh told Byron about the gruesome murder of the liquor store and then about him killing the teenage dope boy for the 8 stacks.

After hearing Lil' Pooh's deadly secrets, Byron was shocked. "Nigga, is you crazy? You out here tripping?" All his time knowing his friend, he never knew him to be aggressive, let alone a killer.

"I was sick and tired of being sick and tired, you feel me?"

"Yeah, I guess you had to do what you had to do to survive, huh?"

"No doubt." Lil' Pooh replied. "But anyway, I see you need some cash. I got a lil' spot in Oak Park I just opened up pushing heroin. The traffic starting to pick up a lil' bit and the fiends know I got that work. In about a week or two, it should be a ten thousand dollar a night spot. You can get on your feet."

Byron thought about Lil' Pooh's proposition. He had just come from the military fighting for the right thing. Now back in the United States, he was thinking about doing the wrong thing. He knew firsthand what came with selling drugs but right now, he needed the money and 10,000 sounded real good to him. He was in a concrete jungle and it was all about survival. At that point, he made up his mind.

"Listen Lil' Pooh, if we do this we gotta do it the right way, or no way. Ten toes down."

"I dig you bro, like the old days. Me and you against the world." Lil' Pooh said before him and Byron shook hands the Mafia way.

"What about that goofy, Funk?" Lil' Pooh questioned.

"Let's just hope he stay in his lane; because if he don't, we gone make him pay. For the old and the new.

Macio sat in his pearl white Lexus ES 300 with a dime piece occupying the passenger seat. He was the top lieutenant and ran the operation on Kedzie and Springfield. Before he met Mr Biggs, he was just a corner look out for a drug boss named Big Kenny. Big Kenny, like many other major dealers on the Westside, had been propositioned by Mr Biggs and the Body Snatchers for a piece of his lucrative empire. He refused and was met with his grim faith, death.

Immediately after, Mr Biggs had his own staff on Kedzie and chose Macio to run the block and conduct his affairs. It was these duties that Macio failed. He had been late handing Mr Biggs his money. In his pursuit for nice cars, clothes and hoes, he messed up Mr Biggs's money. Thirty thousand of it and he was trying to get it back. Don't know why he was on the block at this moment, watching his workers grind and at the same time trying to impress a local gold digger named Rachelle. Little did Macio know, the money meant nothing to Mr Biggs. With him it was all about principle.

"Damn, baby, I thought you said you was taking me to the Cheesecake Factory?" Rachelle said rubbing Macio's crotch.

Looking at his diamond Rolex he replied, "Shorty, we got time. It ain't even seven. What you need to worry about is how you gone ride this anaconda tonight."

She squeezed his manhood even harder. "Boy, you know I got you."

Macio's attention on Rachelle was diverted by a homeless man pushing a shopping cart full of cans up the street. The block was pumping as the workers served a line of fiends. By the way the traffic was moving, he figured he would have the 30 geez he owed Mr Biggs by the morning. Macio watched as the bum walked up to his Lexus and tapped on the window before he snapped.

"What the hell you putting your dirty ass hand on my window for? Get the fuck outta here." Macio spat.

"You got some change, youngster?" The bum begged.

"Naw, I ain't got no change. Now move around."

"Boy, give them man a dollar or something." Rachelle said feeling sorry for him.

"I ain't giving him shit."

"You shouldn't be like that, Macio. What if that was you in that position? You would want somebody to look out for you." Rachelle said crossing her arms over her chest with much attitude.

"First and foremost, bitch, I'm a boss, and sincerely I would never be in that position. As you can see, I'm the dealer not the user." Macio went on with his big dope boy talk until Rachelle begin to scream at the top of her lungs as if she was watching a horror flick. "Bitch, what's wrong with your bird ass?" Macio turned to see what caused her to go left field and was met with the nose of a 223 short-barrel assault rifle.

The bum squeezed the trigger and brought the automatic weapon to life as he sprayed the driver's side of the Lexus. Slugs hit Macio in the head, chest and upper torso. The thunderous gunshots from the rifle caused the dealers and the fiends to run for cover. A 100-round drum attached to the gun did hellacious damage while the gunman kept firing. Rachelle continued to scream until she was shot in the face and her freshly done weave was put on the dashboard. After the last shell hit the concrete, a van pulled up and the shooter hopped in. The van sped from the scene, leaving a 100 brass shell casing and a double murder.

Killa Fred took off his wig and laid the smoky, hot rifle on the floor of the van. It was just the beginning and the Body Snatchers were about to play a vicious game. The murder game.

Young Rudy stood on the corner of Polk and Lawndale hustling. He had another hour or so before he closed shop. Rudy was a certified hustler, always the first on the block and the last to leave. He was knee-deep in the game and had experienced more in 20 years than a lot of guys would ever. Even the murder of his first cousin Toto at a Red Lobster a few years back. Seeing his family murdered right before his eyes changed him dramatically. He now knew that nobody was exempt to death in the drug game, but that didn't deter him from the block and making money. Even though he loved hustling, he hated hustling for Mr Biggs and the Body Snatchers. He felt he was pressed to. That's why every time he turned in the daily profits he would cuff a thousand or two. Only Rudy knew the exact numbers the block was doing.

A Shooter's Ambition

So, he saw it was close to quitting time. "Shop closed! Shop closed." Rudy yelled letting the workers know to start thinning out the crowd. He had already confiscated 3 stacks of Mr Biggs's money that was now in the pockets of his jeans. Looking up and down the block he saw a black Benz pull up and park at the curb. He knew all too well who the luxury car belonged to. Mr Biggs's henchmen. Body Bag.

Dressed in a black hoodie, black Dickie shorts and a pair of Retro 4 Jordan's, Body Bag got out his whip. His diamond encrusted cross shined, as the light from streetlight shined off the expensive necklace. "What's up, thug?" Body Bag said greeting Rudy.

"Ain't shit. Just trying to make a dollar."

"Yeah, so I hear."

Rudy was taken back from Body Bag's sarcasm.

"Y'all got the count right?" Body Bag asked getting straight to the business.

"Yeah, they getting it together right now. You kind of early."

"Oh yeah?" Body Bag replied with his hands in the confines of his hoodie. Stepping up on Rudy he said, "You know, Rudy, ever since your sucka ass cousin got killed, I told Killa one day you was going to be a pain in the ass, but naw, they ain't listen. But I'm a firm believer in what's done in the dark will come to the light, and right now your deceitful deeds have come to the light."

"Why you say that?" Rudy was as nervous as a hoe in church.

Body Bag laughed wickedly in his face. "Ain't no way on this God-given earth nigga blow my family brains out right in front of me then I work for them. Ain't no way, fam. If that ain't no coward, spineless shit I don't know what is. Now, listen, we know you been cutting bread on the side and the boss man is very displeased with your actions. He actually sent me over here to bust your head, but I'ma give you an opportunity of a lifetime."

"Come on, Body Bag. I wasn't getting paid enough. I got a family. My rent due. I was just trying to make a way for myself." Rudy pleaded.

"Excuses, excuses. Like I said, I'ma give you a chance to save

161

your life. You don't." Body Bag shook his head. "You die."

"Come on, Bag, don't do this. I can pay y'all back."

"If I was you, I would start running before I start shooting."

Rudy took off like Carl Lewis going for the Olympic Gold Medal. Body Bag pulled his .380 from his hoodie and squeezed the trigger. The bullet hit Rudy in the leg. The small compact gun jerked in Body Bag's hand a second time as the bullet found home in Rudy's lower back, causing him to fall.

"Just when I thought you was faster than a speeding bullet." Body Bag said walking up on a crawling Rudy. Body Bag turned Rudy over so he could look him in his eyes and aimed the pistol at his head.

"Please, please don't kill me, bro. You already shot me. Please don't take my life." Rudy's pleas fell on deaf ears as Body Bag dumped hot led in his face, thus silencing him forever.

Chapter 23

"Watch carefully, Byron, because you gone have to start helping me out once the block pick up." Lil' Pooh told Byron while he mixed up some crushed pills and added to a few grams of heroin. The pills stretched the heroin, thus stretching the profit of the drugs. They were in Lil' Pooh's hotel room cutting and packaging heroin, getting it ready to distribute on the streets.

Byron watched intently as Lil' Pooh mixed the drugs. "So, this the shit that got my mama out here like that?"

"Unfortunately, it is, bro. Since you left, a lot of things changed. When you was last out here Billy Good had us moving the coke. Now, since heroin hit the scene, the fiends no longer want crack, they want this dope." Lil' Pooh informed.

"What's the difference?" Byron asked full of curiosity.

"The difference between a crack addict and a dope fiend is crack is a mental high, this dope is more physical. You can go three days without smoking crack, but not with this dope. You on this shit and you go three days without it, you gone be feeling like you about to die; straight up." Lil' Pooh educated Byron as he put some heroin in a piece of aluminum foil and folded it into a small square. "You see this piece?"

Byron nodded.

"This a twenty dollar blow." Lil' Pooh handed it to Byron.

"How much we gone make off all of this?"

"This, what I'm bagging up, is two ounces, close to fifty-six grams, but with the cut we putting on it, we gone make more, so I say with the dope we pass out, maybe twenty-thousand at the most."

"Twenty thousand is a lot of bread, but why we gotta pass it out?" Byron asked.

"It's part of the dope game. It's a lot of competition on the Westside and we gotta let the fiends know we got the best shit, or they gone go cop from somebody else. Like Funk."

Byron watched as Lil' Pooh handled his business. He felt a little uneasy about pushing dope for the simple fact his mother was strung out on the drug. Telling his mother to stay away from it while he sold it made him a hypocrite, but times were hard, and at this point it was about survival. $20,000 was a lot of paper, and he wasn't going to turn it down.

"Aye, Byron, what was it like being over there in the army?" Lil' Pooh asked, tying a knot on a plastic baggie full of 20's.

"It' was crazy, Lil' Pooh. I learned a lot about myself and life."

"Oh, yeah? Like what?"

"I learned that the value on human life is very low."

Lil' Pooh looked up from what he was doing before he asked, "You ever kill somebody when you was over there?"

"Yeah, Lil' Pooh. I did my share."

"How many bodies you got?" Lil' Pooh probed.

"Too many to even count," was Byron's reply.

"And you call me crazy? I'm just glad you back in one-piece, homie."

"Yeah, me to, Lil' Pooh. Me too. Aye, you ever see ol' girl I used to talk to before I went to the army?"

"Who?"

"You remember, the lil' red bone. I used to holler at Carmella."

Lil' Pooh let a smile creep across his lips. "Oh, yeah, I forgot. You never got a chance to hit that pussy. Did you? Yeah, I seen shorty a few times recently. She look like she got her shit together too! Matter fact, she work at the Ford City Mall."

"Straight up?"

"Yeah. Aye, tomorrow we gone shoot to the mall and get you a few new outfits. You can't be walking around looking like Damon Wayans on I'm Gonna Get You, Sucka!" Lil' Pooh joked

"Man, fuck you. It's all I got." Byron said.

"Don't trip. Tomorrow, we gone jump fresh. We back in the game. We must shine."

Byron and Lil' Pooh finished conducting their business before hitting the streets to hustle. Tonight, they were going to pull an all-nighter. They weren't coming in until the last bag was sold. Both had something in common. They were official when it came to the grind.

The next day Byron and Lil' Pooh stepped through the food

court of the Ford City Mall. They were exhausted from staying up all night hustling but their pockets where stuffed like turkeys on Thanksgiving. At the sight of all the people in the mall and all the noise, Byron felt a bit uncomfortable in the environment.

"What's wrong, bro?" Lil' Pooh asked noticing Byron's change in demeanor.

"Ain't nothing. I'm cool!" Byron lied.

"Well, come on. Let's go get right."

Ever since he came home from war he didn't like being around big crowds, and he definitely didn't like all the loud noise. While walking through the crowded mall he couldn't help but notice all the beautiful women strolling around carefree. At that moment he started to think about how Carmella would react to seeing him. He didn't even know what he would say when he saw her. All he knew was that while he was in the battlefield, he constantly thought of her. And the very thought of being able to finally talk to her had him nervous.

"Come on, Byron, this that store I was telling you about that got the fresh shit." Lil' Pooh said leading Byron into the Lark Fashion store.

Walking in the store, the first thing Byron noticed was all the designer clothes on the walls and on the mannequins. After he and Lil' Pooh stashed their re-up money from last night's hustle, they were able to pocket two geez a piece.

"Check these jeans out, Byron. These the Ed Hardy ones I was telling you about." Lil' Pooh held up the expensive jeans for Byron to see.

Byron grabbed the jeans from Lil' Pooh and admired the denim. They had a skull with red rhinestones on the back pockets and they were a stone washed color. The price tag read $250.00 dollars. "Joe, these pants two hundred fifty dollars!" Byron said in shock, can't believing the price on the tag.

"So, what, fam? We getting dope money. Whatever you spend in this today, you gone make back by the end of the night; trust me." Lil' Pooh retorted.

"I guess."

"Aye. Ol' girl look familiar to you?" Lil' Pooh nodded in Carmella's direction.

She was helping a customer but when Byron glanced in her direction, he knew at that moment the woman was indeed Carmella.

"What you just sitting there looking love-struck for? Go over there and holler at her. Let me find out while you was over there in the war, you lost your game." Lil' Pooh teased.

Byron gulped and tried to walk over to holler at her. His only problem was that his feet wouldn't move. Lil' Pooh had to literally push him in her direction.

"So what's up? I see you don't have a ring on your finger, so I take it that your fine ass is single."

"Boy, please. I already told you that I have a man." Carmella said to the guy who was trying to spit game to her.

She had been a cashier at the Lark Fashion store for the past two years and was almost up for a promotion. She liked her job; it was easy and laid back, and not to mention she got a 30% discount on all the clothes. The only thing she didn't like about the store was all the drug dealers that shopped there and how they always hit on her. The majority of them were always trying to get her phone number. She had, had her fair share of dating street hustlers and quickly learned that they were only after one thing. Sex. Carmella would be damned if she would be known as the Lark's Whore.

"If you gotta man, why you working in here? If I was your man, you wouldn't have to work at all." Everything the young hustler spoke she heard it all and it was going in one ear and out the other.

Carmella was about to respond with something slick, but at the sight of the man walking her way her words got caught in her throat. It had been three long years since she last saw him, before he just vanished out of her life without warning. She thought of him a lot and then cursed herself for being so weak, for letting her guards down to him so quickly. The short time she spent with him, she knew he would be the one. She loved everything about him, and for him to just up and leave to the military without telling her broke her heart. Now the sight of him aroused her emotions to go into overdrive and her eyes began to water.

Carmella couldn't contain herself any minute longer as she ran towards him. "Byron! Oh my God!" She screamed as she swung her arms around his neck with joy.

"What's up, lil' mama?" Byron said. He was shocked at her reaction but was loving every minute of it while he hugged her tightly. Byron felt his t-shirt dampen and noticed that it came from the tears Carmella was shedding.

Carmella wiggled out of Byron's embrace and slapped the shit out of him. "How could you do that to me? I can't believe you just left and didn't tell me. That was lame as hell." Carmella cried.

"I'm trying to put you on the winning team and you over here crying over this dusty-boot wearing ass nigga." The guy who had been trying to holler at Carmella intervened.

Byron ignored his comment and kept his focus on Carmella and what she was saying.

"Fam, I think you need to find some business and get in your lane before you get crushed in here." Lil' Pooh said with his hand on his waistline.

Seeing that Lil' Pooh was about that life, the guy decided to leave the situation alone. "Alright, you got that. If she like it, I love it." The guy said and walked out the store.

Carmella stood there with her arms folded over her chest and tears running down her eyes.

"Carmella, I didn't have time to tell you. I had so much going on at the time. I just had to get away." Byron said pulling her back into his arms.

"Byron, when I found out you was in Iraq, I worried about you so much."

"Well, you don't have to worry anymore. That chapter of my life is closed now." Byron assured her.

Wiping her tears from her face, Carmella said, "So, what brings you to the Lark anyway?"

"Shit, look at me. Don't you think I need a makeover?"

Carmella stepped back to get a good look at him. He had grown since the last time she saw him. He no longer sported his long braids. He now rocked a shiny, clean baldhead that fit him well. His chest and arms looked as if he had been spending countless hours in the gym, but the thing that changed the most was the look in his eyes. When she last saw him, he was full of life. When they spent time together he would always have that glossy look in his eyes. That look was now replaced with a serious evilness; something she couldn't explain; yet she was still very much attracted to him.

Looking him up and down she let a smile come about. "Well, you do look like you can use a makeover, looking like you about to do roll call." Carmella joked.

"Since you got all the jokes, why you don't do your job and help a good brother out?" Byron replied.

"Byron, you do know these clothes are a little expensive. But don't trip, you can use my discount." Carmella wasn't sure if Byron could afford these designer brands that the Lark sold, but he surely changed her doubts when he pulled out a thick stack of 100's, 50's and 20's. "Looks like somebody been up to something." Carmella said looking at Byron's bankroll suspiciously.

For the next hour Byron and Lil' Pooh shopped with Carmella helping them along the way; showing them the new clothes that had just been put out on the shelves. Carmella started to ring up their items.

"So, what's up?"

"What's up with what, Byron?"

"What's up with me and you getting up tonight? I'm trying to see you."

"See me for what? So tomorrow you can go to another country without telling me?" Carmella answered with much attitude.

"I guess I had that coming. Listen, Carmella, I know I was wrong, but for real, I miss you. You was a friend to me, and I want to make it up to you."

Carmella saw the sincerity in his eyes. "With my discount, your total come to thirty-seven hundred. Y'all want your items in the same bags or no?"

"It don't matter." Lil' Pooh said counting out his half.

"Yes or no, Carmella?" Byron said frustrated, handing her a stack of bills.

Carmella remained silent until she finished bagging up their items. "Listen, Byron, I'ma give you one more chance. You blow it, I'm done messing with you."

Byron was all smiles. After writing her phone number on their receipt she handed to Byron. "I got you, shorty." Byron said.

"You messing up already, soldier boy. Don't be calling me shorty."

"You right, ma. From this point, I'm acknowledging you as wifey."

"Whatever."

"Be ready at nine, wifey." Byron said as he and Lil' Pooh left the store, and leaving Carmella excited and wet between the legs.

S. Allen

Chapter 24

Later that night Byron pulled up in front of Carmella's home that she shared with her grandmother. He had gotten Lil' Pooh to let him use the car while he stayed at the hotel to serve dope fiends. Byron had plans for Carmella, but Lil' Pooh wasn't going to let that deter him from clocking some dollars. He understood how his man felt about Carmella and wanted to see him pursue her, so he was cool, staying back to hustle off the work.

When Byron pulled up Carmella was sitting on the porch with a few of her girlfriends. They all wanted to see in person who Carmella was making all the fuss about. Stepping out the car, all of Carmella's friends were in awe as Byron walked up to the porch fresh to death. The Ed Hardy jeans fit him just right, while the tight v-neck Prada T-shirt hugged his frame, and the shiny patent leather Jordan's gave his outfit a thuggish touch.

"Damn. Ask that nigga do he got a twin brother." Niece asked, drooling over Byron's appearance.

"Whatever, girl. My man an only child." Carmella laughed. Even Carmella couldn't believe how good Byron looked. She thanked herself for picking out Byron's attire.

"What's up, Ms. Lady? You ready to go?" Byron asked.

"Ummm, excuse me, baldhead. Ain't you gone introduce yourself? Just walking up on people's porch like that." Monique said putting Byron on the stage.

"My fault, sister. My name Byron."

"Well, my name Monique. Nice to meet you, Byron."

"Byron, don't pay them no mind. These just my girls. They harmless; trust me." Carmella said stepping off the porch. "Let's go. I'm starving."

"Well, nice meeting y'all." Byron replied.

"You too, sweetie. Next time bring one of your boys." Monique said hi-fiving Niece.

Byron walked to the car and opened the door for Carmella.

"Damn, they teach y'all this in the Army; how to treat a lady?"

"Nah, it taught me some things, but definitely not that." Byron said and slid into the driver's seat.

"Oh, so what they teach you then?" She asked giving him a seductive look, loving the smell of his Issey Miyake cologne.

"You got a nice lil' group of protective friends." Byron said totaling ignoring Carmella's question as he pulled off into traffic. "So, where do you want to eat?" Byron snuck a glance at Carmella's voluptuous figure as he stopped at a red light.

"It don't matter, bae."

"So, McDonald's it is."

Carmella playfully punched him in the arm. "Boy, don't play with me." She said with fake attitude.

"Okay, Ms. Feisty. I'm just tripping. I figure we go to Pepe's on Ashland. You like Mexican food?"

"I'm down with that. I love Mexican food."

"Mexican food it is." Byron said headed to the best Mexican restaurant in the city.

"Why didn't you ever try to contact me when you was over there?" Carmella asked getting straight to the point.

"Carmella, I thought about you a lot. It was so much going on every day, I had to stay focused and committed on what I was doing if I wanted to have any chance of staying alive. A lot of people was dying over there, boo."

Carmella caressed that back of Byron's neck as he drove. "Baby, I'm sorry for thinking and being so selfish. I never stopped to consider what you was going through. All I knew was that when you left, a piece of my heart left with you."

Byron thought about what Carmella was saying. He had thought of her many times while he was in the trenches, but couldn't bring himself to sit down and write her. The only thing his time permitted him was avoiding the dangers that surrounded him and his men.

After eating a fantastic meal at Pepe's, Byron and Carmella found themselves walking hand in hand by the beach of Lake Shore Drive. The cool breeze felt good coming off Lake Michigan. Pulling Carmella close, Byron whispered in her ear. "Carmella. I promise as long as I'm breathing I will never leave your side again."

Carmella blushed like she was a freshman in high school from

Byron's kind, sincere words, Byron's tone and the way he held her; she felt so protected. She was where she wanted to be. In his arms. Without saying a word, she stood on her tippy toes and kissed him. Putting his arms around her waist, he kissed her back, letting his tongue explore hers. After the intense electrifying lip-lock Carmella backed away from him.

Out of breath Byron asked, "What?"

Carmella grabbed his hand. "Come on baby. This is well overdue."

***

"So, you mean to tell me you giving me this whole gram for free?" Ilena said as she stared at the plastic bag containing the powdery substance. She was in the back of Funk's Escalade.

Funk saw her walking down the street and pulled over, bearing gifts. "Yeah, ma. I have some new product I just got. It's fresh off the brick so be careful with that shit." Funk said with a devilish grin.

"Okay, Funk. When I get my check, I'ma give you some money for this; don't even trip."

"Nah. You don't trip. You been a loyal customer so this one is on the house."

"Well, thank you, Funk." 10 minutes later Funk pulled up in front of Ilena's home. "Tell your son I send my love and respects to him." Funk said.

Ilena didn't respond to Funk's comment because she knew the ill feeling he had for Byron so she didn't entertain it. She just got out the expensive SUV and walked in the house, praying Byron wasn't home. Funk honked the horn and pulled off from the curb.

"You know you crazy right?" Meathead said from the passenger side of Funk's truck as he took a pull from a blunt.

"Fuck that bitch and her son. I'm playing Chess and he playing Checkers. I'ma teach that nigga about his disrespect without me laying a hand on him; feel me?"

"Hell yeah, you doing this shit like the real Mafia."

"Nigga, we is the real Mafia." Funk replied as he turned left on

Augusta.

Ilena had just wrapped a leather belt around her upper arm tightly. At the same time, she had some drugs and a lil' water in a big tablespoon. Sweat poured from her forehead as the anticipation of her getting a fix was overwhelming.

Holding her lighter under the spoon, the drugs began to turn into a bubbly liquid. While cooking her drugs she heard a knock at the front door. Whoever it was, was definitely trying to get in. Ilena paid the door no mind. Nothing or nobody was going to get in her way from getting her fix. Ilena grabbed the syringe on the table and stuck the needle into the spoon, injecting the potent narcotic.

After finding a good vein in her arm, she penetrated the greenish cord and injected the heroin. After untying the belt, the drug began to rapidly flow into her bloodstream. At that point she knew something was wrong. She started to feel extremely hot, like her blood was boiling, then she started to lose breath while white foam protruded from her mouth. Her body began to jerk in violent convulsions as she knocked over a table. Ilena's eyes rolled to the back of her head as the battery acid Funk mixed with the heroin caused her heart to erupt. When the spasms subsided, she was sprawled on the floor with her soul traveling to the afterlife.

***

Boom! The sound was deafening as the planted roadside bomb exploded under the military Humvee, flipping the vehicle over. Coming up out of his momentary coma, Byron felt as if his chest had been caved in with a baseball bat. While smoke invaded his lungs, he looked to his left and saw Juice with blood pouring from the side of his head from a piece of metal embedded in his skull. He knew that his potna was dead.

The driver of the vehicle was twisted in the front seat with his right leg severed at the thigh. He looked to be trying to hold on to his lifeline. The passenger of the Humvee was non-responsive from the destruction of the LED. Byron knew he had to get out the vehicle, and quick. Using all the strength he could muster, he found the door handle, pulled it and pressed his body weight against the door frame. The back door opened and as painful as it was, he climbed out the truck. Once outside he took a few steps back before he collapsed on the ground. Byron knew he was in a deadly situation and he had to make a move, laying down dying was not an option. Attempting to get up and walk, the sound of a vehicle coming to a screeching halt caused him to be on full alert.

Three men jumped out the Jeep speaking in a fast language that Byron knew to be Arabic. He was hurt as well as unarmed while he faced his enemies, who were holding AK-47's. As an Islamic terrorist placed his boot on Byron's neck, he pulled the slide back on his rifle, chambering a round. Byron looked at him in fear as he made his last prayer to his maker. His killer said something in Arabic before pulling the trigger, sending Byron into complete darkness.

"Ahhhhhh! Shit!" Byron screamed, awakening from his nightmare he was having.

"Baby, are you okay?" Carmella asked jumping out of her sleep, scared to death.

Byron sat up in the bed drenched in his own sweat.

"Bae, what was you just dreaming about?" Said Carmella, pulling the covers over her naked breast.

This was just one of the many nightmares Byron experienced since being back from the military. "Damn, that shit be feeling so real. Every time I think they stop, they come back."

"About what you was doing over in the army?"

"Yeah," Byron replied, wiping sweat from his forehead.

Carmella kissed him on his lips. "Well, maybe we can get you some help, boo. They can probably give you some kind of medication to make them stop."

Byron spent the night with Carmella. They explored each other's mind, body and soul and was now laying in the bed as naked as the day they were born. Everything felt so right to Byron until his demons awoke him from his sleep. "I don't know, baby. Maybe I do need some help, because it don't look like they are going to just stop on their own." Byron replied.

"Well, I'm no pharmacist, but I can give you a dose of medication." Carmella said putting her hand under the cover and squeezing Byron's manhood that quickly became erect in her soft hands. After stroking on him Carmella put her head under the cover and took him into her mouth.

Feeling the warmth and sensation from the head Carmella was giving him caused him to relax and temporarily forget about his murderous demons that haunted him from the Middle East. Byron laid his back against the headboard and removed the covers from her head. Eyeing his pole going in and out of Carmella's mouth made him want to explode right then and there, but he had to hold back. He wanted to feel her hot, juicy insides.

"Come here, baby." Byron said in a deep baritone-fill voice that was full of lust.

Carmella gave the tip of his dick one last suck while staring him in his brown eyes, saliva running out the corner of her mouth that dripped onto her 36 double D's. Using her hand to guide his thick 9-inches into her love canal, she straddled him backwards, Cowgirl style. She loved how Byron filled her walls to capacity. In a rhythm that was sync she rode him as Byron watched her voluptuous ass checks bounce each time she went up and down. The smell of sex was strong. They were in a perfect rhythm. Reaching around, Byron grabbed her brown nipples and gave them a squeeze.

Carmella went crazy from the feelings of pain and pleasure. "Baby, I'm cumming. I'm cumming, Byron." Her and Byron were on the same page as he pumped in and out of her with a faster pace. "Oh my God, baby!" Carmella yelled as she coated Byron's dick with her love.

Byron's veins in his meat began to swell as he continued to punish her pussy until he released his seeds deep inside of her being.

After the intense love making session, Carmella got up to take a quick shower. It was 7:30 in the morning and she had to be at work, and messing around with Byron she was running late. Sliding on a pair of Dereon jeans Carmella turned to Byron who was pulling his wife-beater over his head. "So, what's your plans for today, boo?"

"I got some running around to do with Lil' Pooh. He probably tripping because I didn't come back last night." Byron said.

"Well, I get off work at four today and I'm definitely trying to see you tonight." Said Carmella as she put on her earrings.

Byron walked over and hugged her from the back, kissing the nape of her neck. At that moment his dick began to stiffen again.

Carmella felt it poking her butt. "Boy, chill before I get fired messing with you."

After giving her a smack on the ass they made plans to see each other later on. Byron left Carmella's house and went to go get up with Lil' Pooh. He wanted to take a quick shower and change his clothes so he figured he would swing by the house. Plus, it had been two days since he walked Mighty. When he turned down his block, he was shocked to see all the police activity.

Driving down the street Byron saw an ambulance in front of his home. A feeling of nervousness took control of him as he got closer to his mother's house. There was a large crowd of people standing on the sidewalk and across the street. All attention was directed to his crib. Pulling over in an empty parking spot he hopped out the car. His head began to race as he saw police and paramedics in front of his home. Something was definitely weary. The only person who was supposed to be there was his mother. His worst fear was confirmed when the paramedics came out with his mother on a stretcher.

S. Allen

Chapter 25

"We are gathered here today in the loving of a child; a child of God. Psalms one-forty-one says deliver us o' lord, from evil, from violence, from those who plan evil in their heart's; they continually gather together for war. They sharpen their tongues like serpents with poison on their lips. Keep us o'lord from the hands of the wicked, preserve me from violent men, who have purpose to make my steps stumble." The reverend preached at Ilena's funeral. It was held at the First Baptist Church on the Westside.

Byron sat in the front row as the words the preacher spoke went in one ear and out the other. He couldn't bring himself to pray to a god who had just taken the only thing he had to live for. Seated next to him was Lil' Pooh and Carmella, the only family he had left. With tears staining his eyes the only thing his mind was focused on was revenge, he could care less what the preacher was speaking on. Byron found out that Funk sold his mother the drugs that claimed her life at only 47 years old.

Dope Fiend Calvin walked up on the porch of Ilena's home the day after she over-dosed. Byron was clutching a bottle of Gin, drinking his pain away when Calvin walked up on crutches, still in pain from the ferocious bite Mighty had given him. Calvin told Byron that in fact he was dating Ilena even though they shared a common love for heroin. He saw Ilena get out of Funk's truck that night, he said he knocked on the door, but she never answered. The next morning, he came back and she still didn't answer the door. He felt something wasn't right, so he breached the home only to find Ilena dead in the living room. He then went to the payphone and called 911. After hearing that information, he had already made up his mind. He was going to kill Funk.

That night, Byron buried his mother at the Burr Oak Cemetery. Tears dropped from his cheek while Carmella held on to his waist. Wiping the last tear away Byron silently vowed he would shed no more, he would make others feel his pain. Watching the last shovel of dirt thrown on his mother's grave Byron walked away, and at that point in time America's worst nightmare had been birthed into the streets.

The next night, Byron and Lil' Pooh were at Lil' Pooh's hotel room. Two bottles of Grey Goose sat on the table as the room was polluted with potent weed smoke. Byron took a pull from the Blue Berry Kush and held the smoke in his chest. Ever since his mother passed he had been doing nothing but smoking and drinking. Lil' Pooh knew that his man was grieving hard, so he did his best to give him his space, while he took to the streets to hustle the work off. The traffic on the block that Byron and Lil' Pooh set up shop on was picking up, so the money was definitely coming in. But the only thing Byron could seem to focus on was finding and killing Funk. Nothing else mattered, not even the money.

Byron passed the blunt to Lil' Pooh. "Man, I'm tired of looking for this nigga. The cat and mouse shit getting real old, real quick. When I see that clown I'ma do his ass." Byron said holding the 38 Special Lil' Pooh had given him.

"Bro, on some real shit, that nigga Funk caked up."

"What's that supposed to mean? That supposed to change the fact he killed my momma?"

Lil' Pooh put his hands up in surrender. "Not at all, fam. Trust and believe I'm on your side. All I'm saying is why just kill him when we can rob him to?"

Byron thought about what Lil' Pooh was saying. If Funk was holding like Lil' Pooh said, then he was definitely going to come up off it before he died.

"This nigga move the dope for the dude Mr Biggs I was telling you about. The out of town nigga. The only thing that might come back to bite us in the ass is if the Mafia's find out we slumped him, they might come gunning for our neck; feel me?" Lil' Pooh said as he passed the blunt back to Byron.

"Funk ain't feeding the Mafia's like he supposed to. After we kill him we gone expose the fact that he was an imposter, and we gone put the Mafia's on like they supposed to be. The way Billy Good and Rico would have had it."

Lil' Pooh let what Byron spoke ponder on his brain. "You know that nigga got shooters. We gone need more than that Thirty-Eight."

Not disrespecting the pistol he gave Byron, the gun had sentimental value to Lil' Pooh. It was the gun he caught his first body with, but he knew if they came at Funk they were going to need more than 6 shots.

A wicked smile came across Byron's face. "I just might know where we can get some hammers from."

Byron and Lil' Pooh sat at the table putting a play together that would bring Funk down to his knees, and at the same time put them at the top of the food chain.

***

Mr Biggs sat at his Oakwood desk inside of his mansion going over his inventory sheets. The blocks he had on the Westside were drying up fast, and he was down to his last 5 keys of dope. With the demand he had from his block lieutenants, the 5 kilos would be gone shortly. His drug supplier was still at war with another cartel and wasn't able to supply Mr Biggs at the time which had him furious. Feeling betrayed, he wanted blood. He even asked the connect to aid and assist him. In addition, he offered to send his men to come and get the work, but Castilino declined him, saying all distribution were on hold until further notice. Mr Biggs felt he had played by the rules and brought the connect millions, and for him to feel a drought from another man's war was a slap in the face.

"So what's up with the Mexican muthafucka?" Asked Killa Fred, pertaining to the plug.

"I come to him with the proposition, yet he still talking about we on hold 'til further notice."

"What he mean we on hold? We down to our last breaks and this nigga playing. So what's the next move?"

"Remember, Killa, what I always told you about patience? These cartel mutherfuckas have to be handled with care, but this is the business." Mr Biggs looked his henchmen in the eye before he said, "I'ma bake this nigga a cake, and when it's done I'ma send you over to Mexico to blow out the candles."

Killa Fred was amped up at the moment. He hadn't split a

nigga's wig since he plastered Macio's brains inside his whip. His thirst for blood was at its peak and needed to be quenched.

Mr Biggs lit his Cuban cigar and took a long pull and blew out the sweet, pungent smoke before he said, "But on another note, we need some more dope and fast."

"How we gone get some more dope with no connect?"

"We don't have a connect. We need work so get it."

Killa Fred knew exactly what Mr Biggs meant. They faced this dilemma before in the streets of Milwaukee when they encountered a drought in cocaine, and at that time the Body Snatchers had to put on masks and gloves and go to work. The mission was get down or lay down.

Chapter 26

"That's right boy, get 'em! Get 'em." Byron commanded Mighty, watching him sinking his teeth into a used tire in the middle of the yard. The rubber tire would strengthen the dog's teeth as well as his neck. After letting Mighty exercise for about an hour, Byron fed him a bowl of Eukanuba and tied him to a fence.

"That dumb ass dog gone kill somebody." Lil' Pooh said as he rolled a fresh blunt of Loud White as he sat on Byron's porch.

"Yeah, I know. That's what Mighty do. Mighty kill shit. Ain't that right, boy?" Byron said patting Mighty on the head.

"What's up with your mans? You think he gone come through for us or what?"

"I don't know. I called him, now all we can do is sit and wait." Byron said and grabbed the blunt from Lil' Pooh.

An hour or so later, a yellow cab pulled up and parked in front of Byron's house.

"You called a cab, bro?" Lil' Pooh asked with his eyes glossy from the weed he had been smoking.

The cab parked and a man with dreads stepped out.

"What's up, Rasta Boy?" Benji greeted, showing his gold teeth.

Byron smiled and hopped off the porch to holler at Benji. "What's good, Joe?" Byron shook hands with Benji.

"You know, ma boy, same ting. Trying to make some mula."

"That's what's up. Ain't we all?" Byron replied.

"I gotta few tings for you my friend. Take a lil' time but I'ma make it happen." Benji said walking to the back of the cab before popping the trunk.

"Don't trip, mi friend, I'ma make it worth all your troubles." Byron replied trying to mimic Benji's Jamaican accent.

Once Benji popped the trunk he pulled back a blanket that revealed an assortment of guns. Byron mentioned for Lil' Pooh to come over. "This my brother, Lil' Pooh. Pooh, this Benji." Byron said introducing the two men. Lil' Pooh shook Benji's hand. "Aye, Lil' Pooh, check these out!"

Lil' Pooh looked at the various weapons that laid before him.

Byron picked up a funny looking handgun that had a clip longer than O.J. Simpson's prison sentence. By him being in the military he knew that he was holding a FNH automatic that fired 30 rounds of 5.62 caliber rounds. He knew that the FNH was deadly, as it was a handgun that penetrated bulletproof vest.

Lil' Pooh picked up a Springfield Armory 45 ACP with a 20-round extended clip. "This pretty as shit and it's light." Lil' Pooh held the plastic Glock-style weapon in his hand admiring it.

"What you want for both these, Benji?" Byron asked.

Benji did some mental math in his head. "Give me one thou for the tings."

Byron went in his pocket and pulled out a wad of dead presidents, counted out a $1,000 and handed them to Benji.

After thumbing through the currency, a look of greed was on Benji's face. "You do good business, mi friend. I like yi style." Benji pulled the blanket all the way back and grabbed a rifle that looked to be an historic item.

"What the hell is that?" Byron asked looking at the old war weapon.

"This thee real ting. This here a IK Forty-Three Snipa rifle. ZF-Four scope let you hit a target at twenty-five hundred meters with ease, me boy."

Byron grabbed the rifle and released the 10-shot magazine that was loaded with high-grade 3.08 ammunition. "How much?"

"Byron, like I say, I like yi style. I see warrior in your eyes from thee first day wi meet. I know yi on mission. For what mi no know, real reckonize real, soldier. That rifle yi hold have many tales of blood. Mi gift to you, mi friend."

Byron held the rifle in his hands as a feeling of power rushed through his bloodstream. "Thanks, Benji, I appreciate this."

"No problem, mi friend. You ever need mi assistance, call." Benji said before he hopped back in his cab and pulled off from the curb.

Byron and Lil' Pooh sat in Byron's house. They had the plan and now they had the tools to execute them. The only thing left now was to start head-bussing.

A Shooter's Ambition

***

It was 4:00 in the morning and Funk had just dropped Meathead off at his baby mama's house in a section of K-Town. They had been on the Southside smoking, drinking and freaking with two chicks they met at a club earlier that week. Funk was high and drunk as he swerved his Escalade in and out of traffic on the way to his crib on Chicago Avenue. Pulling up in front of his house he grabbed his Glock from under the seat and stuck it on his waist. After taking the keys out the ignition, Funk got out the truck and stumbled up his driveway. When he got to the door, he went in his pocket to retrieve his keys until he felt cold steel on the back of his neck.

"Yeah, what's up, potna? Talk that gangsta shit now." Byron said through clenched teeth.

At the same time Lil' Pooh relieved Funk of his gun that was on his waist.

Funk recognized the voice of his captors and knew it was Byron. "Damn, GI Joe, what's all this about?"

Byron, not in the mood for games, struck Funk in the back of the head with the butt of the FN, causing blood to leak from his wound profusely. "Open the door, nigga, ain't this where you live?" Funk remained silent as blood covered his face. "Oh, you want to do this the hard way, huh?" Byron snarled.

Lil' Pooh snatched the keys from Funk and after 3 tries the lock mechanism turned, and the door opened.

"Get your bitch ass in there." Byron said as he aggressively pushed Funk in the house.

After locating the light switch Lil' Pooh turned it on.

"Now, we can do this the easy way or the hard way. The choice is completely up to you."

"What the fuck you want? You know you a dead man walking, right?" Funk stuttered.

Byron walked up and slapped him across the face with the gun. "I see you like that gangsta shit, huh? Where the money and drugs at?"

"Fuck you!" Funk replied and spat blood on Byron's hoodie.

Byron smiled at his antics. "Let's tie 'em up. Lil' Pooh."

Byron and Lil' Pooh used some sheets to tie Funk's arms and legs, securing him from any escape. Byron then told Lil' Pooh to go to the van and get Mighty. Funk's interest was peaqued as he wanted to know who was Mighty.

"I told you to stay away from my momma, Funk, but no, you didn't listen. You always thought shit was a game, even when we was shorties." Byron said before he ran over and kicked Funk in the face.

Funk spat his front tooth out before he said, "Man I ain't seen your mother since then." He lied.

Just when Byron was about to assault Funk again, Lil' Pooh come in the house with Mighty on a leash.

At the sight of the menacing looking dog, Funk's tough guy persona was out the window. "What the hell y'all gone do with that dog?"

"Where the money and drugs!" Byron yelled, causing Mighty to get on attack mode.

Lil' Pooh had to use all his strength just to hold Mighty back.

"The dope behind the stove and the money in the cabinet over the fridge." Funk revealed, terrified of the pit bull that was looking to devour him.

Byron grabbed the leash from Lil' Pooh as Lil' Pooh went to get the load.

"Watch 'em, boy, watch 'em." Byron sneered in Mighty's ear.

Mighty growled, showing his sharp fangs as saliva fell from his mouth, excited at the opportunity to spill some fresh blood.

Lil' Pooh came back with three freezer Ziploc bags full of money and a grocery bag full of $20 blows. "Jackpot, nigga." Lil' Pooh said smiling from ear to ear.

Byron looked at Funk who had tears in his eyes. He knew what fait awaited him.

"Get 'em, boy!" Byron yelled as he let Mighty's leash go.

Mighty pounced on Funk's face and lock his jaws on his face. Funk yelled in agony while Mighty crushed him. Tasting blood,

Mighty went for the kill and went for the neck, tearing the flesh from Funk's jugular, blood sprayed from his deafening wounds that Mighty was inflicting. The vicious canine had even managed to tear Funk's left eye from its socket as well as his nose.

"Come here, boy. Come here, boy."

Mighty obediently obeyed Byron's command, ceased his violent assault and returned to Byron's side, blood covering his snout and upper torso. Funk, barely alive, moaned in pain while his breaths became shorter and shorter.

Thinking about his mother Byron chambered a round into the of the FN and stood over Funk. "Look at me. Look at me!" Byron yelled pointing the gun at Funk's dome.

"Please. Please, fam, take the money and dope. Don't kill me, Byron." Funk pleaded.

Byron's finger tightened on the trigger as he thought about his mother, Billy Good and Rico, how Funk treated him when he got his violation, how he pistol whipped Lil' Pooh, and whatever other disloyal, deceitful deeds Funk did. Byron pulled the trigger and the gun jerked in his hand. The bullet hit Funk in the forehead, blowing his brains on the wall. The smell of blood and gun-smoke put Byron back in an element he knew way too well in the bloody streets of Afghanistan. The murder game. Byron continued to pull the trigger until the 30 rounds where emptied into Funk's face. After the last shell fell to the ground Byron and Lil' Pooh wrapped the body up in a sheet and carried it back to the van. Driving the corpse to the southside they turned into a dark alley off of 51st and Elizabeth, threw Funk's body behind a dumpster and pulled off into the darkness of the night.

Back inside of Lil' Pooh's hotel room, Byron and Lil' Pooh were sitting at the table, counting up the money they got from Funk. The murder they had just committed had them both in a serious mind state, while they counted through the large denominations of blood money. Byron would have never thought that after coming back from the army he would be put in a position to take another man's life. He was wrong.

After counting $300,000 a feeling of power overwhelmed the

two as they had never seen so much money at one time. The grocery bag full of 20's came out to be 2,000 bags of heroin with a street value of $40,000. Each bag had a stamp of the Grim Reaper.

Looking at the strange stamp on the bags, Byron asked Lil' Pooh, "What's up with these stamps on the bags of dope?" He held the bags, admiring them.

"Bro, that stamp on it means that's that Body Bag. It's a few blocks on the westside that got those stamps. Byron, that means it's Mr Biggs's dope."

"Funk was serving for Mr Biggs?"

"That's what I been trying to tell you. Funk got on fucking with dude and this is probably his work." Lil' Pooh said putting a rubber band on a $1,000 bundle.

"Fuck it, bro, it is what it is. We all the way in, now; ain't no turning back. What's done is done."

"So, what now?" Lil' Pooh asked still counting money.

"First thing first, we get up with the Mafia's and let 'em know what it is with this nigga Funk and that I'm stepping up to be supreme Chief."

"And what if they not with that demonstration?"

"Lil' Pooh, we entering this with love and loyalty. Funk was out here eating, but his team was starving. What nigga you know wanna be broke? We gone feed the wolves." Byron said.

"What about Meathead? You know that was Funk's mans. If we don't kill him, he gone end up being a problem later; feel me?"

"Meathead not loyal. Never was. That's not his style. We'll put him on and use him for our benefit, and when he no longer any use to us or our program, we gone crush him. Trust me on this one, Pooh." Byron said helping Lil' Pooh rubber band the money.

Byron had been gone for a few years, but he was now headfirst in the dope game. Lil' Pooh knew that Chicago was vicious when it came to drugs and money, and one accumulated a mass of either two. Integrity and dignity changed in men, as well as principals. Byron's plans were to rule with love instead of fear. Lil' Pooh was riding with him at all cost. He just prayed their hearts didn't get them killed.

Chapter 27

Pulling up on the blocks on Avers and Augusta, Byron and Lil' Pooh were about to put the first part of their plan in motion as they parked on the side of the curb where 15 or more young Mafia gang members where posted.

"Now, listen, Lil' Pooh. Let me do all the talking. I got this."

"I hope so because shorty and them don't look like they into a lot of talking." Lil' Pooh noticed the youngsters gripping the hammers on their waistlines.

Byron smiled. "Yea. Remind me of myself when I was about that age." He retorted before he got out the car.

All Lil' Pooh could do was just shake his head, follow suite, and pray like hell he didn't have to use the 45 he was clutching.

As they approached the crowd of youngsters, a brown skinned dude with short braids pulled a gun from his waist. "What's up, niggas? Y'all know somebody over here or something?" The youngster asked with a mug on his face, wanting to know what their business was in their hood.

Lil' Pooh threw up the five with his right hand. The Mafia sign.

"Oh yea? What block y'all from?" The youngster questioned.

"We from Avers and Augusta; this block right here we standing on." Byron replied.

At the moment, five more Mafia drew guns.

"Man, we don't know you old niggas. Y'all ain't off this block and I advise y'all move around from this corner before you get your head bust, you dig?" The youngster threatened pointing the gun in Byron's direction.

Byron knew that this was the moment of truth. If he didn't succeed in his proposition then the situation could get deadly real quick. "Listen, fam, it's a new day for the Mafia's. Funk is no longer the active Chief for the Mafia's. My name Byron and I'm now the supreme Chief in this area."

"Where Funk at? And who the fuck appointed you Chief?" One of the Mafia's asked stepping up to Byron. Lil' Pooh tightened the grip on his 45. Byron remained calm and in control of the situation.

189

"Funk is no longer with our glorious organization. I murked his ass, and he in the grave with the rest of the rats where he should be."

"Funk ain't no rat, and who he rat on?" The youngster with the braids asked, still pointing the gun.

"He told on the king of the Nation. Y'all familiar with our king Billy Good?"

At the sound of the name the youngster's jaw dropped in disbelief, as he couldn't believe what he just heard. He lowered his weapon to the side. Something was definitely familiar about Byron to the youngster. The way he walked and the look in his eyes. He knew that by how Byron carried himself with authority and power that he was Mafia. Only one other person carried themselves with such integrity and that was his father. The Chief of Chief's, Billy Good. The youngster stared at Byron with his lips in a snarl. "Billy Good is my father, Joe."

Byron looked at the youngster and knew that what he spoke was true as his features showed of his mentor. Byron smiled and extended his hand to the youngster.

Looking at Byron a few seconds longer, the youngster shook hands with him the Mafia way.

"My name Noody," the youngster introduced himself.

"Aye, Lord, why don't you bend a block with us real quick. I got a proposition for you and your men."

Noody looked back at his click who was willing to bust shots at his command. "I'm a hit a block with fam and them real quick. I'll be right back," was all Noody said before he hopped in the car with Byron and Lil' Pooh.

***

"Come on. I gave y'all the work, why don't y'all just get up outta here?" Hennessy pleaded. He was tied to a chair in his kitchen along with his baby mama, Tanisha.

Hennessy was from the Wild-Wild Hunnids on the far southside. He was a baller in every aspect of the word. The Bently GT coup along with his various diamond chains were all due to his hustle— heroin. Even though Hennessy sold drugs, he was not what many would label a drug dealer as he lacked the smarts that came with being one in the murderous game, and often made mistakes, like the one he made at a club called Arnie's when he approached Killa Fred. Sitting at a bar drinking on a bottle of 1800 Tequila draped in jewels, Killa Fred was on a mission when Hennessy approached him.

"What it do, my nigga? I see you rocking that Cervelix Rolex. That musta cost you a pretty penny. What it hit you for? Fifty or sixty bands?" Hennessy asked admiring the iced-out time piece.

Killa Fred smiled. "You know when you getting money this lil' shit ain't 'bout nothing." He replied. He had already sized Henessy up and put him in a category of being a clown and a potential lick, as he eyed the 40 inches of clear diamonds and the Gucci outfit he was rocking.

"The name Hennessy." Hennessy said extending his hand.

"Killa." Killa Fred said and shook Hennessy's hand.

Seeing what Killa Fred was sipping on Hennessy signaled for the bartender and ordered a bottle of 1800. "Where you from, bruh?" Hennessy asked pulling a thick wad of money from his pocket to pay for the bottle.

"Milwaukee." Killa Fred replied eyeing the money in Hennessy's hand.

"I hear y'all niggas up there getting to that papa. What them blocks of diesel going for up that way?"

Knowing that Hennessy was talking about a kilo of heroin he said, "Like a hundred-thousand."

"That's kind of high don't you think?" Hennessy retorted looking at Killa Fred to be a potential customer. Hennessy told Killa Fred he could get him bricks of dope for $70,000 a piece, and that started their business relationship. Killa Fred purchased a kilo from Hennessy for $70,000 about a week ago and then called him and wanted to secure an order for five bricks.

Hennessy met Killa Fred in the parking lot of the Evergreen Plaza Mall to conduct the transaction, with Killa Fred telling him to be expecting him real soon. Leaving the plaza $350,000 richer, Hennessy's thoughts were on balling out of control and not the Cadillac DTS that was tailing him, which brought him to his current situation.

"Where the rest of the dope and money at, nigga?" Killa Fred asked him, holding a Kel-Tec PMR-16 assault rifle.

"That's all I got, fam, I swear to God." Hennessy replied sweating profusely.

"Just give them that shit, Hennessy." Tanisha cried as her tears fell like the Nile River.

Hennessy shot her a look as if to *say bitch shut the fuck up.*

Killa Fred walked over to a bonded, terrified Tanisha and stroked her hair from her tear-stained face. "Baby girl, where the shit at?"

"It's in the bedroom. It's a suite case with some money in it and the other stuff is in a safe in the closet in the far-left side in the corner."

Killa Fred smiled. "What's the combination, sweetie?" Killa Fred probed.

Tanisha looked at Hennessy. She didn't want to reveal their fortune but at the same time she didn't want to die for it either. "I'm sorry, Hennessy," she said before she gave Killa Fred what he asked for. "It's ten, six, twelve."

Killa Fred looked at Body Bag who went to go and get the stash. "Now, that wasn't so hard was it, sweetie?"

"Now, please let me go." Tanisha pleaded.

"I'ma let you go, baby girl. Just give me a minute to make sure everything is everything."

A few minutes later Body Bag came back in the kitchen with two Louis Vuitton travel bags. "Alright, let's bounce, bro."

Killa Fred raised the chopper to Hennessy's dome and pulled the trigger. Blood and brains plastered the side of Tanisha's face as she let out a piercing scream. Body Bag looked on in amazement at the sight of the gruesome murder.

"I thought you said you was going to let me go. Please, don't kill me." Tanisha begged looking down the barrel of the smoking rifle Killa Fred had pointed in her face.

"I am going to let you go, sweetie. I'm going to let you be with your Lord." Killa Fred said before he blew Tanisha's brains out.

With no connect to supply Mr Biggs and The Body Snatchers, the team had to resort back to the game that made them who they were. They now had to embrace their first love. Robbery and murder.

S. Allen

Chapter 28

Byron and Lil' Pooh brought Noody up to speed on the Funk situation. They told him how Funk set up Billy Good as well as being responsible for Rico's death. Noody was enraged while he sat in the backseat listening to Byron tell him how Funk sent his father to the FEDS. Noody never really liked Funk or Meathead, he felt they used the Nation for their own personal benefits. The only reason he dealt with Funk was because he had no family, and to find out Funk was the reason for his father's absence had him perplexed. Funk fed Noody to a certain extinct, but all of that meant nothing and he was glad Funk was dead. With Funk out the way Byron was now Supreme Chief and had plans on rebuilding the Mafia Nation. Noody listened attentively as Byron laid out his plans for the future of the Mafia's.

Looking in the rearview mirror Byron locked eyes with Noody. "Noody, it's a new day for the Mafia's'. There's no more big I's and little you's. We all have a voice and are outstanding members of this organization. Noody, your father taught me a lot, and ruled with an iron fist, and even enforced crucial discipline, but he gave everybody a shot, and that's what I'm doing with you."

"A shot at what?" Noody asked.

"A shot to make some money, and to aid me in the reconstruction of this Nation. I'm about to flood these streets, but unlike how Funk did it, we gone do it with structure and everybody is going to reap the benefits. Lil' Pooh gone oversee the operation and make sure everything is running how it's supposed to. I'm appointing you to be first in command. Your job is to make sure that money is right and all the packs get to your workers. Lil' Pooh gone show you how to set up your security."

Noody nodded in understanding. At the thought of making some money Noody got amped up. "So, when do I start?" Noody asked ready to get it cracking.

"You start now." Byron replied.

Byron took Noody to Lil' Pooh's hotel room and gave him the grocery bag full of $20 blows. Noody had never seen so much dope

S. Allen

at one time, and at the sight of the stamps on the bags he knew in fact that Funk was no more amongst the living.

"Now, Noody, that's forty thousand dollars' worth of dope in your possession. Bring back twenty thousand and use the rest to pay your workers and security personally. Each of your workers should get a hundred dollars a day to work the spot, and the rest is yours to do as you please. My advice is that you use your share to reinvest and get more work from us. It's a lot of money to be made and you are in the position to get it."

Noody was all smiles as a chill came over his body. He was now in a position to eat and that's exactly what he planned to do. "You got that, Chief, and I appreciate this chance you giving me." Noody said acknowledging Byron as his superior.

"Just make the Nation proud, Noody." Byron retorted and shook Noody's hand the Mafia way. The seed had been planted and now all Byron had to do was sit back and watch the Mafia organization flourish into something great.

***

It had been a week and Meathead still hadn't heard from Funk. Every time he dialed his number he was hit with the voicemail. Something was definitely wrong, so Meathead decided to jump in his whip to investigate and head toward Avers and Augusta. Turning down the block in his BMW 745 Meathead was shocked to see the block in full swing as the traffic was congested and the line of dope fiends waiting to get served was thick. Seeing Noody on the corner with a few Mafia's, he pulled up to the curb and rolled the window down. "Y'all seen Funk come through here?" Meathead asked aggressively.

"Nah. Ain't seen 'em and ain't looking for him." Noody responded with ice dropping from his tone.

Noticing Noody's challenging demeanor, Meathead put his car in park, got out, and approached the corner. "What's with all that slick shit, lil' nigga?" Meathead sneered.

Feeling cocky, Noody swung a right hook that connected with

Meatheads jaw line, dropping him to the pavement. The other Mafia's joined in the assault and together they stomped Meathead on the corner. After the vicious beatdown Meathead got up with his head the size of a pumpkin as he staggered to his car.

"Yea, nigga, it's a new day for the Mafia's. This ain't Funk block no more. Byron our Chief, so watch how you come through here on that tough Tony shit." Noody grilled.

Meathead couldn't believe what he just heard as he jumped in his car and pulled away from the crowd of violent youngsters. Using his bloody hands, he grabbed his cellphone and dialed a number. The phone rang three times before it was answered. "Mr Biggs, this Meathead. I need to holler at you ASAP." Meathead said through his swollen lips he received from the beatdown. Mr Biggs gave him an address and told him to meet him in an hour.

***

Lil' Pooh was in the middle of the block overseeing the Mafia's conduct they're operation. It was almost 9:00 and they were about to shut the block down for the night. Dope fiends lined up like zombies as they knew it was last call for alcohol. Noody had reported to Lil' Pooh that they had stomped Meathead out on the block due to his disrespect. Lil' Pooh then called Byron and informed him of the incident. Byron responded by telling them next time they saw Meathead to put him under Mafia arrest so that he could holler at him.

With the traffic the block was bringing in Lil' Pooh knew they were on the road to riches. He set up a meeting with his Gangster Disciple potna Carlos to see if he could plug him with some heroin. Carlos agreed to supply Lil' Pooh and the Mafia's with dope. Lil' Pooh saw the sky as the limit.

Lil' Pooh's thoughts of balling was ceased when a dark blue Aevra with tints pulled up and stopped in the middle of the street. The driver of the vehicle lowered the window. Potent weed smoke escaped from the interior. "What's good Lil' Pooh?" The driver yelled out the car.

Lil' Pooh looked at the driver who was brown skin with shoulder-length dreads. He had never seen the guy but nodded at him anyway. "What's good?" Lil' Pooh said throwing his hands in the air.

The driver rolled the window back up and sped down the block recklessly. Lil' Pooh watched the Aevra turn the corner in confusion but thought lightly about the dude. Maybe he knew him from somewhere or maybe he didn't. After shaking off his paranoia Lil' Pooh walked down the block to help Noody shut it down.

***

Slap! The sound of Mr Biggs' palm connecting with Meathead's check echoed through the empty, dense basement sounding like a gunshot. Mr Biggs told Meathead to meet him at a location on the city's Northside. After telling Mr Biggs about his assumption of Funk being dead and Byron running the block on Avers and Augusta, to say Mr Biggs was displeased would have been an-understatement.

"Who the fuck is running you lame ass niggas and that block is no concern of mine. Funk owe me a hundred thousand, and I'm not taking no losses. You his right-hand man and you was in the loop with that nigga. He dead or missing, whatever the fucking case maybe, I'm putting you responsible for that bread; you dig?" Mr Biggs sneered.

Meathead knew it was close to impossible to come up with that much money. Funk had always spoon-fed him, not letting him make money on his own. He was treated and carried how he was in character—Funks flunkie. Now he was praying for it by being forced into a situation he had no control over. At that moment he cursed his self for calling Mr Biggs.

"What you just standing there for? Go get my money, nigga, and I'm letting you know, you got two weeks; you hear me? Two weeks."

Meathead held the side of his swollen face and nodded in understanding before he made an exit from the basement.

Mr Biggs pulled a cigar from the front pocket of his Armani button up and set a flame to the tip. The expensive nicotine seemed to temporarily calm his nerves.

"You want me to go over there on Avers and lay them bustas down or what?" Body Bags asked.

Mr Biggs blew out a thick cloud of smoke before he said, "Not yet, Body Bag. We have to first see what enemy we are up against, go over there and investigate, and find out everything you can about the boy Byron. In war we must know our enemies, and as of right now we not in a position to war; you understand?"

"Yea. I feel you, Boss."

"We might be able to finesse this Byron character out of his block."

"And if we can't?" Body Bags questioned.

"Then we go and take it." Mr Biggs said taking a pull from his cigar.

Body Bags smiled at the thought of homicide and left the basement to carry out the orders he was given.

***

"Here. Take this hundred dollars and go cope five blows from them niggas." Body Bags said to a slender dope fiend who sat in the passenger seat of his Dodge Magnum.

"After I get them, den what?" The dope fiend asked scratching her arms of getting a fix.

"Then bring them back to me and I'ma take care of you." He said and slid her a crisp 100-dollar bill from his thick wad of cash.

The fiend slid out of the Magnum to handle the task.

Body Bag sank low in the seat of his Dodge Magnum, the brim of his Milwaukee Bucks fitted hat pulled low over his eyes while a Sig Sauer P92 rested on his lap. From his location he could see the drug traffic on Avers and Augusta, and could tell that the Mafia's were moving differently. They had security on the corners and had all the dope fiends standing in a single file line to get served. To some form he was impressed by the structure they were moving.

Body Bag knew it was just a matter of time before Mr Biggs gave them the green light to take over the block. And when he did, he intended to show the Mafia's what the Milwaukee Murda game was all about.

Body Bags's thoughts of mayhem was intercepted when the fiend hopped back in his whip. "Here, baby. Now what I get for doing that?" the woman said switching around in her seat. Looking at the aluminum foil bags with the Grim Reaper stamp on them caused a look of pure to pleasure across his hardened face.

After giving the fiend the potent drugs back, he said, "That's you. Now get out my shit."

Ignoring his rudeness, the dope fiend did as she was told and got out the vehicle on a mission to get high.

Body Bag pulled off into traffic while grabbing his cellphone. Dialing a number, he pressed send and put the phone to his ear.

Mr Biggs picked up on the second ring. "State the business, youngster."

Body Bag proceeded to tell his boss what became of his investigation. Somebody had definitely violated, and for that violation, somebody definitely had to die.

Chapter 29

It had been 6 months since Byron and Lil' Pooh brought Funk the deadly move that put the Mafia's at the top of the dope game. The money was coming in mass quantities and everybody on Avers and Augusta were feasting off the proceeds. Lil' Pooh tried to convince Byron to relocate for security reasons, but Byron refused. Instead, he opted to redo his mother's house since that was where he held all of her memories.

The traffic stayed consistent on the block due to the good quality of dope that Carlos and the GD's where blessing them with. Formally a few thousand dollar a night block was now bringing in no less than a $100,000 a night, and that was on an off night. Everything was going well for Byron. He had money, cars and clothes, not to mention the love of his life Carmella was two months away from giving birth to his child. The world was in his palms and with the dollars he was getting his opportunities were limitless.

Sitting in his cocaine white Mercedes MG Cabriolet, smoking on a blunt of Purple Haze, Carmella nodded her head as she sat in the passenger seat. It was a humid 96-degrees so Byron had the top down on the luxury vehicle. The dope game had been good to him, so it was nothing to drop 10 bands on the $200,000 car. Byron was making $300,000 off each kilo of heroin and that was after he paid the Mafia's; and he was going through two kilos in bags a week. Looking at his diamond flooded Rolex he saw that it was 3:00. He was expecting Lil' Pooh and Noody to meet him on the block to discuss the latest issue.

A few weeks ago, while Byron and the Mafia's were posted on the block getting to the money, a Chevy Tahoe pulled up and two men got out. One of the men introduced himself as Fred while the other one remained silent with a mug on his face. Seeing the attitudes of the strangers on their block, the Mafia's pulled guns.

"No need for all that, playas, we come in peace." Killa Fred said with a sly smile.

"So, state your business." Lil' Pooh said menacingly.

"Well it seem we have a lil' issue. Nothing we can't fix. You see, a few months ago y'all smoked a nigga name Funk."

At the mention of Funk's name Lil' Pooh reached for the gun on his waist.

Killa Fred was unmoved and continued speaking. "Now we can give a fuck about Funk and why y'all killed him, but y'all took some money and drugs that didn't belong to him. It belong to Mr Biggs. My Boss."

"So, you come over here trying to collect some money or dope you assume we got from a dead nigga?" Byron asked agitated at the disrespect.

"Come on, big homie. We know what happened. We know about y'all lil' beef and we know y'all got on with our shit. His right-hand man already gave us the rundown." Killa Fred said throwing Meathead under the bus.

"Check this out, my nigga. I don't know where you got your information about us killing somebody and taking some money or whatever, but you got the wrong idea and the wrong niggas, so I advise y'all move around." Byron said stepping up in Killa Fred's space.

Body Bags, tired of playing games, pulled a baby tee from his Tru Religion jeans, as the Mafia's pulled out enough artillery to ignite a world war. Byron held up his hand to tell the Mafia's to stand down.

"Not now, bag." Killa Fred said, patting Body Bag on his back. Body Bag lowered his gun with a wicked grin. "Y'all got that, playas, but trust and believe we gone keep in touch." Killa Fred replied as him and his goon got back in the truck. They knew they were out manned and out gunned. If they would've pepped off on the corner they would've surely been killed. Killa Fred knew it would be another place and another time.

Byron watched the truck bend the corner before he turned to address his men. "If them clowns come back through here, kill them niggas."

Noody and one of his security stepped off to let the rest of the Mafia's know the situation.

"I want Meathead dead, ASAP." Lil' Pooh nodded in

understanding. If they was looking to war with the Mafia then war it would be." That was three weeks ago.

Carmella turned the volume up on the sound system inside Byron's Benz and let Mary J Blige pour through the speakers. "Real love. I'm searching for a real love." Carmella sang, bobbing her head to the music. Her Prada sunglasses covering her eyes, blocking them from the hot Chicago sun, as well as the haters who wished they could be in her position. She had a man that loved her, she was two months shy from giving birth to a healthy baby boy, and wanted for nothing.

Byron looked at his queen and smiled. He was happy to be in the position he was in. He was Chief of the Mafia's, a loyal crew that was making plenty of money. At the sound of Mighty barking in the backseat, Byron turned to the right just in time to see the Dodge Magnum come to a screeching halt on the side of his Benz. The tint made the occupants undetectable. Seeing the back window roll down, everything from that point was in slow motion as a Draco AK-47 was stuck out the window.

"Noooooooo!" Byron yelled as the gunman pulled the trigger on the assault weapon.

Boc! Boc! Boc! Boc! Boc! Boc! Boc! Boc! Boc!

Byron yanked Carmella to the floor of the Benz. The 7.62 rounds rocked the car, penetrating and shredding the exterior of the vehicle. After the thunderous gunshots ceased, Byron could hear the sounds of tires squealing off. The Magnum raced down the block as the shooter left a mess of shell casings and the air polluted with gunsmoke.

"Get up, baby, we gotta get up outta here." Byron said pulling at Carmella's limp body.

She was unresponsive from the bullet that made contact with her head. At the sight of the large wound in her cranium Byron knew it was over. There would be no wedding, no raising a family together or parenthood, because Carmella was gone. Byron looked in the backseat of his car and saw his pit bull holding on to his life with short breaths from getting hit from gunfire. Grabbing his phone Byron dialed 911 in attempts to get some help, while a crowd started to form around his car.

"This is nine-one-one, what's your emergency?" The dispatcher asked.

"My girl just got shot." Byron said losing his breath and his blood from being shot in his stomach.

"What's your location, sir?"

"Ten-forty-eight North Avers." Byron replied.

"Paramedics are on the way. Please, stay on the line with me, sir."

Byron never heard her. His phone slipped from his blood-soaked hands as he became unconscious.

"That was some good shooting you did, playa," Body Bag said, sitting in the passenger seat of his Dodge Magnum.

Meathead sat in the backseat holding the hot Draco. Mr Biggs wanted him personally to do the hit since he was Funk's right-hand man, and it was Funk's fault he was 100 bands short. Not to mention Byron and the Mafia's disrespect to Killa Fred and The Body Snatchers as a hole. A message had to be sent, and Meathead was the chosen one to send it. Being promised Funk's position, Meathead was willing to ride for the cause, and accompany 8 Track and Body Bag on the mission of homicide. "Yea, that ain't 'bout nothing. I'll kill anything to get to this money."

"Yea, I can dig it, killa." Body Bag said sarcastically before he turned around and shot Meathead in the face.

8 Track wiped some blood from the side of his face from the explosion of Meathead's cantaloupe while he turned into a deserted alley. "Damn, goofy ass nigga, why you ain't warn me before you did that shit?"

"Warn you for what? I couldn't wait to bust that nigga head." Body Bag arrogantly said, tucking the Glock 14 back on his waist

8 Track pulled the whip behind a garbage dumpster where he and Body Bag got out. "I'm just saying, my nigga, next time give a nigga a wink or something."

"Man, shut the fuck up and help me with this punk," Body Bag replied and opened the back door. The two goons grabbed Meathead's corpse out the Magnum and tossed him in the dumpster.

"Trash ass nigga." Body Bag said noticing the blood stains on his Gucci khakis. After disposing the body, they got back in the car and pulled off to go get the car detailed, leaving Meathead the city's 400th murder victim.

S. Allen

Chapter 30

Laying in a bed in Cook County hospital Byron had awakened from his 16-hour coma. The bullet from the AK caused him to lose a severe amount of blood and severed a portion of his intestines. After surgery, the surgeons were able to patch him back together, but he would be forced to wear a colostomy bag. Byron tried to sit up but the pain in his stomach told him to do otherwise.

Dr. Rodneal had just come in to check on Byron. "How are you doing, Mr. Hobson? I am glad that you are awake." Dr. Rodneal said handing Byron a plastic cup of water.

Byron drained the water in one gulp. It had been 16 hours since he had any liquid and his mouth. Felt like the Sierra Dessert. "Thank you."

"You're welcome. You should consider yourself a lucky man. With the amount of blood you lost, it's a good thing the ambulance got to you in time." Said Dr. Rodneal, taking the cup back from Byron. Byron looked under the cover and saw the plastic bag on his stomach, covering a piece of his intestines. All he could do was shake his head. "How long I gotta wear this?"

"Well, Mr. Hobson, you will probably have to wear the bag for about four months. Maybe longer depending on how well you recover, but we will monitor to you on a regular." The doctor informed.

At that moment all Byron could think about was Carmella's brains in the interior of his car and the gunshots that rang from the tinted vehicle. "Did my girl make it?" Byron asked, already knowing the answer to his question.

The doc put his head down as he hated to be the bearer of bad news. "Mr. Hobson, we couldn't save Ms. Green. Her wounds were fatal. We could do nothing to save her. I'm sorry."

A tear fell from Byron's eye. "Well, were you able to save the baby?" Byron's heart began to race. "Where is he? Can I see him?"

"Mr. Hobson, your son is fine. He is two months early, but he is in healthy condition. We have him in a nursery as of right now for premature children. We will have to monitor him closely."

Byron thanked God that his son was okay. "When will I be able to take him home?" Byron was anxious to take on the responsibility of fatherhood.

"Mr. Hobson, due to the incident and the violence that claimed the mother's life, DCFS has stepped in, and as of right now they have legal guardianship of the child."

"Who the fuck is DCFS?" Byron asked confused.

"Department of Children Family Services. As of now the child belongs to the state of Illinois. You will have to go to court and show that you are capable of taking care of the child. At that time, they will make a decision and placement for the child."

Byron couldn't believe what he was hearing. First, he lost his mother, then Carmella, and now they were saying he couldn't see his son. It felt as if somebody had just dropped a 200-pound plate on his chest. Just when he thought his situation couldn't get any worst, it did.

There was a knock at the door and two white, uniformed officers walked in. "Excuse me. Chicago Police. We would like to have a few words with the *victim*, please." Detective Calhoun said in a sarcastic tone.

The doctor looked the two officers up and down with suspicion, and then looked at Byron whose thoughts were of his son and nothing else. "Very well. Just know that Mr. Hobson needs some rest and is really in no condition to talk, so can you please hurry with your investigation so he can get some rest?"

"No problem, doc, we just have a few questions; this won't take long at all."

The doctor turned on his heels and left the detectives with Byron.

Detective Calhoun waited until Dr. Rodneal left before he walked over to Byron's bed. "Long time no see." He said taking a sip from his coffee.

"What you want, man?" Byron was in pain and was already annoyed with the detective.

"I have a few questions and I need some answers. First, do you know who just tried to murder you?"

"Nope. I don't know shit." Byron replied playing ignorate.

"Oh, I see. This the part where you stick to the code of the streets and refuse to cooperate. We'll let me tell you something, dummy. Your pregnant girlfriend was just shot with a AK-47 in broad daylight with you getting hit in the process, all because of your drug-dealing."

"I don't sell drugs. You got the wrong dude."

"Oh, I do? You got shot sitting in a two hundred thousand dollar car and you don't have a job, a paycheck stub, or nothing to show how you can afford that kind of vehicle, but you don't sell drugs? Byron, we know all about your dishonorable discharge from the military, your mother over-dosing on heroin. We also have reason to believe that you and an associate were involved in the murder of Rashad Banks, also known as Funk. You know what makes me sick to my stomach? Niggers like you serve our county and then the first sign of trouble resort back to this ghetto, hoodlum mentality. But I tell you this, were watching you, and as soon as you slip, your ass is grass and I'm going to be the lawn mower. When you ready to give up the shooter, give me a call, because I doubt who ever fired those fatal shots in broad daylight is finished." Detective Calhoun threw his contact card on Byron's chest. "Enjoy the rest of your day, soldier," Calhoun said and left the room.

Byron balled up the card and threw it across the room. He lost everything he had to live for as his sadness quickly turned to anger. He was set on revenge, and all involved would feel his wrath. The tears were dried up and the focus was on his enemies. In his heart he knew he was going to kill Mr Biggs as well as his cronies. Mr Biggs's life was on borrowed time. Byron's thought of homicide was broken when Lil' Pooh walked in the room. A smile came across Byron's face at the sight of his comrade. Lil' Pooh was his brother from another mother and his only family.

"What's up, bruh?" Lil' Pooh said, dressed in a black tee, army fatigue shorts and black Reebox Classics.

Byron could tell Lil' Pooh was in murder mode noticing the bulge on his waist. "What's up, thug?" Byron shook Lil' Pooh's hand the Mafia way, as Lil' Pooh took a seat in the chair next to

Byron's bed.

"Ain't shit. Just came to check on your well-being. I been back and forth to this hospital since you been in that coma. Now that you out that shit, what's the business?" Lil' Pooh said ready to bust his guns.

"You know that cracker detective from back in the day just left here." Byron informed him.

"Oh, yea? What he say?"

"He came in here on some one on one. Want me to snitch shit."

"Word?"

"He say he think I got something to do with that Funk situation."

"They got any proof?"

"My nigga, if they had proof he wouldn't be asking questions, it would be Cook County Jail and then Statesville Penitentiary, you dig? What's up with Mighty?" Byron inquired.

Lil' Pooh put his head down. "I buried Mighty behind your mama's crib, fam. They found that nigga Meathead in a dumpster off of Kedzie Avenue." Lil' Pooh told Byron.

Byron's heart went out to Mighty. Mighty was his soldier and his love and loyalty would be dearly missed. Meathead was murdered and if the Mafia's had nothing to do with it, then who? It was a lot of shit going on and Byron knew it was time to lace his boots and step back into the field. "Lil' Pooh, these niggas just violated the wrong one. They shot and missed. Now their proper punishment will be perused. I'm about to touch these niggas in a way they never been touched."

"Yea. That's what I'm talking about." Lil' Pooh said itching to blow the 45 on his waist.

Byron shook his head. "That's where you wrong, Lil' Pooh. This time I'm a need you to stay in your lane."

"And what lane is that?" Lil' Pooh asked in confusion and slightly offended.

"The lane of getting to the money, Lil' Pooh. You can't war and get money at the same time. I need you to step up and lead the Mafia's. You a leader, Lil' Pooh. You got this dope game shit down packed. Continue the operation and stacking geez. That what I need you to do."

"So, while I'm doing that, what you gone be doing?" Lil' Pooh asked trying to get some understanding of Byron's logic.

Byron looked at Lil' Pooh through bloodshot eyes. "Killing, fam. That's what I'ma be doing. Now help me get up outta here."

Lil' Pooh passed Byron his clothes. After painfully getting dressed, Byron held on to Lil' Pooh's shoulder as he and Lil' Pooh snuck out of the hospital. Byron was now mentally back in the bloody war grounds of the middle east. The death mission he was attempting was unavoidable. Blood had been spilled by the hand of Mr. Biggs and The Body Snatchers, and now Byron was going to soak the streets of Chicago with theirs.

S. Allen

Chapter 31

"Bet a hundred I roll six-eight since you talking all that G-Shit." Kadafi said shaking the two-red dice in his hand. He and his Body Snatcher associates where involved in a heavy dice game on the corner of Homan and Ohio.

"Bet, nigga. You ain't hit a point all night. You might as well donate to the Brave Heart trust fund." Brave Heart said throwing a crispy $100 bill into the gambling pot. He was a 17-year-old thug who stayed in trouble. He had been hitting Kadafi by making side bets. To these young men getting money, shooting dice and fucking with hoes was all part of the game, but they failed to understand. Games were meant to come to an end.

Byron sat in an abandoned building 6 city blocks from his intended targets. It was a quiet night and only a few fiends and bums roamed the streets. A black Carhartt hoodie covered his head as black gloves covered his hands. Byron zeroed in on his targets with the ZF-4 scope. He assumed his range was about 800 meters. This would be an easy shot as he had hit targets in Iraq at a 1,000 meters with ease. Putting his index in the trigger well of the rifle and the butt of the gun in his right shoulder, he sat and waited for the right moment.

"Six-eight, running mates! I fold, you goofy ass nigga." Kadafi laughed picking up the pot of money after hitting his point on the dice.

"Lucky ass nigga." Brave Heart said pulling a cigarette from his pocket to roll a blunt. After rolling the blunt, he lit it and inhaled the smoke in his lungs.

Kadafi was on a roll and his pockets were getting fat, all to Brave Hearts expense. "You know what's up. Put up," Kadafi, said shaking the dice, challenging Brave Heart to put some more money up.

"You ain't said nothing." Brave Heart retorted and threw another C-note on the ground.

"You sweeter than bear meat." Kadafi said and rolled the dice. The dice landed on ace-trey. "Foe, nigga, and I bet another hundred

I hit my point."

"Bet." Brave Heart replied and put another Franklin in the pot. At that point something zipped passed his face and then his blunt was split in half. "What the fuck?" Brave Heart said examining his blunt with confusion, and then his head exploded; putting his thoughts on the dude next to him. Brave Hearts body hit the concrete with a loud thud.

A chick who was watching the game let out a horrific scream. Kadafi looked up to see what had happened when he was met with the same fate. A 3.08 bullet hit him in the face. He died instantly as crimson oozed from the hole in the center of his forehead leaving a larger hole in the back of his head. The same whole his brain exited from. The crowd at the dice game took off running in opposite directions, leaving the two bodies sprawled out on concrete in a bloody mess.

Byron saw his deadly work through the lens of the powerful scope that mounted his rifle. He had ended the life of two of Mr Biggs's cronies with just two steady pulls of a trigger. After grabbing the spent brass shell casings, Byron fled from the abandoned building undetected. Nobody saw or heard a thing due to the silencer attached to the murder weapon. Chicago was known for its reputation of violence and gangsta warfare, but what Byron just began would forever haunt the city of the Chi. By hand, he launched an act of pure terror.

***

"Man, bro, we clocking good today. We already ran through sixty packs and the night still young." Noody said to Lil' Pooh while they stood on the corner of Avers and Augusta. It was early in the day and the Mafia's were running through dope like water running through a well.

"It's definitely moving. You know how the block boom on the first and the fifteenth of the month." Lil' Pooh said taking a pull from his Newport.

"What's good, Noody? Lil' Pooh?" A guy with shoulder-length dreads said stopping in front of them on a 10-speed.

"What? You trying to cop some work? If so, you need to go over there and stand in line with everybody else," said.

"Nah, I was just checking up on y'all. Making sure y'all straight." The dude on the bike replied before he peddled away.

"Man, you know that nigga?" Lil' Pooh asked Noody, seeing that it was the same dude from the Aevra.

"Hell naw. I thought you knew him." Noody responded.

"I don't know that joker either. Make sure you tell the guys to stay on point." Lil' Pooh said feeling that something was in the air. It was something up with the dude in the Aevra, and Lil' Pooh was getting a bad vibe from him. Next time he saw him, he would be ready to get to an understanding.

"I got you, bro." Noody replied.

Lil' Pooh jumped in his Buick Lacrosse and pulled off.

***

"So what, Brave Heart and Kadafi got shot on the block. Things happen when you out here living that life. Ain't no telling what they had going on. Them two stay in some bullshit." Said Mr Biggs.

Body Bag had just informed him about the situation that happened on Homan and Ohio. The Body Snatchers were still looking for a heroin connect and were robbing drug dealers just to maintain. Now two of their lil' soldiers had been shot. Bullshit was definitely in the air.

"You not understanding me, Boss. Niggas that was out there said that shit was crazy. One minute they shooting dice and talking shit, then they laid down with they bodies blowed out."

Mr Biggs rubbed his thick goatee as he was in deep thought. What Meathead told him about Byron being in the military and been deployed to the middle east had him thinking hard about if it were possible he could have been the shooter, and was running around the hood on some DC Sniper shit. They had underestimated their enemy and that mistake cost them two of their young soldiers. The soldiers were replaceable, but his money and reputation wasn't as he knew it took years to build a reputation and only one second to

215

destroy it. They sent shots at a veteran and missed, and if it was Byron who did the hit on Homan and Ohio, they had a helleva problem on their hands.

"When I sent y'all to dead that nigga, y'all missed, so Brave Heart and Kadafi's blood lays on your hands." Mr Biggs said looking Body Bag in his eyes. "I want Byron in the cemetery by the end of the week. Them blisters on Avers and Augusta. I want all that shit dead. You understand me? Dead." Mr Biggs sneered through clenched teeth.

Body Bag grabbed his phone off the clip on his belt and dialed a number.

"What up?" Killa Fred answered.

"Meet me at the spot in thirty minutes."

"One," was all Killa Fred said before he gave Body Bag the dial tone in his ear.

The Body Snatchers were now at war, and it was the element he loved to be in. Body Bag left Mr Biggs's crib excited at the thought of some vicious gunplay.

"Many men wish death upon me. Blood in my eyes, dog, and I can't see I'm trying to be who I'm destined to be, but niggas wanna take my life away." 8 Track bobbed his head to 50 Cent as Many Men blasted through the 4-125 from the inside of his conversion van, turning into the King gas station on Homan and Lake Street while a Mac-11 occupied his passenger seat. 8 Track had been riding around looking for Byron or any of his soldiers, so he could give them all of the 50 shots that were in his mac. Mr Biggs put a hit out on Byron, and The Body Snatchers had a green light to shoot on site.

Pulling in the gas station, he parked on the side of a pump and got out. After going in the store to get some blunts and paying for his gas, 8 Track grabbed the nozzle on the pump and proceeded to pump his gas, all the while scanning the streets for his enemies, not noticing the yellow cab that was parked down the street.

Byron had 8 Track in his scope as he was ducked low with his silenced rifle hanging discreetly out the window of the backseat of the cab. At that moment Byron had a flash back of when he was in the battlefields of Afghanistan, and he was the chosen one to send a Nato round into the head of an Islamic terrorist who was trying to plant a roadside bomb. Looking through his scope, 8 Track was doomed to face his death. As if he was taking a picture, his head now in the cross-hairs. Byron applied a slow and steady squeeze to the trigger, causing the rifle to jerk in his hands. After refocusing his sight back in the scope, he saw 8 Track grasping at his throat while blood squirted from the gap in his neck profusely. Byron pulled the trigger again, sending a 3.08 to 8 Track's chest, blowing his heart through his back. Nobody heard a sound as the congested Westside traffic muffled the silenced rifle.

Seeing 8 Track's body stretched on the side of the van leaking, Byron patted Benji on the back.

Benji turned to face Byron and asked, "You good, me boy?"

"Yea, let's get up outta here, Benji."

Byron replied. Benji put the cab in drive and pulled into the hustle and bustle of the mid-day traffic.

***

"I'm Todd Jhensen."

"And I'm Vanessa Wilbert, and you're turned in to WGN news at Nine. On today's top story, a rash of shootings have been taking place on the city's Westside. Witnesses say no gun fire was heard during these daylight murders. Let's go to Dionte Collings who's live at the scene of one of the recent shootings, at the King Gas Station on Homan and Lake, just a few blocks away from where two young men were shot in the head on the block of Homan and Ohio. Dionte, can you tell us what's going on, and is it possible we have a sniper on the loose?"

"Well, from what we know at this point, the victim was standing right here pumping his gas when he was shot. A witness says she saw the victim grasping at his throat while he was shot again. The witness says there was no sound of gunfire at the time of the shooting. Three nights ago, two men were shot on the block of Homan and Lake. Both men were shot in the head from what police say was a high-powered rifle. Witnesses also say no gunshots were heard at the scene. Authorities are not releasing the names of the deceased, but are saying the murders to be gang related.

"Is it any reason for the citizens of Chicago to be worried?"

"Well, at this point, I would advise the people of Cook County to be alert and take precaution. If they see any suspicious activity to please contact the police."

"Alright, thanks, Dionte."

"No problem."

"In other news—"

Byron turned off the TV and continued wiping down the rifle. In the last week he had shot three people in cold blood, and it was just the beginning. Byron was not going to rest until Mr Biggs and his squad of killers were resting in peace.

Chapter 32

Noody guided his '79 Chevy Caprice that sat on 28-inch Davin's, down State Street, on the city's Southside. The green candy paint shined like an apple Jolly Rancher in the sun. His music pounded through the speakers in the confines of his trunk, setting off car alarms as he drove past. Noody was on his way to the infamous Robert-Taylor projects on 49th and State to pick up some heroin from their connect, Carlos. A lot of guys from the Westside would have been nervous to travel the streets of the Southside; it was the motherland for the GD's who ruled this area of the city with an iron fist. Noody wasn't like the rest of the the young thugs from the Westside, he was an elite member of the Mafia's, and the Mafia's and the GD's were eating together, so he wasn't worried. But the Glock 26 on his waist was comforting.

Turning into the parking lot of the Robert-Taylor's Noody noticed all the GD's posted up in front of the building. All of them had their attention on the clean Chevy Caprice. Grabbing his cellphone, he called Carlos to let him know he was downstairs. This was Noody's second time picking up work from Carlos. Normally it would have been Lil' Pooh, but Lil' Pooh had a meeting with Byron, so Noody had to handle the function. Noody watched a young GD closely as he walked up to the Chevy. His hair was in 6 long braids, while a T on a shoestring hung on his right shoulder. Noody kept his hand on the handle of the Glock. The youngster tapped on Noody's window.

"What's good, Joe?" Noody said rolling the window down.

"What's up, big homie? Folks Carlos sent me down here to escort you in the building."

Noody took the keys out the ignition and reached in the backseat and retrieved the two Loui Vuitton handbags that contained $120,000 of re-up money. Walking up to a red brick building with number 4950 on it, a guy with a walkie talkie was posted.

"What's the deal, family? With all due respect we gone have to pat you down."

Noody knew this was protocol, so he didn't feel disrespected as he put his hands up to get searched.

The Chief of security searched Noody, relieving him of the hammer that was on his waist. "We gone have this for you when you come back downstairs." The security said and put Noody's Glock in the small of his back. After finishing the pat search, the guy allowed Noody and the lil' dude with the braids to enter the building.

Entering the building the stale smell of urine evaded Noody's nose as he was led to the 8th floor, were 16 GD's were in the hallway. Including Carlos.

"Glad you could make it, my nigga." Carlos said dressed in a navy-blue Pelle-Pelle short set. The diamonds in his six-point chained lit up the hallway.

"Glad I could make it; I got a gift for you from Lil' Pooh."

"I have something for him as well." Carlos said and handed Noody two leather bags. "It's seventy ounces in each bag, fam."

Noody looked in the bag and saw the neatly wrapped ounces of raw heroin and smiled. "Looks good to me." Noody gave Carlos the Loui bags. The two shook hands.

"Tell Lil' Pooh I'm trying to get his numbers up and he bullshitting." Carlos said with a chuckle, but was dead serious. Carlos had enough weight to flood the city, and he wanted Lil' Pooh to up his orders.

"That's a bet. I'ma let him know." Noody left the building with his palms itching, ready to get to the money.

"Look at this lame. He been riding around the city all day in that loud ass car, ain't even on point. Don't he know this Chi-Raq?" Body Bag said while him and Killa Fred watched Noody's Chevy pull out of the Robert-Taylor projects. They had been tailing him for hours waiting for the perfect time to execute their plan.

"That nigga just a pawn on the chess board; he's a nobody. We want Byron, but we gone send him a message to let him know he in the big leagues. Understand, Body Bags, in war when somebody attacks you either mentally or physically or threatens your being in anyway, as a man you make sure it's clear they will suffer in return.

He may be able to win a fight, but he will pay for each victory." Killa Fred schooled Body Bag as he pulled the antenna up on the remote control which was a detonator. "Now make sure you stay six cars behind him." Killa Fred instructed.

Body Bag followed Noody who was now getting on the Dan-Ryan Expressway headed west. While Noody had his car parked in front of a hood rat's house, banging her back out, Killa Fred was planting a block of C-4 under his Chevy. Killa Fred was exactly that. A killa.

Coming up on the southside of Milwaukee, a Mexican hitman by the name of Alex Lopez showed him the way of murder through lethal demolition, and car bombs was just another tool in Killa Fred's war chest, as Noody would soon find out.

Noody hit the ATT button on his Sony sound system, turning the music down, before grabbing his cellphone. He sent Lil' Pooh a text to let him know the pickup went well and he was on his way back to the block. Lil' Pooh returned the text saying he would meet him in the hood in about an hour. Noody threw the phone in the passenger seat and turned the music back up, bobbing his head to Twister's *Komakazi*, as he got off the exit on Independence Avenue.

"You want me to get off the exit with him?" Body Bag asked as they watched the Chevy get off on Independence Avenue.

"No, keep going." Killa Fred replied.

Body Bag did as he was told as Killa Fred pushed the red button on the detonator. A loud explosion could be heard from behind them. Killa Fred turned back in his seat to see a huge ball of fire in the air. The hit had been a success. They had just sent a message to Byron and the Mafia's that when you come at The Body Snatchers, don't come playing.

***

"Bro, you look like shit." Lil' Pooh said noticing Byron's appearance.

Byron and Lil' Pooh were at a bar called Tonie's on the Northside. He told Lil' Pooh to meet him at the bar so he could bring him up to speed on what was going on in the trenches. Ever since he snuck out the hospital he had been putting in blood work— he didn't have time to shower, shave or sleep. All his time was permitted to stalking and killing his enemies.

"So what's the word on the street?" Byron asked Lil' Pooh.

"To be real, fam, these niggaz is terrified, talking about it's a sniper running around the Westside. After that demo on Homan and Ohio, them niggas stopped hustling on that block. They moved to Christoona Street."

"Oh yea?"

"And niggas don't even go to King Gas Station no more, ever since dude got slumped. I don't think nobody get gas right there no more. That shit look abandoned. Nigga, you crazy." Lil' Pooh said downing his shot of Grey Goose.

"Lil' Pooh, I need to find Mr Biggs. I need to know where he resting his head. Killing his men is getting me nowhere. You kill the head, the body will follow. You dig?"

"I'ma get on it ASAP," Lil' Pooh replied.

"I need an address in the next few days. I'm trying to end this with these busters. On another note, what's up with the operation?" Byron asked pertaining to the business side of the organization.

"Everything going according to planned. Noody on his way back right now from seeing Carlos. We grabbed two kilos, and should reach to go back in a few weeks." Lil' Pooh informed.

"What's the daily numbers looking like?"

"No less than a hundred geez," Lil' Pooh said, looking at the time on his Frank Mueller time piece.

"That's what's up. When I'm finished cleaning up this mess, I got a cat in Cali I met in sniper school. Big things popping; feel me? We gotta expand from this Chicago shit. We trying to take this Mafia thing nationwide."

"I feel you." Lil' Pooh replied seeing Byron's vision.

Byron and Lil' Pooh were still at Tonie's conducting Nation business and making plans for the future of the Mafia's when Lil' Pooh's phone vibrated in his pocket. Grabbing it, he answered,

"Yo. What? Calm down, I can't hear you. When? Alright, say no more. I'm on my way." Lil' Pooh hung up the phone with a perplexed look on his face.

Byron noticed it immediately. "What's good, Lil' Pooh? You alright?"

Lil' Pooh swallowed the spit in his throat before he spoke. "Noody just got killed."

"What?"

"They say his car blew up on Independence."

"You serious?"

"As cancer," Lil' Pooh said in disbelief.

"Man, let's get up outta here." Byron and Lil' Pooh left the bar headed toward the block. They needed answers, and they needed them quick.

S. Allen

Chapter 33

It was two weeks later when Lil' Pooh was standing on the corner of Avers and Augusta, a bottle of Remy OX in his hands. He had just come from Noody's funeral that was held at the Gatlin Funeral Home on the southside. The entire Mafia organization was in attendance as they came to show their respects to a fallen soldier. Noody lived fast and died young in the name of the streets. At only 18 years of age, the wicked streets of the Chi claimed his life. With so much that he had done in the hood, from bang-banging, robbing, selling drugs, to murder, his grieving grandmother couldn't even see his face before he was laid in the ground. The explosion that caused his death did him wrong as the morticians weren't able to reconstruct him. Noody's limbs were missing along with his head, so his funeral was a closed casket.

Lil' Pooh took a swig from the bottle before he poured the rest on the ground. "We gone miss you, lil' homie. Rest in peace." Lil' Pooh couldn't understand how death could come so fast. One minute you were here, the next minute you were gone.

Looking at the blue sky, Lil' Pooh started to think of his own life. The streets of Chicago had turned him into a savage. He went from being a drug dealer, to alcoholic, to a cold-blooded murderer, all in just a few years. He grew up looking up to Billy Good and Rico, and was disturbed on how their outcomes were. He thought about how he shot an innocent Mr. Alam in the head. A man who only lived to love and support his family. He died for a few hundred dollars and some cheap liquor. Closing his eyes to stop the tears from escaping, he visualized Byron emptying his clip into Funk's dome, how Byron's mother had been strung out on the very drugs that they stood on the corner and sold.

Byron had enough money to get out of the game, but Byron was set on revenge. Lil' Pooh knew that this war he was involved in was real, and he wanted to make it out alive.

Lil' Pooh had given an assignment to one of the Mafia's to find out the location of Mr Biggs. On a humbug Mr Biggs was at a club called the Luther's House of Blues in downtown Chicago. Sabrina, who was at the club at the time, saw Mr Biggs and a few of his men at the establishment and called Lil' Pooh, who sent some soldiers to the club. After leaving the club intoxicated with a few females, Mr Biggs slipped as he didn't notice the car that followed him to a building on 15th and Kedzie. That mistake would cost him dearly.

The day was still young, and Lil' Pooh had to get his thoughts together. Noody was gone and it was nothing he could do about it but move forward with his life. It was time to prepare for his exit out of the game. Lil' Pooh was so caught up in his emotions he never heard the individual creep up behind him.

"Lil' Pooh, what's up?"

Lil' Pooh turned around, only to see the guy from the Blue Aevra. A mean mug appeared on Lil' Pooh's face. "Nigga, do I know you or something?" Lil' Pooh asked, not noticing the 44 Bulldog the guy held.

The guy smiled before he raised the gun, pointing it at Lil' Pooh's face. Lil' Pooh looked in horror as he made an attempt to reach for his 9. His attempt was futile. His exit out the game had come sooner than he had expected.

The loud boom from the hand cannon could be heard from three blocks. The first slug hit Lil' Pooh in the stomach, forcing him to the pavement. The gunman shot two more times hitting Lil' Pooh in the head. Laying on the ground with his brains leaking into a sewer, Lil' Pooh traveled into darkness as the gunman walked up and shot him once more for good measure before he spat on Lil' Pooh's stiff corpse before he said, "That's for my lil' brother, you bitch ass nigga." Tucking the hot burner in his pants, the gunman ran to an awaiting vehicle, leaving Lil' Pooh with his head split.

Lil' Pooh never thought the robbery and murder of that 16-year-old boy would come back to haunt him. Had he been more on point he would have noticed Fontanes brother discreetly parked across the street, witnessing his brother's execution. That mistake had cost him his life.

***

Detective Calhoun pulled up to the scene on Avers and Augusta and parked his Crown Victoria at the curb. He got the call 30 minutes prior and put the peddle to the metal. Detective Calhoun was doing surveillance at Noody's funeral and watched as the Mafia's payed homage. He was watching Byron in particular. Something in his gut was telling him that Byron was the one doing the killings on the Westside and was possibly using his sniper skills to carry out the murders.

"What do we have here?" Calhoun asked walking up to the scene of the shooting just as they were zipping Lil' Pooh up in a body bag.

"Well, Detective, seems like this one here was gunned down on this corner. A witness says a guy with dreadlocks just walked up and shot him three times." Homicide detective Tolbert informed.

Detective Calhoun walked up and unzipped the body bag and almost puked when he saw Lil' Pooh with his face missing.

"You alright, Detective?" Tolbert asked.

"That's Eddie Montgomery."

"You know the victim, Detective?"

"Yea, I do. I arrested him and a few friends a few years ago in a raid on this very block. Another one of them was killed earlier this year; a Rashad Banks." At that moment a light went off in Detective Calhoun's head. His thoughts were on Byron. The murders had to be connected but he just didn't know how, but they had Byron's fingerprints on them, he was sure. Detective Calhoun zipped up the Body Bag. "I got a pretty good feeling these boys are engaged in some kind of drug war. I think we can get the answers we need from Byron Hobson. I want him apprehended and detained as soon as possible. Get him off the streets now!" Calhoun yelled over his shoulder as he ran to his car.

"On what cause, Detective?"

"On homicide investigation." If they didn't get Byron off the streets, he had a strong feeling more people were Going to die by his rifle.

***

After getting the information on Mr Biggs, Byron was on a

mission. He figured that Mr Biggs beefed up his security due to 8 Track losing his mind a few days ago. Byron proved, in Guerilla warfare, the hunter could easily become the haunted. He got up with Benji for some more firepower. The GK43 was a good accurate rifle, and its low recoil made it a beast, but he needed something with a little more power and more shots, so Benji had given him a fully automatic Mak 190 assault rifle, that was now resting on his backseat.

Byron was on his way back from Noody's funeral. He talked to Lil' Pooh who left the funeral early. He couldn't stomach to see Noody put in the ground. Byron knew Lil' Pooh was drunk when he talked to him, so he was on the way to pick up his grieving homie. He was about to turn down Avers and Augusta until he saw all the police activity on the block. Slowing down he could see a body on a stretcher being loaded into an ambulance. Byron grabbed his cellphone and dialed Lil' Pooh's number. It went straight to voicemail. *What the fuck*, Byron thought then dialed Sabrina's number.

"Hello?" Sabrina asked on the second ring in tears.

"Sabrina, this Byron. What just happened on the block?"

"He gone, Byron."

"Who gone?"

"Lil' Pooh, Byron. Lil' Pooh just got shot in the head." Sabrina sobbed into the receiver of the phone.

Byron began to beat on the steering wheel. "Fuck, fuck, fuck!" Byron yelled at the top of his lungs and let his phone fall to the floor. He couldn't believe this was happening. First Noody, now Lil' Pooh. Byron pulled his car over to the curb; his tears wouldn't let him see the oncoming traffic. He just came from burying Noody not even an hour ago, and now Lil' Pooh was gone just like that. He saw plenty of people killed, and had issued his fair share of death, but Lil' Pooh was his family; the only family he had left; so his heart was crushed. Byron looked at the paper Sabrina had given him with the address 1517 Kedzie written on it. Byron was playing a game of life and death. Pulling his car back into traffic he was headed to put the game to an end permanently.

Chapter 34

"On today's stop story, the Chicago police have released the name of a murder suspect, suspected to have been involved in at least five homicides. Let's go to Dionte Collins who is live at the scene at the Kedzie and Harrison Street Precinct. Dionte, can you tell us what's going on in the case of Byron Hobson? Is he charged with the murders?"

"From what we know, Byron Hobson has been sought by Chicago police for five homicides. Standing right here with us is the Chief of Police. Chief, can you tell us what's going on in this case?"

"Byron Hobson is in question. He is ex-military, has extreme sniper training, and has been named to the best sniper the United States of America has produced. We have evidence that says these shootings were executed with someone who has official accuracy or rifle training. Mr. Hobson is considered to be armed and dangerous, and we'd like anybody who knows the whereabouts of Byron Hobson to contact the police immediately."

"Alright, thanks, Chief."

"No problem."

"And you have heard it right here from Chicago's Chief of Police. If you see Byron Hobson, contact police immediately or crime stoppers, at 626-0693. Back to you, Vanessa."

"You see that shit?" Killa Fred said turning down the volume on the 70-inch plasma TV that was mounted on the wall.

Mr Biggs and his goons were at a building on 15th and Kedzie, one of their strong holds on the city's Westside. They were about to take over the Mafia's block on Avers and Augusta. Mr Biggs scheduled a meeting with the rest of the membership at a warehouse on 95th and Jeffery. If they were to come at Byron and the Mafia's, they had to come hard as the news had revealed that their enemy was not the average Joe but a cold blooded assassin. It was time to get active and Mr Biggs needed all his men on point and ready for war.

"Yea, I see it, but I don't. This nigga definitely been cruising for a bruising. That's why we gotta find him and kill 'em." Mr Biggs replied.

"I think he just on a suicide mission. We gone show 'em he faking with this murder shit." Body Bag said, putting a 30-round clip magazine in a MPS machine gun. At the same time Killa Fred was pulling a Kevlar Vest over his chest.

"After tonight I want this shit done and over with; you understand?" Mr Biggs said checking the clip to his 911 .45.

Mr Biggs and his henchmen continued loading their weapons, getting ready to bring the drama to Byron and the Mafia's. Tonight, they were going to rush Avers and Augusta with all the soldiers and pistols they had. In the end, Mr Biggs would have taken over a $100,000 a night heroin block. The money was his motivation, and he was willing to put his life on the line to obtain it. Mr Biggs and his men left the building on their way to 95th and Jeffery to meet up with the rest of his army, and then to Avers and Augusta to eliminate his enemies.

***

Byron sat in his black T-top '87 Monte Carlos SS. He was in a murderous mind state parked across the street in front of the 1514 building on Kedzie Avenue. His palms sweaty as he gripped the Mak 190 that rested on his lap. Now was the moment of truth; it was either kill or be killed, and Byron wasn't in the mood for dying.

Byron counted four of Mr Biggs security standing in front of the building. His initial plan was to run up kamikaze style, but the activity in front of the building looked as if Mr Biggs would come out soon, so he patiently waited. Sunk low in the seat of the SS, Byron watched the front of the building. He could see that the individuals in front of the building were armed. Byron's patience paid off as he noticed Mr Biggs and three more men exit the building. After calmly pulling down his black ski-mask, he pulled the slide of the Mak 190, injecting a round into the chamber and then stepped out the whip.

Cha-cha-cha-cha-cha! Byron squeezed the trigger, lighting up the dark street. A few of The Body Snatchers returned fire. Byron ducked behind the SS and applied relentless pressure to the trigger. *Cha-cha-cha-cha-cha-cha!* Hot shell casings covered the pavement as Byron continued to fire. Killa Fred pulled Mr Biggs down behind a parked car to shield him from the assault of the 7.62 rounds being sent in their direction.

Body Bag sprayed led from the MPS, which made Byron get low but continuing to fire, hitting one of the bodyguards in the face, leaving him sprawled out on the concrete. Byron focused his aim on Mr Biggs who was pinned down behind a car. *Cha-cha-cha-cha!* The loud rifle barked and jerked in Byron's hand. After emptying the 30-round magazine Byron jumped back in his car. He pulled off, leaving a bloody mess. He would get at Mr Biggs's cronies another time. Getting the head, he knew the body would crumble.

"Two-two-three, we have a report of shots fired on Fifteenth and Kedzie. I repeat, Two-two-three, we have a report of shots fired on Fifteenth and Kedzie." The dispatcher said over the radio.

Detective Calhoun was in the McDonald's on Kedzie and Roosevelt, getting a cup of coffee when the call came over the radio. "Got-dammit." He cursed as he raced out of the McDonald's parking lot. He was only a few blocks away from the shooting as he gunned his Crown Victoria down Kedzie. Detective Calhoun put the police light on top of the hood and activated it. He had a feeling that Byron had something to do with the shooting. He wanted nothing more in life than to deliver Byron personally to the Menard Penitentiary with a fresh 100-year sentence. Detective Calhoun saw a shiny black Monte Carlos speeding toward his way on the other side of Kedzie. When the car passed him, he looked to the left and got a view of the driver. He couldn't believe his eyes as he slammed on the brakes, bringing his car to a screeching hault before he made a U-turn in pursuit of the SS.

Byron had just crossed the bridge on Kedzie and Roosevelt when he looked in his rearview mirror and saw the Crown Victoria with the sirens blaring. "Fuck!" Byron cursed as he slowed his car down at a traffic light on Kedzie and Madison. He was in a jam as he was behind 3 cars. The police car pulled beside Byron, and once Byron saw the pale-faced cracker Detective Calhoun screaming for him to pull over he knew he had to make a move. Turning the wheel to the right Byron pulled carefully out of the box he was in and stomped on the gas pedal, shooting the car across the intersection on Kedzie and Madison like a rocket.

Looking in his rearview he saw that Calhoun was still in hot pursuit. Byron's main objective was to ditch the cop and make it back to Avers and Augusta. A stinging sensation on the side of his stomach caused him to feel it. What he felt was wetness, and after examining his hand he knew now that he had been shot.

Byron raced down Kedzie Street as the 600 horsepower under the hood had him leaving the Crown Victoria in the dust. Byron made a quick right on Franklin Street and smashed the gas. The Magnaflow pipes howled as he made a left on Trey. Looking in the rearview, the Crown Victoria was nowhere in sight. At that moment Byron was glad he invested the $9,000 on the Monte Carlos, as the car was made for sticky situations, and eluding Detective Calhoun was definitely a sticky situation.

Byron grabbed his cellphone and dialed a number. He had been reluctant to use the number but now he had no choice. The phone rang as Byron glided down Chicago Avenue. He was only a few blocks from his home, then the person on the other line answered.

"Hello."

"Sergeant Hobson, how's it going?"

"You still calling me Sergeant, huh?" Byron said with a slight chuckle, the pain in his stomach becoming unbearable. "Listen, I need a favor. You told me to call if I ever needed one, and Commander Sanchez, I really need one."

"Anything, Hobson," Comander Sanchez replied.

Byron proceeded to tell him what he needed, until he pulled in front of his home. After giving Byron his word he would take care of it, Byron grabbed his Mak 190, got out the SS and painfully walked inside his home.

"I need all units to the block of ten-forty-eight North Avers. I repeat, all units to the block of ten-forty-eight North Avers." Detective Calhoun said over the radio. He was pissed that he had lost Byron, but his Crown Victoria was no match for the Monte

Carlos. Detective Calhoun knew Byron was on the way to Avers and Augusta. Tonight, Byron was going either of two places. To jail or the morgue, and Detective Calhoun was adamant about being the one to send him to either of the two. He was headed to Avers and Augusta to confront one of Chicago's most wanted.

Byron sat in his mother's home loading a 100-round drum for the Mak 190. The pain from his gunshot wound was excruciating. He took a swig from a bottle of Bacardi 131 that Lil' Pooh left, to ease the pain. He was in war mode as he was on a mission. A mission to kill. He was riding for his mother, for Juice, for Lil' Pooh, for Noody, for Carmella, Billy Good and Rico, and the Mafia's organization as a whole. After loading the last shell into the drum, he stuck it under the rifle, locked it and loaded it.

"Byron Hobson, this is the Chicago Police Department! We have your home surrounded! Come out with your hands up! I repeat, come out with your hands up!"

Byron got up and peeked out the curtain, seeing what looked to be at least 5 squad cars on the block with officers standing with AR-15's and shotguns pointed at his house. He knew he had a decision to make. Everything he had loved was gone, he had nobody; it was him against the world. Byron hit the liquor one more time before he stuck the Mak 190 out the window. And fired.

To be Continued!
A Shooter's Ambition
Coming Soon

Submission Guideline

Submit the first three chapters of your completed manuscript to ldpsubmissions@gmail.com, subject line: Your book's title. The manuscript must be in a .doc file and sent as an attachment. Document should be in Times New Roman, double spaced and in size 12 font. Also, provide your synopsis and full contact information. If sending multiple submissions, they must each be in a separate email.

Have a story but no way to send it electronically? You can still submit to LDP/Ca$h Presents. Send in the first three chapters, written or typed, of your completed manuscript to:

LDP: Submissions Dept
Po Box 870494
Mesquite, Tx 75187

DO NOT send original manuscript. Must be a duplicate.

Provide your synopsis and a cover letter containing your full contact information.

Thanks for considering LDP and Ca$h Presents.

A Shooter's Ambition

<u>**Coming Soon from Lock Down Publications/Ca$h Presents**</u>

BOW DOWN TO MY GANGSTA

By **Ca$h**

TORN BETWEEN TWO

By **Coffee**

BLOOD STAINS OF A SHOTTA **III**

By **Jamaica**

STEADY MOBBIN **III**

By **Marcellus Allen**

BLOOD OF A BOSS **VI**

SHADOWS OF THE GAME II

By **Askari**

LOYAL TO THE GAME **IV**

By **T.J. & Jelissa**

A DOPEBOY'S PRAYER **II**

By **Eddie "Wolf" Lee**

IF LOVING YOU IS WRONG... **III**

By **Jelissa**

TRUE SAVAGE **VII**

MIDNIGHT CARTEL

DOPE BOY MAGIC

By **Chris Green**

BLAST FOR ME **III**

DUFFLE BAG CARTEL **IV**

HEARTLESS GOON **III**

By **Ghost**

A HUSTLER'S DECEIT III

KILL ZONE **II**

BAE BELONGS TO ME III

S. Allen

SOUL OF A MONSTER III

By **Aryanna**

THE COST OF LOYALTY **III**

By **Kweli**

THE SAVAGE LIFE II

By **J-Blunt**

KING OF NEW YORK V

COKE KINGS IV

BORN HEARTLESS II

By **T.J. Edwards**

GORILLAZ IN THE BAY IV

De'Kari

THE STREETS ARE CALLING II

Duquie Wilson

KINGPIN KILLAZ IV

STREET KINGS III

PAID IN BLOOD III

CARTEL KILLAZ II

Hood Rich

SINS OF A HUSTLA II

ASAD

TRIGGADALE III

Elijah R. Freeman

KINGZ OF THE GAME IV

Playa Ray

SLAUGHTER GANG IV

RUTHLESS HEART II

By Willie Slaughter

THE HEART OF A SAVAGE II

By Jibril Williams

FUK SHYT II

By Blakk Diamond

THE DOPEMAN'S BODYGAURD II

By Tranay Adams

TRAP GOD II

By Troublesome

YAYO II

A SHOOTER'S AMBITION II

By S. Allen

GHOST MOB

Stilloan Robinson

KINGPIN DREAMS

By Paper Boi Rari

CREAM

By Yolanda Moore

SON OF A DOPE FIEND II

By Renta

FOREVER GANGSTA

By Adrian Dulan

LOYALTY AIN'T PROMISED

By Keith Williams

THE PRICE YOU PAY FOR LOVE

By Destiny Skai

THE LIFE OF A HOOD STAR

By Rashia Wilson

<u>**Available Now**</u>

RESTRAINING ORDER **I & II**

By **CA$H & Coffee**

S. Allen

LOVE KNOWS NO BOUNDARIES **I II & III**
By **Coffee**
RAISED AS A GOON I, II, III & IV
BRED BY THE SLUMS I, II, III
BLAST FOR ME I & II
ROTTEN TO THE CORE I II III
A BRONX TALE I, II, III
DUFFEL BAG CARTEL I II III
HEARTLESS GOON
A SAVAGE DOPEBOY
HEARTLESS GOON I II
By **Ghost**
LAY IT DOWN **I & II**
LAST OF A DYING BREED
BLOOD STAINS OF A SHOTTA I & II
By **Jamaica**
LOYAL TO THE GAME
LOYAL TO THE GAME II
LOYAL TO THE GAME III
LIFE OF SIN I, II III
By **TJ & Jelissa**
BLOODY COMMAS I & II
SKI MASK CARTEL I II & III
KING OF NEW YORK I II,III IV
RISE TO POWER I II III
COKE KINGS I II III
BORN HEARTLESS
By **T.J. Edwards**
IF LOVING HIM IS WRONG…I & II
LOVE ME EVEN WHEN IT HURTS I II III

A Shooter's Ambition

By **Jelissa**
WHEN THE STREETS CLAP BACK I & II III
By **Jibril Williams**
A DISTINGUISHED THUG STOLE MY HEART I II & III
LOVE SHOULDN'T HURT I II III IV
RENEGADE BOYS I II III IV
By **Meesha**
A GANGSTER'S CODE I &, II III
A GANGSTER'S SYN I II III
THE SAVAGE LIFE
By J-Blunt
PUSH IT TO THE LIMIT
By **Bre' Hayes**
BLOOD OF A BOSS **I, II, III, IV, V**
SHADOWS OF THE GAME
By **Askari**
THE STREETS BLEED MURDER **I, II & III**
THE HEART OF A GANGSTA I II& III
By **Jerry Jackson**
CUM FOR ME
CUM FOR ME 2
CUM FOR ME 3
CUM FOR ME 4
CUM FOR ME 5
An **LDP Erotica Collaboration**
BRIDE OF A HUSTLA **I II & II**
THE FETTI GIRLS **I, II& III**
CORRUPTED BY A GANGSTA I, II III, IV
BLINDED BY HIS LOVE
By **Destiny Skai**

S. Allen

WHEN A GOOD GIRL GOES BAD

By **Adrienne**

THE COST OF LOYALTY I II

By Kweli

A GANGSTER'S REVENGE **I II III & IV**

THE BOSS MAN'S DAUGHTERS

THE BOSS MAN'S DAUGHTERS II

THE BOSSMAN'S DAUGHTERS III

THE BOSSMAN'S DAUGHTERS IV

THE BOSS MAN'S DAUGHTERS **V**

A SAVAGE LOVE **I & II**

BAE BELONGS TO ME I II

A HUSTLER'S DECEIT I, II, III

WHAT BAD BITCHES DO I, II, III

SOUL OF A MONSTER I II

KILL ZONE

By **Aryanna**

A KINGPIN'S AMBITON

A KINGPIN'S AMBITION **II**

I MURDER FOR THE DOUGH

By **Ambitious**

TRUE SAVAGE

TRUE SAVAGE II

TRUE SAVAGE **III**

TRUE SAVAGE **IV**

TRUE SAVAGE **V**

TRUE SAVAGE **VI**

By **Chris Green**

A DOPEBOY'S PRAYER

By **Eddie "Wolf" Lee**

A Shooter's Ambition

THE KING CARTEL **I, II & III**

By **Frank Gresham**

THESE NIGGAS AIN'T LOYAL **I, II & III**

By **Nikki Tee**

GANGSTA SHYT **I II &III**

By **CATO**

THE ULTIMATE BETRAYAL

By **Phoenix**

BOSS'N UP **I , II & III**

By **Royal Nicole**

I LOVE YOU TO DEATH

By Destiny J

I RIDE FOR MY HITTA

I STILL RIDE FOR MY HITTA

By **Misty Holt**

LOVE & CHASIN' PAPER

By **Qay Crockett**

TO DIE IN VAIN

SINS OF A HUSTLA

By **ASAD**

BROOKLYN HUSTLAZ

By **Boogsy Morina**

BROOKLYN ON LOCK I & II

By **Sonovia**

GANGSTA CITY

By **Teddy Duke**

A DRUG KING AND HIS DIAMOND I & II III

A DOPEMAN'S RICHES

HER MAN, MINE'S TOO I, II

CASH MONEY HO'S

S. Allen

A Shooter's Ambition

By Destiny Skai & Chris Green
KINGZ OF THE GAME I II III
Playa Ray
SLAUGHTER GANG I II III
RUTHLESS HEART
By Willie Slaughter
THE HEART OF A SAVAGE
By Jibril Williams
FUK SHYT
By Blakk Diamond
DON'T F#CK WITH MY HEART I II
By Linnea
ADDICTED TO THE DRAMA I II III
By Jamila
YAYO
A SHOOTER'S AMBITION
By S. Allen
TRAP GOD
By Troublesome

<u>BOOKS BY LDP'S CEO, CA$H</u>

<u>TRUST IN NO MAN</u>
<u>TRUST IN NO MAN 2</u>
<u>TRUST IN NO MAN 3</u>
<u>BONDED BY BLOOD</u>
<u>SHORTY GOT A THUG</u>
<u>THUGS CRY</u>
<u>THUGS CRY 2</u>
<u>THUGS CRY 3</u>
<u>TRUST NO BITCH</u>
<u>TRUST NO BITCH 2</u>
<u>TRUST NO BITCH 3</u>
<u>TIL MY CASKET DROPS</u>
<u>RESTRAINING ORDER</u>
<u>RESTRAINING ORDER 2</u>
<u>IN LOVE WITH A CONVICT</u>

<u>Coming Soon</u>
BONDED BY BLOOD 2
BOW DOWN TO MY GANGSTA